Paper Sparrows

Paper Sparrows

Nathalie Abi-Ezzi

www.hhousebooks.com

Paperback ISBN: 978-1-910688-89-2

Cover design by Ken Dawson Creative Covers and Emily Nash
Typeset by Polgarus Studio

Published in the UK

Holland House Books
Holland House
47 Greenham Road
Newbury, Berkshire RG14 7HY
United Kingdom

www.hhousebooks.com

For Raymond and Hala

Chapter One

Layla looks down at the carpet of clouds and watches the aeroplane's bird-like shadow. She is somewhere between England and Lebanon. Back in London are her friends and university; ahead, Beirut and her family. The word "home" is no longer so clearly anchored to one place.

Her brother would love it up here. Ziad has never been on a plane, and if he could see this, he would think … what would he think? The truth is, she no longer knows. At thirteen, he might have thought one thing, but Ziad is sixteen now, and the silence between them has thickened. The texts and e-mails have dried up, they rarely talk on the phone and, when they do, he avoids saying much about himself.

Still, she makes a mental note of the food she has been served, the bumps of turbulence, the moustache on the man asleep in the seat beside her, splayed back across his cheeks as if he were walking into a gale-force

1

wind. She will tell Ziad everything. And not only about the flight, but about London too: her college, her hall of residence, the buses plastered with advertisements, pelican crossings, stormy skies like something out of the Bible, the way women change into trainers before they head home from work, how in summer it stays light till nine at night. She will use such pieces of information to build a bridge between them again.

It has been three years since she saw her parents and brother. Term only ended yesterday, so she could not have come a single day sooner; she might well have put off coming for a couple of days if it hadn't been for Maria's wedding.

She looks across at the newspaper on her sleeping neighbour's lap. _UN Secretary General Kofi Annan demands that Israel take urgent action to prevent a humanitarian disaster in the Gaza Strip._ As Israeli jets continue to pound Gaza in operations aimed at securing the release of a soldier captured by Palestinian militants, supplies of food and fuel have been cut off. There is now no access to drinking water or medicine, and no electricity, while the situation in the sewage plants has become critical.

Glancing at their watches, women begin to troop to the bathroom carrying hairbrushes and make-up cases. On their return, they leave trails of perfume.

'Ladies and gentlemen, we shall shortly be starting our descent to Beirut Rafiq Hariri International

Airport. The local weather is dry and fine, with a temperature of twenty-nine degrees.'

The setting sun stains the clouds purple and orange. Down there is the sea and the airport. Her stomach churns. She has waited so long for this moment; yearned to be in her own country, a place where she belongs. Now at last she will be able to lie back, close her eyes, and be cradled by her family. From them, she will draw strength enough to go back and face her struggles in London.

'… and please make sure that all electronic devices are switched off. Thank you.'

She checks the time. By now she has missed the wedding ceremony, but there is still the reception to attend. She can hardly wait to see Maria. They have been friends since Kindergarten.

Smiling, she slips her shoes back on, finds the ends of her seat-belt and clicks them together.

With one final scrutiny of her face and hair, the man at passport control nods her through.

The airport gleams – the polished grey stone floors, the walls of steel and glass, the terminal newly completed and spotless. The luggage from her flight is already on the carousel. A Louis Vuitton suitcase goes past. Next to it, an old battered case tied shut with rope. Then her blue pull-along with a red ribbon on the handle.

Going outside is like strolling into an oven, the same heat that smacked into her face when she stepped out of the plane; that created a haze on the tarmac and a blur of humidity over the sea. Headlights flash. Taxis wait to carry passengers onwards. There are shouts from porters, and people jostle to greet friends and family. She scans around at the faces with features and colouring that are like her own: a small girl dragging an even smaller sister behind her, a man hoisting a suitcase, a woman struggling on stilettos, another wrapped in a headscarf.

'Madame?' Two porters stretch out their arms to take her luggage.

'No thank you. I can manage.' She has dragged and carried her case all the way from halls in London, she really doesn't need the help – but she hands the porter a couple of thousand *lira* anyway. The man opens his mouth in surprise. One doesn't get tipped for doing nothing. But then he shrugs and turns to another traveller.

Layla hails a taxi.

At the hotel, she leaves her suitcase at the reception desk, and a woman with orange lips and a big smile ticks her name off a list, then directs Layla outside to a large manicured garden with in-ground lighting, flowers, tables, chairs, and a swimming pool lit from beneath. The water's reflection shimmers on walls. The bride and groom have not yet arrived. A band of five men dressed in traditional costume plays in one corner, their baggy trousers, sash belts and fezzes a contrast to the well-dressed people who are milling, chatting and observing each other.

There is an Italian theme: several draped flags and a mock gondola (God only knows where they found it) floating in the pool. She wanders over to have a look, enjoying the warmth of the evening. The beat and rhythm of the *dabke* music fits into her body, intrinsic as her heartbeat.

'Hey, Layla!' An old school friend, Rima, comes towards her. There are smiles, hugs and kisses. Rima looks a little shocked by Layla's hair. 'Wow.' She shakes her head, mini shakes, as if she can't think of what to say. 'But I didn't know you were coming back.'

'Well, it's the end of term.' She smiles at Rima. 'You look great!' Rima has always looked great.

'You too.'

'Now you're being nice. I've put on so much weight.'

'Noooo.'

'Yes.' Twenty pounds, to be exact.

'Well I like your hair. Maybe I should do something like that with mine.'

After watching Breakfast at Tiffany's, Layla had dyed a streak of blonde into her black hair, then decided that a streak of pink on the other side might be interesting too.

'But tell me,' says Layla, 'why is everything Italian?'

Rima laughs. 'The football, dear girl, the football! God, it's been nothing but football around here for weeks. Haven't you seen the graffiti? Maria was supporting Italy to win in the World Cup, and—'

'Wait. Maria was supporting Italy? I don't even remember her liking football.'

'Okay, so maybe it's her husband. Either way, yesterday Italy won, and I don't know which Maria was more pleased about, that or getting married.'

'But … well, that was taking a chance, wasn't it? I mean, what if they'd lost?'

Rima laughs again. 'She probably thinks Italy won it for the sake of her décor!'

They talk a little more about Rima's job, then about Layla's studies, London, the cold, the food. It's good to speak Arabic after so long, to make sounds she does not make in English. In London, she only had to speak and she was instantly a foreigner, her r's too rolled, her syllables too pronounced.

'Have you got a boyfriend?' asks Rima.

'No.'

'Oh.' There is pity in both her face and voice.

'Are you still with Elie?'

'Oh yes. To the death. And one day, before I shrivel up, he might even propose.'

Two fifty-something women, coiffed and glittering, are giving Layla looks. And for the first time, encapsulated in those glances, it dawns on her that she is not dressed for the occasion – not by Lebanese standards anyway. Around her, the place is awash with designer clothes and handbags, yet her own outfit ... The skirt is the one she wears to work, and her white shirt has been washed so many times that it's no longer white. Her shoes are flat and worn, and don't match her handbag. She is wearing stud earrings and a watch – neither of which count as jewellery – and no make-up except for some tinted lip-balm. How could she have forgotten about the excesses required for occasions like this one? Suddenly she feels all wrong.

The band breaks off mid-tune and starts to play *Volare*. There is whooping and clapping.

Rima grips Layla's arm. 'They're here.'

Fireworks go off: the sky explodes into pink and green. On the other side of the garden, Layla spots Maria laughing. She is a beauty, small in every respect except for a slightly too-large nose; and today she's heavily made up, her hair forced into ringlets that bounce gently on either side of the tiara— Because naturally there *is* a tiara, and a veil, and a long white dress, and white shoes on tiny feet. At her side, his arm through hers, is a brand-new husband with gelled hair, bronzed skin and a sheen of sweat that makes him gleam like a terracotta statue dipped in water.

Dry ice is released over the pool. The gondola drifts like a casket across the smoky water.

The bride and groom start to dance. The groom's arm is raised up and keeps beat with the music. Others begin dancing too. Layla claps along. There are more fireworks, and bottles of champagne are being carried out in football-trophy cups. Corks pop and champagne foams into glasses.

When the dancing is done, she sits at a table with Rima. There are a few familiar faces, but no one she knows well. She makes polite conversation, but the other guests mostly chat and laugh among themselves. It strikes her, as though observing it for the first time, how hand gestures accompany all talk, like a conductor leading his orchestra.

Then the food comes out. Bread rolls, raw vegetables, dips and mixed nuts to start. Smoked salmon, prawns, a large stuffed fish. Then chicken and gnocchi, or beef fillet and mashed potatoes. Vegetables aplenty.

Rima mentions to the young man next to her that Layla is studying in London.

'Oh really?' He turns to Layla. His eyes are almond-shaped, with long lashes. 'What are you studying? Law? Medicine?'

'Music.'

He looks surprised. It is not one of the worthy professions. The money-makers.

'But tell him where,' insists Rima. 'Not just anywhere. At the Royal College of Music.'

Layla laughs, embarrassed. 'Has my mother been talking again?' Her parents are so proud. She can just see her mother's face. Her daughter at the *Royal* College. She tugs at one of her earrings until it begins to hurt.

The man smiles politely, then turns to watch the desert arrive.

Desert is vanilla ice cream and tiramisu in burnished teacups. In the centre of the table is a plate of *petit fours*, and another of chocolates filled with cheesecake, all interspersed with tiny roses twisted out of sugar. Someone must have taken out a loan to pay for all this.

'It all looks so delicious,' says Rima.

Layla ladles a spoonful of tiramisu into her mouth. 'Mmm.' A few more spoonfuls and it is gone.

Rima is smiling, but has pushed her desert away.

'Don't you like it?' asks Layla.

'Too fattening.' Rima glances covertly down at Layla's stomach and spreading thighs. 'But don't worry, you can diet once the summer's over.'

Layla knows this is meant kindly. It is the sort of comment that people here make as a matter of course, but she isn't used to it any more. 'Well, if that doesn't work, there's always liposuction.'

Rima snorts. 'You joke, but Beirut's bursting with plastic surgeons. Whatever you want done, they'll do it. Girls get nose jobs for their sixteenth birthday presents. Maria's considering one.'

'Really?' Layla tries to locate Maria again, as if seeing her might dispel this possibility.

Rima changes the subject. 'I wish you'd been there for the ceremony.'

'You weren't there?' asks someone at the table.

Layla explains: a long flight, etcetera, etcetera.

'It was beautiful,' says Rima. 'Them holding hands, the white train. Afterwards they released two white doves from the church steps. It was already dark, but they flew off.'

'It sounds perfect,' says Layla.

'Although you have to wonder what'll happen to those two birds. I mean, you know, will they starve, or get shot … or maybe they'll be caught again for another wedding.'

The image is ruined, but she knows that Rima's probably right. The tiramisu has left a sickly taste in her mouth. Someone at the next table leans forward, and Layla glimpses Maria clinking glasses with her husband. It's strange. Maria looks different, someone else entirely.

Now the wedding cake is wheeled out. The wedding cake: not white or cream but lime green. Surely that can't have been Maria's choice. Or perhaps it was, Layla doesn't know any more.

The bride and groom stand together, his arm around her waist, both gripping the hilt of a sword. An actual real sword. Then, to clapping and cheering and yet more fireworks, they execute that lime green cake.

A photographer is busy bobbing like a prize-fighter around them, occasionally calling out instructions. The overhead lights change colour, turning the wedding dress pink, blue, orange. The gel on the groom's hair gleams.

There is more music and dancing, then the screech and bang of more fireworks, blossomings of enormous fire-flowers in the night sky. People start getting up to dance, and before long Layla is alone at the table. She glances at her watch. A man with dyed hair and sagging cheeks asks her if she'd like to dance. She can't be bothered to holler over the music, so mimes something, she doesn't even know what, with an apologetic expression, and he wanders off again.

She gets up and makes her way towards the bridal pair.

'Layla!' Maria spots her. 'You came!'

'Of course I did.' Three kisses, left cheek right cheek left cheek, and she congratulates them both. There's a little small-talk, then she thanks them for a wonderful evening, but explains that she's tired from her long flight. Gazing at Maria, Layla cannot see in her the girl who, when they were little, used to skip rope and cheat in tests and whisper secrets. They say their goodbyes, and as Layla turns away, the loss makes her feel hollow.

There's no one behind the hotel desk, so she finds her suitcase herself and bumps it down the steps. Taxis are already queued up outside. She promised Baba that she would get a ride with someone who was going the same way. Even though she's been living alone in a foreign city these last three years, Baba would still object to her taking a taxi home by herself. But Baba is not here to see. She climbs into a taxi and gives the man the name of her home town.

Her thighs stick to the faux leather seat of the taxi. Everything – the seat, the door, the dashboard – is hot to the touch. Or perhaps it is only her fingers that are too hot.

'It's nice, going to a wedding,' says the driver, a man in his sixties with one gold tooth and several missing ones.

'Yes, it was lovely.' She wonders what his own wedding day must have been like, what his wife is like. The two boys whose photos are sellotaped to the dashboard must be grandchildren. For all she knows, this might be the happiest man in all of Lebanon.

'It's a new beginning, isn't it? We need new beginnings. It's like this country, we've waited long enough for a fresh start, and now look at us.' The car swerves as he points to the newly cobbled avenues, Parisian-style cafes, and rows of baby Aleppo pines in pots. 'Downtown, downtown, everyone wants to go to downtown. Tourists straight from the airport. But I can't blame them.'

She tries to take it all in. It doesn't look like the same Beirut. 'It's amazing! None of this was here when I left.'

'How long?'

'Three years.'

The driver sucks in his breath. 'Three years.'

It feels like longer.

'A lot can change in three years,' he says. 'They'd barely started rebuilding it back then. They only finished a month ago.'

He points out Nejmeh Square, a giant four-faced Rolex clock tower in its centre, beautifully lit and made of the same gold-coloured stone as all the other buildings in this part of Beirut. While she was up in the plane, floating across a heavenly strata of blue and white, the world really had changed, and now she feels like a tourist.

'I can't get over how different it is,' she says.

'Yes, all new. A miracle of money. And now there are global firms, there's business, investment. Everything's on the up.' He sings a snatch of a song as they drive through Martyrs' Square, the giant blue domes of Mohammad Al-Amin mosque lit up against a black sky. 'The whole of Beirut was like that once,' he says as they leave the district.

She's not sure whether he means like downtown, or like the pock-marked building they are passing now, a remnant of the civil war. Both statements would be true.

13

They fall silent as they drive through the city, past Brazilian and Portuguese flags and football slogans, handcarts positioned beneath floodlamps selling pottery, fruit and nuts; ice-cream shops still open for business, and office blocks and company signs that certainly weren't here three years ago. Then they begin the ascent into the mountains. One hairpin bend follows another, the automatic drive clicking into a lower gear each time, and her stomach drops again. Of course, she knows it is only that her intestinal tract, relatively loose and mobile inside, is for a moment no longer being held up by her body. You don't grow up in the same house as Baba without learning The Facts. That the brain works harder at night than in the day; that the nail of the middle finger is the fastest-growing; that pine needles are richer in vitamin C than any citrus fruit; that the left lung is smaller than the right to make space for the heart.

Finally, with the lights of Beirut laid out below them, the road levels out.

'There's nothing like coming home, is there?' says the driver at last.

She smiles, her insides fluttering. 'That's true.' A unique feeling, like putting on a glove already moulded to the shape of your hand, while at the same time recognising that when you last wore it, you were a younger, altogether different person.

'Your family, the land you were born on: there's

nothing like that. You can keep your Paris and London.'

London. The street lamps. The tube trains. The buses. The timetables. The way everything simply runs. The way this is expected. But it is not home. This is home. And here is Baba's pharmacy, just the same as it has always been except that the sign is hanging down a little on one side.

Further into the town, though, things have changed. New shops and restaurants have sprung up. The few old shops that remain – a greengrocer's, a bookstore – look like bullied boys in a playground.

'Just down that road,' she says. Her road. The road she and Ziad grew up on.

The taxi driver turns into it and pulls over where she points.

'I thought that you'd been living abroad when I saw you put that on,' he says as she unfastens her seatbelt.

She thanks him, pays and gets out. He lifts her suitcase out of the boot, gives a nod and gets back into the car. The door is slammed, the handbrake released; he does a U-turn and drives away. The brake lights glow red when he reaches the end of the road. Then he turns right and is gone.

Chapter Two

Layla drags her case behind a parked car and sits down on the low wall that surrounds their building. She needs a few moments to gather herself. Even after so long, the bumps and edges of the rough-hewn limestone, still warm from the day's sun, are familiar beneath her fingers, and the dirt verge familiar beneath her feet.

Across the road is a new four-storey block of flats, squat and angular. She knew it would be there – Mama talked about it when it was being built – yet she can still see what used to be there: the two old cypress trees, the morning glory, the wild grasses they used to play among as children; now there is laundry hung out to dry, a satellite dish, potted geraniums. It is like glancing down and finding that she is wearing someone else's shoes..

She turns to look at her family home on the ground floor of another block of flats. Cracks of light shine through the slats in the wooden shutters. Mama and Baba are still up then, waiting for her. They have been

16

waiting these three years. And Ziad will be waiting too, his thirteen-year-old body recast as a sixteen-year-old one.

Down the street a short way, a pine tree leans out into the road. Using a sharp stone, Ziad once dug out a hole in that tree's bark. Slowly, it wept a sticky resin that moved almost invisibly down the trunk, hardening as it went. 'Breathe into that hole,' he told her.

'What?'

'Go on. Breathe into there.'

She didn't understand. His mind worked differently to hers. But she put her mouth up to the tree-trunk, the scent of resin sharp in her nostrils, and breathed out. At the same time, she felt her brother's face suddenly close to hers, his breath warm against her nose. Then quickly, before she knew what he was doing, he pushed some of the pliable resin back into the hole.

'There. We're in there, your breath and mine. Sealed in the tree. It'll carry on growing and we'll be in there, a part of it, forever.'

They were close then, and had remained that way until the day when, beneath another tree, the bond between them had been severed. But it can be repaired. She wants that connection with her brother back: the familiarity not only of someone who is genetically fifty per cent identical to her, but who has shared the minutiae of her formative years.

She shuts her eyes, trying to settle her nerves and

relishing for a minute longer the anticipation of stepping into her home. Ever since she left, she has been balancing on unstable ground, but now at last she will have the solidity of her family again. Scaffolding. No, more than that. A foundation.

She pictures her parents in the living room, Mama on the sky-blue sofa, Baba in his armchair. On the floor beside Baba is the tall Mother-in-Law's Tongue plant, its long stiff leaves pointing to the ceiling. In the dining-room is the piano: hers and Mama's. Her bedroom door is open, the room dim in the light from the hall, and inside it are her bed, her books, the print of Monet's water-lilies on the wall.

A car approaches, then passes on. She gets up and drags her suitcase onto the porch, stops outside the door and inhales the brightness of jasmine, then steps onto the sunken centre of the doorstep, worn down by countless entrances and exits. She rings the bell. The door opens. Mama is there, smiling, revealing the gap between her front teeth that makes her look like a child. 'Layla.' She hugs her tight, as if she wants to absorb her. 'Layla, my Layla.'

She hugs Mama back, and in that moment, standing in the threshold within her mother's arms, slips backwards through time and slides, curved, into a shell that fits her perfectly. The years evaporate and she is a child again, here in this instant where nothing has changed.

Over Mama's shoulder, she takes in the living room: the sofa and rug, the tiled floor, the television and bookshelves. Low down on one of the white walls is a faint blush of pink where she once painted a large red circle. It was washed off, but is not gone. It hovers there like a memory, and incites a rush of warmth and safety, like a linking of arms with a childhood friend.

When she and Mama finally part, there are tears on Mama's face. But now that Layla looks at her properly, she sees that her mother is different. It's a shock, because a parent ought never to change. Yet Mama's hair, thick and wavy, has threads of white in it, and there are crows' feet at the corners of her eyes. A surge of love – swaying in the shallows, Layla is lifted off her feet by a wave and floats, powerless.

Mama wipes the tears from her cheeks and peers at Layla. Instinctively, Layla realizes that she too is searching for her three-years-ago daughter, trying to reconcile the person who left with the person now standing in front of her.

Mama closes the door. 'God, how I've missed you.' The sound of her mother's voice, not on the telephone but here in this space, is textured, like wood that has started to split from lack of oil. 'Your hair. I didn't know you'd coloured it.' Smiling, she touches Layla's streaks. 'But I can't believe you're home again, *habibti*.' She hugs Layla again, blinks away more tears and wipes her nose. 'Your father's nodded off. Fadi! Fadi!'

Some sounds – a murmur, her father's footsteps on tiles, on hallway rug, on tiles again – and he comes into the dining room that adjoins this room. Layla puts him together piece by piece: leather slippers, brown trousers, belt, shirt, his face, red on one side from sleep. He rubs one eye and puts on his glasses. When he sees her, he brightens as if from some internal light.

She goes to him; then somehow her head is against his shoulder and he is kissing her temple. He is sleep-warm and solid, abrasive with the day's growth of stubble, and she cannot speak, only hold onto him and inhale the scent of soap and the faint remains of his aftershave.

'You've grown,' says Baba. 'I knew you would have, of course, but to see it … to see you …' He tightens his grip.

Her eyes prick with tears and she is heavy with contentment. Home. Her family. From her resting-place against him, she can hear his heart, *thud-um*, *thud-um*, and see the upright piano, a Yamaha U1, its walnut case shining, in front of her.

'Where's Ziad?' she asks.

Mama clears her throat. 'He's out. But he'll be back soon.'

Layla pulls back from Baba. 'Out?'

Mama smiles appeasingly. 'He's gone out in Beirut with his friends.'

'But … didn't he know I was coming tonight?'

'You know what boys that age are like,' says Mama. 'All they want to do is be with their friends.'

'Didn't he want to see me?'

'Of course he did, darling.' Mama takes Layla's hand. Her wedding ring, warm and hard, digs into Layla's palm. 'It's just—'

'The boy's out of control, that's what,' says Baba. 'I told him not to go out, but he won't *be* told any longer.'

This doesn't sound like the brother Layla knew.

Mama lets go of Layla's hand and turns to Baba. 'His friends were having a night out, that's all, and he wanted to join in. Feel like one of the lads. What's wrong with that?'

Layla remembers the way Ziad's classmates used to run past on the way to school, as he limped slowly after. The hares and the tortoise, only this tortoise was never going to win the race.

'He hasn't seen his sister in three years,' says Baba.

'It's okay,' says Layla. 'I don't mind. I'll just see him when he gets here, that's all.'

'Anyway.' Mama puts on a cheery smile. 'Would you like something to eat, darling? Are you hungry?'

'Hungry! I've been to a Lebanese wedding, remember?'

'Yes, yes, tell us all about it. How was it?'

'Oh, too much food. Too much everything!'

They sit and talk for a while about the entertainment

and guests, then Baba checks his watch. 'If you want to have a shower, remember the electricity cuts off in twenty minutes.'

'Oh. Right.' She had forgotten about things like electricity being rationed. 'I'll have a quick one in that case. Ziad'll probably be back by then.'

She pushes her bedroom door open. The bedside lamp is on, and all is exactly as she left it, pink and white and a little shabby. There's the photo-album on the shelf, the pencil in the desk-tidy with a bright pink feather at one end, the necklace hanging from the bedpost. It's as though her sixteen-year-old self has just popped out for a moment.

This is the room she shared with Ziad until the day of her tenth birthday. They would lie each evening in the darkness and chat until Ziad fell asleep. He was always the first to fall asleep, and she would listen to his breathing until she drifted off. It was that sound – his breath and the occasional movement of his head against the pillow – that lulled her to sleep. Standing here now, she feels like a trespasser.

In the shower, she lets the water soak warm through her hair; allows it to wash away the hurt that Ziad wasn't here to greet her, and swirl it down the plughole.

Water fills her ears. She closes her eyes. All that is left is the patter of drops on her head, heard through her skull. It sounds just like applause: the applause of her professors and fellow students a few months earlier after she played Rachmaninov's Prelude in G minor; or when, last November, she gave a Sunday morning recital of Beethoven's Tempest sonata at the Royal Albert Hall.

She moves. One ear unblocks, and she is back under the shower in her parents' house in Lebanon.

When she comes out of the bathroom, Mama is standing beside Baba's armchair. 'You're too hard on him.'

'And you're too soft.'

Ziad is still not back then. Irritation sparks in her, but the next moment she realizes that her parents are in the middle of a quarrel.

'How is he ever going to take over the pharmacy?'

Mama raises both hands high and lets them drop. 'Not this again! So he's not a gifted chemist, we all know that. Is that the end of the world?'

'No, but that's the business that's going to be handed down to him, Meerna. It's ready and waiting, and the boy doesn't even pretend to show any interest.' Baba takes off his glasses and, muttering to himself, starts to polish them with the hem of his pyjama top.

'Well, you can't push him,' says Mama. 'Look where it got you earlier: you insist he can't go out, he insists he will, and off he goes in a huff.'

Baba clamps his lips tight together, a gesture Layla

recalls well. Ever reluctant to upset Mama, he will not say any more now.

She steps into the dining room.

'He's never to be home after midnight, that's one of the rules,' says Baba.

Mama's looking at the clock on the wall. It's a quarter to one. 'What if he's fallen off that scooter of his? The way they ride those things … One way streets don't apply. Nor do helmets. They zigzag along the motorway with as many passengers as they can fit on. What if something's happened?' She tugs at the belt of her dressing gown.

Ziad e-mailed Layla a photo of the red scooter Baba had got him. It was old and nothing flash, bought so that Ziad could get to school and back without it taking him forever.

'I'm sure he's okay,' Layla says. 'He's probably just stuck in traffic.'

'At this time of night?' Mama shakes her head.

'Have you tried calling him?' asks Layla.

Mama shoots Baba an accusing look. 'I would, but he was in such a mood earlier, he forgot his mobile.'

'Well …' Layla twists up her damp hair and ties it back. 'Who was he going out with? Can't we call them?'

'That's true. He was going to Jacques' house, and I've got their home number—'

'You're going to call at this hour?' says Baba.

'Yes, Fadi, at this hour, when my son hasn't got his phone and I don't know where he is! Or should we wait up till dawn?'

'All right, all right.' Baba raises his hands, pacifying, and for a few moments silence falls as Layla's parents stare at each other, a silken web of things that have gone on in her absence hanging invisible between them.

Mama goes and takes an address book out of a drawer. 'Silly boy,' she murmurs as she dials. 'Where are you?'

Fleetingly, Layla wonders if her mother has been this worried about her for the last three years too. But she knows that in this respect things are different in Lebanon: if a young person here goes out at night, his or her whereabouts must always be accounted for. It is one of the many legacies of the civil war. With a sudden itch of worry, she cranes to look down the corridor, as if even now Ziad might emerge from his room.

Waiting for someone to pick up at the other end of the phone, Mama clears her throat, her features already arranged into an apology. When someone answers, she straightens up and uses her speaking-to-strangers voice.

'Hello, this is Ziad's mother. I'm so sorry to call this late, but—' She explains the situation. 'Oh, they have?' Her face relaxes. 'Right, I see. It's just that he left his mobile here, and you know how one worries.' She listens, a polite smile on her face, as if the person at the other end were right here in front of her. 'Yes, if you wouldn't mind. Sorry again to have woken you up. Thank you. Yes, goodbye.' She hangs up.

'Well?' Baba already looks relieved.

'They went out. They'll be back any minute, and Jacques' mother said he can stay over. It's too late for him to be driving his scooter back at this hour. She'll get him to call first thing in the morning.' She gives a tut. 'Typical teenager. Just doesn't think.'

Baba sits back in his armchair, gazing at Mama the way he has always done: as if she inhabits a rarer atmosphere.

'What's the matter, darling?' Mama asks Layla.

'Nothing.'

But Mama can see through her. 'Don't be angry with him.'

'I'm not angry. Only ... he hasn't seen me for three years, but he'd rather be out having fun with his friends. He's not even coming back tonight!' Is she making too big a deal of this? She wanted her family together. Wanted to start mending things between her and Ziad.

'He's growing, and trying to fit into his new skin, that's all,' says Mama. 'Anyway, you'll see him for yourself tomorrow morning. He's practically a man now.' Both pride and sadness infuse her smile.

Tomorrow morning. There will be no faint light leaking in around the brown university hall curtains, no shrill of an alarm-clock from the room next door, no tube journey to South Kensington or walk up Exhibition Road.

'But you look tired, darling, you should go to bed,' says Mama. 'I am.' She kisses Layla goodnight. 'Sleep well.'

Layla notices how soft Mama feels, and how distant. Both Mama and Ziad have always had that quality – the sense that a significant part of themselves, diaphanous and vulnerable, is beyond reach, utterly private and unknowable. Layla herself, on the other hand, is as hard-boiled as Baba.

'Goodnight, Mama.'

'I'll be there in a minute,' says Baba in the gentle voice he reserves for his wife, and watches her leave, in thrall as if even now he can't believe his luck: how a man who is all hard edges like him could have caught such a wondrous creature. Does he still sit and pretend to read his newspaper, never once turning the page, while Mama plays the piano, Layla wonders?

With a deep sigh, he pushes himself out of his armchair and begins to lock up and turn off the lights. 'I'm sorry Ziad isn't here. I know how much it means to you.'

She touches the piano, running her hand lightly over the keyboard. 'It's okay. I'll see him soon enough.'

At the dining-table, Baba gathers together a pile of receipts – the takings of the day from the pharmacy –

and paper-clips them together. 'Rana Hammoud came in today wanting some aspirin for her mother. You remember Mrs Hammoud, don't you?'

'Of course.' An elderly woman in widow's weeds with a walking stick.

'Well, she's got arthritis now, and asked her daughter to buy her some aspirin. Except that she's on blood-thinners too.'

'Warfarin?'

Baba nods.

'God, that could have killed her!'

'Yes, it could.' He gives a sudden laugh. 'Oh, but you're a pharmacist's daughter alright, Layla.' He gives her ponytail a gentle tug. 'God, how I've missed talking to you. You're still the only one in the family who I can—' Just as quickly as it appeared, the smile drops off his face, and she knows he is thinking about Ziad.

He goes into the kitchen, and Layla follows and stands in the doorway. He turns on the tap and runs some water into a glass. The light in here is harsh and bright, and this room, like the rest of the house, is the same as it was three years ago. There are the yellow-brown cupboards, the white tiles, even the same bunch of dried flowers hanging upside down from a nail hammered into the wall.

At one point, Layla had thought she would become a pharmacist too; science had always come easily to her. But then Mama wanted her to follow music.

'Why didn't you want me to go to London, Baba?'

The suddenness of the question startles him.

In the months and weeks before Layla left home, her parents had argued, Mama adamant that Layla should go and study in the UK, and Baba equally adamant that she should stay.

He heaves a sigh, as if this isn't the conversation he wanted to be having at this hour of the morning. Light glints off his glasses as he turns to face her. 'I didn't want to lose you.'

'Then ... why did you agree for me to go in the end?'

He drinks, then puts the glass in the sink with a sad smile. 'Because while I understood that if you went, I would lose you, it also became clear that if you didn't go, I would lose your mother.'

The room is still. The dim light softens Baba's face. There's a rush in her stomach – love, guilt, a clarity of understanding that is only possible after a long absence. But her parents, not together? It is impossible to comprehend such a thing.

'Every parent wants to make the things that were impossible for them possible for their children.' He looks up. 'Don't you see? She couldn't be a musician, but you can.' He comes over and touches her cheek. 'And you know how much that means to her.'

Yes, she knows. The weight of Mama's dreams has lain heavy on her shoulders since she was a child.

29

He embraces her. 'There, you go and get some sleep now.' They say goodnight and he heads off to bed.

On the kitchen wall, the dried bouquet – tiny yellow flowers in it, some stems of lavender that are no longer purple – looks dusty and brittle. As she turns out the light, Layla imagines crushing the whole thing to flakes in her hand.

Chapter Three

She opens her eyes and is a child again, with the summer light shining between the slats of the shutters. The next instant the years return, clicking into place. Sitting up in bed, she pushes the shutters open. The sun is rising and the hills are blue and hazy. There is a clank of goat bells, and further away, a truck's engine roars into life.

She lies back down, and gradually drifts back to sleep with Debussy's *Cathedrale Engloutie* playing in her head. She dreams of the sunken cathedral, watching as, to parallel fifth chords, it emerges from the ocean, barely visible through the mist. It is all there: the chanting of priests, the chime of bells, the faint playing of the organ; she realizes that the building, with its red facade and tower on either side, bears an uncanny resemblance to the Royal College of Music. Even as its true identity is revealed to her, the building begins to sink again. Soon the bells are muffled, the organ recedes beneath the waves, and the entire thing is gone.

When she wakes, the light has changed. She checks her phone. It's past ten o'clock.

In the kitchen, the radio is on and Mama is putting away dishes. 'Good morning.' She says, gives Layla a kiss. 'How did you sleep?'

'Really well, thanks.'

A man on the radio is talking about the intensifying artillery and air strikes on Gaza, and the Qassam rockets that have continued to fall in Israel since it withdrew from Gaza last September.

'Have you been keeping up with the news here?' Mama asks.

'Not really. Well, not at all actually. I know about the latest attack on Gaza, but that's about it. I don't get time to read the news.'

'Operation Summer Rains. In this part of the world where it never rains in summer. Quite the sense of humour.' Mama points at the table. 'I bought you some *knafeh*.'

Layla sits down and unwraps the paper. 'You shouldn't have bothered going to the bakery. I'd have been happy with anything.'

'Oh. There are Rice Krispies if you prefer.'

'No, no, this is great. Only, what I mean is, you don't need to look after me any more. You know that, right?' For the first time, she is an adult in her parents' house.

Mama shrugs. 'It's in the job description.' She waits,

smiling in anticipation of Layla's first mouthful.

When she bites into the *knafeh*, a shocking sweetness floods her mouth.

Mama's smile spreads. 'Good? It used to be your favourite.'

'Mmm.' Layla's taste buds are no longer used to a ring of sesame bread stuffed with soft cheese and syrup. Not first thing in the morning anyway.

'I know it's fattening, but it's a treat.' She hesitates. 'You know, darling, you have put on a bit of weight.'

Layla swallows. 'I know.' Is every single person she meets going to comment on it? She watches her mother measure coffee into a *rakweh* of boiling water on the hob. 'Is Baba at work?'

'Yes. But he'll be back for lunch.'

Until then, he will be standing behind the glass counter of the pharmacy, backed by shelves that rise all the way to the ceiling, each one lined end to end with medicines. Looking over his glasses, he will give a customer more information about his or her condition, advise them on the best course of action, and warn of any possible side effects of the medicine he is about to give them. He is as capable in there as a fish in water or a bird in air. It is his natural environment. His element.

Element, she thinks. *A chemical element is a basic substance made of atoms of one kind, that cannot be separated by chemical means into simpler substances.*

It cannot be changed. The atoms adhere to each other in an unchangeable, unbreakable union. A family of sorts.

Mama holds the coffee-pot to the flame, bringing it to the boil three times before she turns off the gas. Then she carries it to the table and pours coffee into two tiny cups.

'Did Ziad call?'

'Not yet. He's probably still asleep.'

The man on the radio cuts short what he is saying. *'Reports are just coming in that Hizballah has launched diversionary rocket attacks from Lebanese territory into Israel. Simultaneously, Hizballah fighters have attacked two armoured Humvees patrolling the Israeli side of the border fence, capturing two soldiers and killing three more.'* He sounds slightly panicked. *'We will bring you more information as we get it. In other news today, ...'*

Mama has stopped with the coffee-cup halfway to her lips.

'That didn't sound good,' says Layla.

Mama blinks and takes her sip of coffee. 'Oh, there's always something going on down there. It's a never-ending chit-chat between Israel and Hizballah across the border. Like boys taunting each other. Except it's people's lives they're playing with.'

'They don't usually capture Israeli soldiers, though, do they?' She feels stupid for asking, but she's been away from all this for so long.

'That's true. But maybe it wouldn't have happened if the corpses weren't piling up in Gaza, and the world watching in silence.'

Layla is taken aback. Mama has never spoken to her this way before. Then again, she has never sat in her mother's kitchen as a nineteen-year-old before either.

'Well, that's one point of view.' In London, she has met students from all over the world, including Israelis. 'If you'd been born in Israel, you'd think differently.'

Mama looks taken aback. 'Maybe. Maybe not.' For a moment there is silence, then Mama smiles again. 'Now tell me. Tell me everything about London.'

As Mama sips coffee, Layla answers questions about her meals, how she travels, and who lives in her halls. But most of all, Mama wants to know about music. The lectures, the pieces she is learning, the concerts she has been to and the pianos she practises on.

'You must be so good now,' says Mama.

Layla shrugs. It gives her no pleasure to know that she has surpassed her mother's abilities.

'What's it like,' Mama asks, 'to play a Steinway grand?'

'Oh, I don't know.'

But her mother continues to wait for an answer.

'I guess it feels like … like the ends of your fingers are singing.'

Mama's mouth twitches. On the windowsill, geraniums glow orange in the sun. Layla is about to tell her about the Royal Albert Hall, but the expression of longing on Mama's face stops her short.

Layla gets dressed. It's late, and by the time she goes back into the kitchen, Mama is already gathering ingredients, bowls, and a knife to prepare lunch.

'Can I help?'

'Oh, no, darling. Why don't you go and play me something? I can't wait to hear you.'

But Layla doesn't want to. 'Maybe later.'

'Oh.' Surprised. A little disappointed. 'Okay.' She puts some cloves of garlic onto a chopping board. 'Here, you could peel and crush those for me.'

Layla starts to peel. Soon scraps of torn garlic skin lie scattered on the chopping-board. 'Actually, Mama …'

Mama has started washing tomatoes in a plastic bowl full of water. 'Yes?'

'Actually I'm not doing as well as all that.'

'What?' Mama stops what she's doing.

'In my studies, I mean.'

In the bowl, the enormous tomatoes bob and jostle against each other. 'Why not? I don't understand. Why not?'

Through the oblong gap of the doorway, the piano is just visible, its silent presence judging her. 'It's hard work.'

Mama laughs. 'Of course it's hard work. Don't you know that everything worth having takes hard work? We all have to work harder than we'd like.'

Since Layla left, Mama has taken on bits and pieces of work wherever she can get it – doing people's accounts, giving piano lessons, tailoring – but even so, Layla has to waitress late into the night to earn extra cash. Life in London is expensive, and she needs to use public transport, buy course books, eat the odd piece of fresh fruit. It has taken her this long to save up enough money for the flight over here.

'But you,' continues Mama, 'you're strong. You've never found anything too hard.'

Sometimes it feels as if she's ripping herself in two, trying to study, practise and earn money without enough hours in the day to do any of it properly. And then the frustration of performing poorly in front of her teachers. Them thinking that that's the best she is capable of.

She rubs her forehead with the heel of her hand, leaving a trail of antiseptic garlic. 'Is it inconceivable that I'm just not as good as you think I am?'

'Yes, that *is* inconceivable. You have something special. A gift.'

'Oh Mama! What you have to understand is that here in Lebanon I might be something special, but over there, over there where every student is stuffed with talent, I'm ordinary.'

Mama steadies herself, as if the ground has moved beneath her feet. Then, slowly, she shakes her head. 'I don't believe that. And neither do they, or they wouldn't have given you a scholarship to cover all your tuition fees.'

She can't argue with that.

'It's such a chance, darling! And we've all sacrificed so much for you to be able to have it. Not just me and Baba, but you too. You can't mess it up. You can't!'

The door of Ziad's room is ajar. Ignoring the red and white STOP sign, she pushes it open. It's a typical teenager's room: the bed is barely made, the blanket pulled loosely over it; a pair of shoes lie discarded, one on top of the other, underneath; on the desk is a mess of schoolwork and a half-drunk bottle of water. Ziad has pinned pictures cut out of magazines onto a cork board above his bed: an ad for an X-Men film, the Andromeda galaxy, an astronaut on the moon. The little guitar he played briefly when he was younger sits on a high shelf. The furnishings are in blues and greens, Ziad's favourite colours.

He should have called by now, or else be here.

As if in response to her thoughts, she hears the key in the front door.

'Ziad.' She hurries out of the room and down the hallway.

'Hi, *habibti*.' Baba pushes the door shut behind him. 'What is it?'

'Nothing. I thought you were Ziad.'

'Ziad!' Baba scowls. 'Wait till I get hold of him!'

'Why? What's he done?'

Mama comes out of the kitchen, carrying a wooden spoon in one hand and wiping the other on her apron.

'He's only gone and emptied out my wallet. I found out now when I went into the shop for bread on my way home and saw that I hadn't a single lira!' As if to prove the fact, Baba takes his wallet out and opens it for them to see.

'I don't get it,' says Layla. 'Why would he have taken your money?'

'He asked for money to go out with his friends,' explains Mama, 'but Baba said no.'

'He must have done it when he went to fetch his shoes.' Baba takes off his jacket and hangs it on the back of a chair. 'He's become a complete tearaway. *Stealing* now!'

'He mustn't have been thinking,' says Layla. 'Or … or …' She doesn't know what to think.

Baba gives a quick smile. 'You always stand up for him. Always have done, ever since that day.'

They all know which day he means. The day when, in one swift instant, she had felt what it was like to be Ziad, and he had hated her for it.

'He's just going through a tricky patch.' Mama waves the wooden spoon like a conductor's baton as she talks. 'He wants to find something worthwhile to do, but he doesn't know what yet.'

'What could be more worthwhile than being a pharmacist, and helping people when they're ill?'

'Oh Baba!' Layla gives a little laugh.

'What?'

'To you, being a pharmacist is the perfect job. No other job can compete. Dispensing medicine, without the disagreeable bit of having to examine the patient.'

'And?'

But it's not the time to argue the point. 'I thought he was doing okay at school.'

Baba grunts. 'With the grades he's getting?'

'He passed his *Brevet* exams,' says Mama. 'Studied day and night for months, especially physics and chemistry; so hard he almost made himself ill.' She looks at Baba. 'That's how much he wanted to please you.'

All at once Layla feels like a stranger in her own family. She didn't know Ziad had struggled so hard for the *Brevet*. No one had told her.

'If he doesn't want to take over the pharmacy, then there has to be something else to fall back on,' says Baba. 'And in that case, he'll have to be ahead of his friends academically to get a decent job.'

Again, Layla is lost. 'Why?'

'His leg. Disabled people in this country—'

'Don't call him that!' snaps Mama.

Baba takes a levelling breath. 'All right. But it

doesn't change the fact that it'll be an obstacle when it comes to looking for work with a decent salary, and social and health benefits.'

'His leg will?' This has never occurred to Layla. When she left, neither she nor Ziad had been thinking about the job market. 'But that's ridiculous!'

Baba shrugs. 'Maybe. But as it is, half of the unemployed in this country are under twenty-five. Our young people are leaving in their droves.'

Mama tuts impatiently. 'We don't want to hear about the country's unemployment. I just wish you'd given him some money and told him to go out and enjoy himself.'

'Yes,' says Baba softly, 'because that's the way you are about him.' He doesn't need to say any more. Ziad is Mama's baby.

In pride of place on the middle bookshelf is a framed photograph of Baba and Mama on their wedding day. Baba's face is unlined, and Mama is smiling a big smile with that gap between her teeth. They are standing side by side, so close together that there isn't the slightest gap between them.

'So what if I'm a bit lenient?' says Mama. 'He deserves everything we can give him, doesn't he?'

'That's probably why he's turned out this way,' says Baba. 'We've indulged him. Whatever he's wanted, we've always given. He didn't take to the piano but he wanted to try the guitar, so he had guitar lessons. Well that didn't last. Then it was computer programming, so we bought him a computer. Then he needed extra lessons at school to pass his exams. Then he wanted a scooter.'

Mama turns on her heel and goes back into the kitchen. They follow. There's a smell of cooking chicken.

'But none of it has helped,' continues Baba, still in the flow. 'It's just like he said yesterday: he doesn't think his life is fair. He thinks that everything is against him. That Layla's had the better deal in life.'

'What?' She grabs onto the back of a chair. 'Did he say that? But that's not true!' How could Ziad think that having to leave her family and live alone in a foreign country was the better deal? Struggling to succeed for Mama's sake, when she would actually have been more than happy to stay here and join Baba in the pharmacy? If it hadn't been for the fact that Ziad, as the son, automatically earned that privilege?

But, looking from one of her parents to the other, she knows that she can never say any of this out loud.

Seated at the kitchen table, Baba eases off his shoes. 'That dog's hanging about outside again.' He takes a mouthful of garlic chicken and *tabbouleh*. 'I should get Mr Khayyat's son to shoot it.'

Mama looks up. 'You'll do no such thing!'

'You wouldn't, Baba!'

'Don't you know the diseases stray dogs carry? Parvovirus, distemper, mites, fleas. He might be rabid for all we know.'

'Except that he's not,' says Mama. 'He's friendly enough.'

'Fine, fine, if the two of you want a mangy, flea-ridden animal wandering about the place, have it your way.'

They eat in silence for a while. Layla hasn't tasted proper *tabbouleh* since she left home. The stuff they sell in London is all wrong: mainly bulghur wheat and hardly anything else.

'Ziad likes that dog,' says Mama at last. 'Wasn't he upset enough when the last one he befriended got run over? Stray animals don't last in this country,' she tells Layla, 'but this one … he turns up when Ziad's due home. Just sits there and waits.'

'That animal sits outside because Ziad pets it and feeds it,' says Baba.

'Ziad has a heart of velvet.' There's a little shake in Mama's voice. 'Which you'd know if you stopped picking on him long enough to notice.'

Baba chokes on a sip of water.

'Well you know you do! He eats too noisily. He doesn't do that fast enough and doesn't do this slow enough. Why isn't he getting better grades at school? Is it any wonder the boy doesn't want to be here!'

'Please, can you two stop arguing?' This is not the

43

way it was meant to be.

Her parents fall silent, and Layla runs through the telephone conversation she had a few minutes ago. Before they sat down to eat, she'd phoned Jacques' number. His mother picked up, but said that Ziad had left the flat early this morning. Layla stabs a piece of chicken onto her fork. He ought to be here by now. Beirut is less than an hour's drive away, hardly the ends of the earth.

Baba takes a mouthful of food and chews methodically. 'He'll be back in a bit. It's just a teenage upset. It'll last a day, and then he'll come back as if nothing ever happened. After all, where else does he have to go?'

Mama laughs bitterly. 'God, Fadi, you're such a realist! You have the measure of everything, don't you? A few milligrams of this, a few micrograms of that. You think you understand everything.'

Baba drags his hand through his hair. Order is what he prizes: cause and effect. 'He'll be back.'

'Maybe it's me he doesn't want to see,' says Layla. In spite of the quarrel with Baba, if Ziad had wanted to see her, wouldn't he have come straight home this morning?

'Of course he wants to see you,' says Mama. 'He's your brother. He loves you. He just feels badly about things.' She twists her wedding ring around her finger. 'We've had to … sell some things to make ends meet.'

An impact runs through Layla, as if Mama has slapped her. 'What things?'

'Your mother's sold some jewellery,' says Baba. 'I sold a silver box. Nothing important. Nothing that's going to change our lives.'

And then it dawns. Slowly. Horribly. 'Did you sell them so you could send me money?'

Mama studies her hands. Baba frowns at the chicken.

'It's not just that,' says Mama. 'The cost of living here has rocketed too. Rent, clothes, food – everything's so expensive now. People are struggling.'

Struggling? But in Beirut there are new gold-coloured buildings, a giant Rolex clock, gondolas floating in swimming pools.

'So Ziad was upset about you selling stuff?' Layla is suddenly aware of the edges of the chair against her legs, the oilcloth table-cover under her hand. He must blame her. He must think it's her fault that they have even less money than they should; that he can't go out and spend the way his friends do. 'Why didn't you tell me any of this?' She ought to have known. But it's like Baba has always said: you have to get right up close to something to understand it.

'He started going on about my father's watch yesterday,' says Baba.

'Wait, wait, wait. You're going to sell Jeddo's *watch?*' It was a wedding gift, and is Baba's most

45

prized, not to mention most valuable, possession.

'We were considering it, yes,' says Baba. 'But Ziad dug his heels in – we mustn't sell it, it's his inheritance ... He said we should sell the piano instead.'

Layla's breath catches. That piano pre-exists her. It is an object from another era, a signifier of her mother's previous life.

'But we couldn't sell it, *habibti*,' says Mama, 'we just couldn't. Some things ... well, some things are worth more than money.'

Over Baba's shoulder, Layla can see it: the shiny case, the eighty-eight keys she has often counted. But it is mute and still. Without anyone playing it, it is dead.

Baba frowns. 'You don't suppose—' He stops short. His chair scrapes back across the tiles and he goes out of the kitchen, heading down the corridor to their bedroom. A minute later he is back. 'He's taken it.' He pads across the kitchen floor in his socks. 'He's taken the watch.'

Mama bites her lip.

'Are you sure?' asks Layla. 'Maybe it's somewhere else.'

'No. It's gone.'

Mama sinks lower into her chair.

'This is the last straw, Meerna!' Baba thumps both palms down onto the table. 'I've had it with him! Money is one thing, but items of sentimental value ...'

Layla can hear Baba breathing in and out; can sense

the anger in that breath. He and Jeddo are no longer on speaking terms, and she suspects this is why the watch means so much to him.

'Well, if he thinks he can behave this way and then just come waltzing back in when it suits him, then he's got another think coming!'

'Calm down, Baba, before you give yourself a heart attack.'

'I don't want to see him, Meerna. He can keep the damned watch and stay out of my sight.'

'He's our son,' says Mama, as if that's the only explanation that will ever be needed for anything.

But Baba doesn't reply. He pushes his feet back into their shoes. He hasn't finished his lunch, but a moment later the door closes behind him. He is going back to the pharmacy to deal with soluble problems like boils and blocked sinuses, diarrhoea and head-lice.

Mama is holding onto her glass. It's about a third full, the water rounded into a hemisphere. She rotates the glass gently, and the water swirls round and round in its prison, given shape by the thing that holds it. Then she stops, tips the water out onto her plate, and gets up.

She is sitting at the piano. Her left arm is resting on the top of the instrument, and her head is resting on that arm. From where Layla is standing, only the top half of her mother is visible, as though she has been sliced clean through. It makes her remember the first time she ever saw Mama cut herself. Blood had poured out, red and bright. Of course, Layla had seen her own blood enough times after falls and scrapes, but it was a shock that her mother should also be filled with the same stuff; that her parent should be so horribly mortal.

With her right hand, Mama touches the keys, pressing them down so slowly that the hammer doesn't hit the strings hard enough to make any noise.

Some of Layla's earliest memories involve Mama shaping her hands over the keyboard and playing, her right foot moving up and down on the sustain pedal, light gleaming on her hair and shimmering on her wedding ring. There was no sheet music: Mama played from memory, a music that seemed to come from nowhere. Her face tightened, twitched, relaxed, and even as a toddler, Layla recognised that this Mama was different to the Mama who walked about the house. This mother's hands moved over the keys and spun worlds from nothing. She was here yet at the same time not here.

A couple of years later, sitting beside Layla, Mama would magic up accompaniments that made Layla's simplest one-fingered tunes sound pretty. Sometimes Ziad, still a crawling baby, would haul himself up, hold onto the keyboard and bang on the keys, bubbling with laughter. Mama would go and peel him a banana, then they would continue to play until he returned, sticky-fingered, to disturb them again.

Sitting at the piano now, Mama starts to strike the notes a little harder. Layla recognises the tune immediately. Bach's *Siciliana*, a piece she and Mama used to play in a duet arrangement. Even now, Layla still likes to start her practise hours with Bach. It puts everything in order somehow, cleanses both her mind and her hands.

She goes to the piano. Mama stops playing. Layla edges onto the piano stool and starts to play one half of the duet, wondering if Mama still remembers her part.

For a few moments, Mama's hands hover above the keys, finding the right notes. Then she joins Layla and they play, following the path of the beautiful, sad piece together. When it is done, Mama kisses Layla on the cheek, gives her shoulder a squeeze and gets up without a word.

Layla finds her lying curled up on her and Baba's bed. Sunlight filters through the half-drawn curtains, tinting the bedspread and walls orange, blue and pink. On the dressing table is a bunch of plastic flowers on a crocheted doily. On one side of it are Mama's hairbrush and bottle of perfume, on the other, Baba's comb, clothes-brush and aftershave. There, too, is a photograph of Baba, so proud, laughing and holding baby Ziad above his head as if he wanted the whole world to see.

Mama is lying facing away from Layla. '"If I could stop just one child from having to limp their way through life, that would be enough." That's what he says. But he'll never make a doctor. Or, at this rate, a pharmacist either.'

A lump rises in Layla's throat. 'He'll find his way. He'll find the thing that's right for him.'

'Golden Girl, he calls you.'

One day when she called home, a stranger answered. It was Ziad, but his voice had broken, and it sounded as if an entirely different person was talking down the phone to her. She hears that voice now calling her 'Golden Girl' – the talented one, the lucky one. Hears the bitterness in it.

'And now even you're struggling with your studies,' says Mama.

Leaning against the handle of the dresser drawer, Layla pushes her hip into it. The pain is somehow comforting. 'Sorry.'

Mama sits up. 'No. Don't you dare say you're sorry. I didn't mean that it's your fault. We're not able to send you enough money, so you have to work. If anyone, it's us who ought to be sorry.' She takes a deep breath. 'But you'll make it work, Layla, I know you will.'

And there it is again: the obligation, the full bloody weight of someone else's unfulfilled life bearing down on her.

'In this country, you wouldn't be able to make a

living out of music. The best you could hope for is to be a piano teacher. If you want to be anything more than that, you'll have to do it abroad.'

'But this is my home. This is where you all are. I don't want to have to be away from you forever.'

Mama gets up and comes over. 'Don't you understand, darling? The day you left, your life opened up. We were left behind. And that's just the way it is.' She says it so simply. To Layla, though, it is anything but simple.

Layla has an alternative life, one in which she never left Lebanon. Instead she stayed here with her parents and brother. She was close to Ziad – went to the same school, shared stories in the evening, made fun of the same teachers. In that life, they are all happier than they are in this one.

Mama touches the photo of Baba with Ziad. 'He's such a sensitive boy,' she murmurs. And she ought to know, because he is like her – delicate, sensitive, someone to be protected. Together, they are like gazelles at a watering-hole. 'Where is he, ha? Where is he? If he left Jacques' house early this morning the way the mother said, then he ought to have been here hours ago.' A moment later, her face crumples and she presses a hand to her mouth, as if preventing words from falling onto the floor and smashing into little pieces.

'Hey.' Layla puts an arm around her shoulders. 'It's

okay. Don't cry.' It feels strange that she should be comforting her mother. She isn't sure she likes this reversal in their relationship. 'Ziad, Baba, me – it'll all be fine.'

But Mama just carries on pressing her hand to her mouth. The curtains bloat in the breeze, and the two of them stand adrift in a sea of diamond-shaped colours.

Chapter Four

'Right.' Layla takes the keys from a bowl in the living room. 'Are you sure Baba won't need the car today?'

'He hardly ever uses it,' says Mama. 'He prefers to walk everywhere.'

'He's going to get in a mood about me going, isn't he?'

'He can get in a mood or not, I hardly care. Ziad's my son too, isn't he? And your brother. Thank you, *habibti*, for going. You know I'd come too if I wasn't up to my eyeballs in work. There's a load of accounts I need to get done by tomorrow morning, and—'

'It's okay, Mama.' Floating in the broken colours of Mama's room, Layla said she would drive down to Jacques' flat in Beirut to find out where Ziad had got to. As she'd hoped they would, the words lifted Mama out of her slump. Of course, in all likelihood Ziad will be back home before her, but it will give her something positive to do in the meantime. And it's got to be better than sitting at home watching Mama be all tragic.

'Have you got your phone, darling?'

Layla checks her pockets for mobile and purse, feeling like a child again. 'Yes.'

Together, they walk out into the mirror-bright day. It is already hot. Two floors up, Mrs Najjar is sitting on her balcony in a dressing-gown with a pot of coffee and a cigarette. She waves. 'Welcome home!' she calls down. 'We've missed you. *Smallah*, how you've grown.'

Layla smiles and waves back. 'I'll come and see you tomorrow.'

'Good. I want to hear all the details.'

They walk to Baba's car. 'Be careful, won't you,' says Mama. 'You know they drive like maniacs here.'

'I will. And I'll see you this evening, okay?'

Mama gives a watery smile. Then she spots something behind Layla. 'Look.'

A little way off, a large dog, white with a splatter of tan, is sitting looking along the road, alert, as if it's waiting for something or someone. It has a long tail and hanging jowls.

'Is that the one Baba was talking about?'

'Yes, that's the one.'

As if they have called it over, the dog gets up and lollops towards them. It heads for Mama first, but she waves her arms – 'No no no. Go away.' – so it swerves round and comes up to Layla instead. It sniffs her, its nose leaving a cool wet streak on her arm.

She steps back. 'Does he bite?'

'No, but … well, at the very least he must have fleas. Go on!' Mama tries to shoo him away again, but the dog doesn't move, looking up at Layla; his whip-thin tail waves slowly from side to side and he whines, a painful metallic sound.

'I haven't got any food, if that's what you're thinking.'

He doesn't look vicious, and on an impulse, she puts out a hand and strokes him.

Mama tuts disapprovingly.

The dog sits down and starts to scratch behind its ear with a hind leg.

'See?' says Mama. 'Like I said: fleas. Anyway, you'd better go, darling, before he gets attached to you too.'

'Right.' Layla gives her mother a hug, unlocks Baba's old Renault and slides in.

The dog puts his head into the car. He puts a paw on the front seat.

'Go on!' Mama pushes him back and closes the door. 'Get away!'

Layla winds down the windows. 'Phone me if Ziad comes home.'

'Of course.'

She starts the engine and pulls away. In the side mirror, she sees the dog walking beside the car. She goes into second gear, then checks her side mirror again. The dog is still there. Third gear. In the rear-view mirror, Mama is shrinking. But in the side mirror …

She stops the car and pulls the handbrake. Gets out. Opens a back door. 'Go on, get in then, if that's what you want.'

The dog doesn't seem to know how to get into a car. With a scraping and scrabbling, he topples in, half on the floor and half on the seat.

'Layla!' Alarm is packed into Mama's voice. 'Layla!' It's all there in that one word: Baba's car, that stray animal; have you lost her wits? Baba will be furious. And anyway, what do you think you're going to do with that dog in Beirut?

One quick glance back, and she gets in and drives away, turns the corner, and Mama's flailing figure is gone.

'Oh why in hell shouldn't I?' she says to the dog. 'You want to know where he is too, don't you? I'll sort it out with Baba when I get back.'

The dog scrambles about in the back from one side to the other, then tries to clamber up into the front with her.

'Oh God.' Perhaps taking him was a moment of madness after all. 'Stop that!'

He retreats.

'It's only a car. A. Car. Okay?'

Panting, he sticks his head out of the window.

'Hey!' The car swerves a little. Is he going to jump out? 'Hey!'

But he doesn't jump out. In the side mirror, she sees

his head – nose up, mouth open, ears flapping, and eyes closed in pleasure.

Standing in the doorway of the jeweller's, the shop-owner stares as she drives by.

She laughs. 'You'd better not have fleas. And you'd better not scratch up Baba's seats. Or pee. Or ...' She takes a deep breath. He'd better not shit in the car.

Baba's Renault is as neat as it ever was. A blue bead and medallion of Saint Maron hang from the rear-view mirror. A box of tissues sits slotted behind the handbrake, as if the manufacturer had designed it especially. All is clean and pristine, except for the large stray dog in the back seat.

Dog's tongue is hanging out, flying sideways in the wind. The sight of him makes Layla smile again, and as they leave town the stress of the day begins to ebb.

They start the descent to Beirut. As the car rounds a bend, a little girl waves goodbye to her. It's as if the child knows something she doesn't, thinks Layla, then pushes the thought away. She tries to remember what Jacques looks like, but all she can see is Ziad, happy, smooth-faced, his big eyes pulled down slightly at the outer corners, making him look as if he's asked a question and is waiting for the answer. Floppy brown hair that refuses to stay combed flat. His narrow face and slender body.

She drives on, trying to ignore the niggle of worry. She's certain there will be a perfectly sensible, even banal explanation for his absence. Perhaps he's gone to the cinema. Or he might be sitting with a friend beneath the palm trees on the Corniche promenade, watching the waves. Yet the further she gets from home, the more Ziad takes over her thoughts – his up-and-down gait, his sudden laughter. Memories scroll through her mind, and he is always there, embedded in each one.

A car overtakes her. A truck is coming towards them. The car speeds up and narrowly misses the truck.

Layla slams on the brakes. 'Idiot!' she screams. She doesn't want to look at what Dog's nails have done to the back seat as he tried not to fall over. Slowly, she pulls away again. A car coming up behind her honks its horn. The driver waves his arm and overtakes her, mouthing something as he passes.

'Oh piss off!' she calls, then bursts into laughter. 'Yes, I'm back in Lebanon all right.' There were things she had never seen before she arrived in London: ducks, a rainbow, body piercings, a baby bird dead on the pavement, grown-ups riding bicycles, a blue-tit, carriage clocks. But in London, she never once saw driving like this.

The roads of Beirut are clogged with cars. There are few street markings or pavements, and no suggestion of safe driving. Hardly anyone is walking. 'It's not done, is it, Dog? I mean, why walk when you can drive?' Except for Baba, she thinks. Baba doesn't care about what people think.

She passes the Sunday market-place and, using the address memorised from Mama's phone-book, heads into Ashrafieh. Twice she has to stop to ask where the road is, but finally she turns into a narrow street with cars parked up on the pavements and electric cables strung between the buildings. The block of flats she is looking for is brown, with two enormous pots of frothing petunias on either side of the doorway. She parks in the shade, leaves Dog in the car with the windows half open, and scans the list of names on the buzzers. There it is, right at the top: Haddad.

She presses the intercom. A few moments later there's a screech and buzz of static as someone picks up. 'Hello?' A boy.

'Hi. Is that Jacques?'

'Yeah.'

'I'm Layla, Ziad's sister. Can I have a quick word? It won't take long.'

Silence. Layla wonders if he has heard her. Then the door buzzes open.

The entrance hall is dark. The electricity has cut out – she can hear the growl of a generator – and there's not enough power to work the lift, so she takes the stairs. On each landing, she presses a button that turns on a light, until she reaches the fifth floor. Here there's a small window where the stairs end, and a miniature view of Beirut: blocks of flats, the odd red roof, a few trees, then the sea.

She heads down the corridor and finds the right

door, but before she can knock, it opens. A fat, curly-haired boy is standing in front of her. He has on baggy shorts, and a T-shirt with a picture on it of a baseball player pitching a ball.

'Hi.' Layla smiles. She vaguely remembers Jacques from school, although he wasn't this soft-looking and glum back then. 'Do you remember me?'

'Yeah,' he says. 'Of course.'

'How are you?'

'I'm good.' He holds the door open and she squeezes past.

Inside, the flat is big and airy, with vases and floral curtains, a peach-coloured sofa and a large TV. Cut glass glints from a dresser. The living room smells of air-fresheners. One side leads to the kitchen, the other to the dining room, and beyond that, presumably, to the bedrooms.

'Isn't your mother home?'

'No, she went out.' Jacques slouches against the back of a peach-coloured armchair, not meeting her eye. His mother would have assessed Layla in a single sweep of the eye. She would have ushered her in, made her sit down, offered her something to drink and eat. This is a must. It is obligatory.

'And how is your mother?'

Jacques gives the back of the armchair little kicks with his bare feet. 'Fine.' He stops kicking. 'You called this morning, didn't you?'

'Yes, I wanted to speak to Ziad. He left his phone at home, and— Look, do you know where he is?'

'Nope.' Jacques shrugs. 'He left.'

'Yes, I know that, but did he say where he was going?' She wishes he would look at her.

'No, he didn't say.'

God, is Ziad really friends with this sullen boy? She must have a word with him about it later.

'Has he got any other friends around here?'

'No. I don't know. Anyway, why are you asking me all these questions?' The hairline near Jacques' dark curls is damp. His frown deepens and he gives the armchair one last kick.

'He's all right, isn't he?'

He darts a look at her.

'He'd had a bit of an argument with our dad – he probably told you – and—'

'I don't know anything about that.' Jacques stands upright and takes a step towards her, as if that might hurry her out. 'Okay?'

'Hey, I just want to know where my brother is.' She's beginning to feel that something isn't right. 'Did something happen? Did you ... I don't know, did you fall out or something?'

'No, nothing happened, okay? He came over, but he's not here now and I don't know where he is.' He doesn't say 'and I don't care,' but it hangs in the air nonetheless.

'All right. Okay then.' She thanks him and lets herself out, pulling the door closed behind her.

In the hallway, she stops and takes a couple of deep, air-freshener-free breaths. Now what?

She checks her mobile just in case, but there are no texts or missed calls. As she starts down the corridor, footsteps sound on the stairs and a boy appears on the landing. He's about her age, tall and slim in a red T-shirt, jeans and trainers.

'Hello,' he says as he passes. A nice voice. Grainy. Skin dark from the sun. And for some reason, she's suddenly aware of every one of those twenty pounds she's put on.

At the end of the corridor she stops and turns. The boy is outside the Haddad's flat. He's taking a key from his pocket and is about to open the door when he sees her watching.

'Can I help you?'

'No. Only … um … I was just in there.'

'In here?'

She nods.

'You're not a friend of Jacques', are you?'

'No. My brother is, though. Ziad.'

'Oh, right.' He smiles.

'Do you know him?'

'Sure, I know Ziad. He's a nice guy.'

Is there pity in that remark? Or condescension?

'So you're his sister.'

'That's right.'

He comes back and stretches out his hand. 'I'm Joe. I'm Jacques' brother.'

His hand is warm. A firm grip. Brother? She barely even remembers Jacques having a brother. 'You don't look much like him,' she says, half to herself. No, there's nothing pasty about this one. He is lean and brown and long-limbed.

'You don't look like your brother either,' he says, which is also true. She has darker eyes than Ziad's, a wide face, black hair. He twists the key in his hand. 'I don't actually live here, you know.'

'No?'

'I'm at the AUB. I spend the week on campus, then come home for the weekend. I'm just passing by today to pick up some clothes.'

Laundry, he means. A Lebanese man wouldn't want to be doing anything as girlie as laundry himself. 'Right.'

They stand in silence for a while.

'Look, er, do you want to come back inside?'

'I don't think your brother's too keen to talk to me any more.'

Joe frowns. 'What do you mean?'

'I just wanted to know if he had any idea where Ziad might be. He spent last night here, you see, and Jacques—'

'Jacques what?'

63

'Well, I wonder if there's something he wasn't telling me. I mean, I don't *know*, it's just a feeling, but ...' She shrugs.

Joe stares at her for a few moments, frowning. Then he goes back to the door and puts the key in the lock. 'Come on in. If Jacques knows anything, I'll get it out of him.'

She follows Joe inside. Somehow the flat looks different, as if in the few minutes that they've been standing in the hallway talking, it has shrunk, and its colours intensified.

'Jacques!' Joe pushes the door shut with his foot. 'Hey, where are you?'

Layla stays by the door. There's a sound from the kitchen, and Jacques comes out. He's eating, holding the last of some bread between thumb and forefinger. There's what looks like jam on one side of his mouth. He smiles when he sees Joe, and she can tell from that one look that they have a good relationship. Then he sees Layla and the smile freezes, then slowly retracts. He looks from Layla to Joe and back again. 'I thought you'd gone.'

'Don't be so rude,' says Joe. 'And it seems she hasn't gone.'

'We already spoke.'

'Yes, but you know what? She's still looking for her brother.' He turns to Layla. 'Come in, come in, please. Have a seat.'

But Layla shakes her head. She prefers to stand.

Jacques shoves the last of the bread and jam into his mouth and licks his fingers. His face turns mulish. 'I already told her: I don't know where he is.'

'Fine,' says Joe. 'Now tell me.'

Jacques laughs. 'Tell you what?'

'Look, it's fine,' says Layla. 'Ziad's probably home by now.' Mama hasn't called, but she doesn't want to cause problems between the brothers. 'I'll just go.'

'No, wait,' says Joe. 'It's okay. I just want to hear what he has to say, that's all.' He goes to Jacques and puts an arm around his shoulders; draws him into the room. 'You and Ziad are friends. And he was here yesterday, right?'

Jacques wriggles free. 'And?'

Standing side by side, Layla can see a similarity in their noses and the squareness of their chins, but that's all. One is tall and dark with a posture like a soldier's, the other short, wide and altogether doughy. 'We're just asking: do you know where he went?'

'I already said, I don't know.'

'Okay. Tell us what happened last night then,' says Joe.

'Not much. We went out. Had fun. Came home.'

Joe faces his brother. 'Is there something you're not saying?'

'No!'

Joe lowers his chin, as if he is talking to a child. 'Really?'

Jacques laughs. 'What is this? An interrogation? I mean, why wouldn't I say?' For a few seconds, Jacques stares at his older brother. Layla can almost see the thoughts flashing through his head. 'Anyway,' he says, 'Ziad's sixteen. He wouldn't want his sister interfering in his business.'

'Interfering!' cries Layla. 'I want to see my brother. Is that interfering?'

But Jacques doesn't even look at her.

'What business?' asks Joe calmly. 'What is there for her to interfere with?'

Jacques squirms, looking down at his feet.

'Well?' presses Joe. 'Go on, tell us.'

It's a while before Jacques speaks. When he does, it is slow and hesitant, as if he is treading on new ground. 'A ... a bunch of us were going out last night to have some food and go to this club, that's all. It was all arranged.'

'And?' says Joe. 'What happened?'

'I'm about ready to leave, and then ... then Ziad turns up.' He shoots a quick look at Layla.

'Weren't you expecting him?' she asks.

'No.'

She feels a stab of pity for her brother. 'Did he go with you?'

Jacques wets his lips and nods.

'Right,' says Joe. 'Okay. Then what?'

Jacques looks hot, uncomfortable. He wipes a

crumb from his cheek with the back of his hand.

'So?' Joe takes the smallest step towards him.

With that movement, something cracks and gives way. 'No one wanted him there, okay?' he says loudly, as if it's a relief to get it out. 'And that's the truth! We were going to a club.' He is belligerent now, self-righteous. 'We wanted to look cool and ... and you know, girls don't like that sort of thing.'

Layla turns cold. Girls. Sex. All at once she sees a whole new set of disappointments laid out for Ziad. 'What did you say to him?'

Jacques shrugs.

'What did you *say*?' she repeats.

'Nothing that wasn't obvious! You know ...'

'No, I don't know.'

Jacques puffs out a breath. 'A night club's just not the place for him, is it? I mean, dancing's not exactly his strong point.'

Layla comes forward, right up to the edge of the rug Jacques' standing on. Somehow, though, she doesn't want to step onto it. 'You didn't want to be seen with him, did you?' Her muscles are tight with anger. 'You thought he'd ruin your image. That's it, isn't it? So you turned him away.'

'So what if we did?' Jacques' face smooths out in defiance.

Until this moment, she'd thought all of that was over, that Ziad had left the taunts and name-calling and narrow-mindedness behind him in the land of childhood.

'We didn't say anything he doesn't already know,' says Jacques.

She wants to punch that fat face of his. But what good would it do? Because once again, she's too late. Just like she was one day years ago, when a similar scene played itself out.

Joe tugs at his T-shirt in an embarrassed way. He is looking at his brother in disgust. 'You're a total idiot, you know that?'

'I didn't know he was going to get that upset about it, did I?'

'How did you *think* he'd feel?' Joe gives Jacques a short, sharp push.

'Hey!' Jacques shoves him back, but Joe is already braced for it and the push has little impact. 'It's not my job to look after him, okay?'

Joe steps forward, forcing his brother back until his legs are up against the glass T.V. table.

'I didn't know he was going to head out and not go home.' He slides sideways until he is clear of the table, and of his brother. 'Anyway ... anyway, maybe he should toughen up.'

Joe raises his palm up. 'Stop! Shut up, all right? Just shut up. Whatever it is you're thinking, keep it inside your stupid head, because no one wants to hear it!' He goes to the French windows and stares out past the balcony at Beirut. On the dresser, a clock ticks, each second precise and brittle.

Layla tries to calm herself. 'Where did he sleep? I mean, there must be some other friends he stayed with.'

'No, they were all there last night.'

'Yeah right. Friends.' She takes a deep breath. 'What time did he leave?'

'I don't know. Ten-thirty, eleven maybe.'

'Which club was it? Had he been drinking?'

'No. Look, we'd barely got there. He got worked up and left. He didn't stop to give us the details. Anyway, what's all the fuss about?'

Layla glares as if she could burn him up with her eyes. Beirut in the middle of the night, an hour away from home, after you've argued with your father and walked out with his money and watch, then been crushed by your friends; when you're disabled and as unhappy as Ziad has been, and when there's the precedent of what happened eight years ago.

She is about to say something to this effect when a key sounds in the lock. The front door opens and a woman carrying a bag of shopping is there, trying to tug her key back out of the lock. She has shoulder-length red-tinted hair, and is wearing a brown skirt and orange blouse. She starts when she sees Layla. Then her eyes sweep across to Joe and Jacques.

'Hello,' she smiles, glancing from one to the other, feeling the mood, trying to gauge what is going on.

'Hi Mama,' says Joe.

Layla tries to look normal but knows that she does not. Her face is tense, her stance awkward. Joe introduces her.

'Oh, of course, of course,' says his mother warmly. 'I knew your face was familiar.' She pulls the key out of the lock and shuts the door. 'Did your brother get home all right?'

Layla isn't sure what to say. 'Well, actually, we were just talking about that.'

The boys' mother puts down her shopping bag. She looks confused. 'Joe?'

Briefly, Joe explains.

'No, no,' she says. 'You're wrong. I heard them come in last night. That is, I was in bed, but I heard the door. And Ziad left this morning. Didn't he, love?' she says to Jacques.

Jacques goes to the window and pretends to look out.

'Jacques? That's what you told me: that he left early. Isn't that right, *habibi*?'

'*I* came back last night.'

'What?'

Jacques mumbles something.

'What was that?' asks his mother.

He turns around. 'I said, Ziad didn't come back with me.'

'You *lied* to me?'

He says nothing, and glances at Layla, flushed with shame. Here he is getting told off by his mother in front of a stranger, and a girl at that.

The mother gives Layla a quick, embarrassed smile. Then, to Jacques: 'Do you want to tell us where he went then?'

Jacques frowns, pressing his knuckles into his cheek.

'*Jacques?*'

He looks up, angry. 'It's your fault! Pushing and pushing, when it was clear I didn't want him to come with me!'

'What?'

'I didn't want him there. None of us did! So when we got to the club, he got upset and left.'

His mother stares, blinking. Jacques stares stubbornly back.

'It's alright, Mama,' says Joe. 'Ziad will turn up. I'm sure he's fine.'

Her hand goes to her mouth. 'But it was late. He was in my house – in my care.'

'Are you sure he didn't mention somewhere he might go?' Layla asks Jacques.

'No.'

'Maybe he spoke to someone before he left?'

Jacques starts to look annoyed.

'All right, all right,' says his mother. 'If he doesn't know, he doesn't know.' She steps between Layla and Jacques. 'Look, I'm sorry about what happened yesterday, I am, but you know, your brother's probably fine, and ...' Her face turns a shade harder. In spite of his lie, she is going to protect her son. 'Jacques doesn't know anything more.'

For five ticks of the clock, they stand face to face. Then Layla gives a nod and starts towards the door. Her throat feels tight, her cheeks flushed. She opens the door and steps into the hall.

'Wait.' Joe's voice.

'Don't, love,' says his mother. 'You don't have to.'

But Joe is coming out after her. 'Wait.'

'Joe,' calls his mother. 'Come back!'

Chapter Five

She's already in the car when he comes out, and watches him appraisingly: his jeans and red T-shirt, the designer logos visible on both (knock-offs are easy to come by here); his inch-short black hair, glossy as a Labrador's; his tanned face. Like most young Lebanese men, he is groomed to within an inch of his life.

She heard a little more of the exchange he had with his mother in the hallway. He said he wanted to help Layla, that it was their responsibility for treating her brother – their visitor – so disgracefully. His mother dug in her heels, was still reluctant for him to go, but he followed Layla out anyway. Now he's standing here looking panic-stricken as Dog pokes his head out of the rear window.

'I don't actually need your help, okay?' she says, still simmering with fury. 'I mean, don't feel obligated. It wasn't your fault.'

'No, but it was my brother's.'

She lets out a laugh. 'And family's family. The actions of one speak for the actions of all, right?'

'That's right. Anyway, I *want* to help.'

She grips the steering wheel. 'Fine.' If he wants to make up for his brother's behaviour, then why should she stop him? What does he think he's going to do anyway, when she doesn't have a clue herself? Still … 'Well? Are you going to get in?'

He's eyeing Dog. 'Is he safe?'

'Who, Dog? Of course he's safe.'

'Doesn't he have a name?'

'He's a stray. You want me to give him a name?'

Joe's mouth sags open. 'You've got a stray dog in your car?'

'In my father's car. What, you wouldn't have one in yours?'

'I don't have a car.'

He has caught her off guard. 'Really?' She hardly knows anyone here who doesn't drive. Someone his age would be driving a fashionable car too or, if not, then he'd certainly be boasting about the one he's planning to buy next week or next month.

'Well, he probably needs to do his business by now, so if you're not going to get in …'

Gingerly, Joe opens the door and climbs in. When Dog sniffs the back of his ear, he shies away.

'He won't eat you.' Layla starts the engine. 'Although having said that, I haven't actually fed him.' Perhaps she ought to let him loose on Jacques.

'Where are you going to take him?'

'I'm not sure.' How should she know where to take a dog to relieve itself around here? Not many people keep pet dogs, let alone take them for walks.

'I know somewhere. It's not far.'

She starts the engine. She wants to get going and leave this block of flats as soon as possible. Plus it's hot, and Baba's car has no air conditioning. The sooner they get moving, the sooner they can get a breeze going. She puts the car into gear and lurches off the pavement.

'Take a left here.'

She takes the corner too fast.

'Calm down, okay?'

She touches the brake.

'There's a park not far from here.'

'A park? What park? There aren't any parks in Beirut.'

He hesitates only for a second. 'There's the Garden of Forgiveness, Gibran Khalil Gibran Garden, the Capuchins Garden, Leila Osseiran Garden, Saint Nicholas Garden—'

'Whoa, stop, stop. How do you know all that?'

'I live here. And I remember things.'

'Right.' But not everyone remembers so much, and in such detail. Or is it just that she has been away so long, she doesn't know her own country?

'Technically, of course, those places aren't parks, just little drops of green. The only real park here Horsh Beirut.'

'Horsh Beirut? Why haven't I heard of it?'

'Because it's closed to the public.'

'The only park in the city is closed to the public?'

'It's on the southern side. Maybe they're afraid there'll be trouble if people of different sects mingle together too much. Take a right turn here.'

She wishes she had known that. She should have known it. As she veers around the corner, she takes another look at Joe. He might be odd, but he has a good face. This close, she can see his black eyes and thick lashes, and a scar on his neck, a tiny pale curve on the dark skin. He has a faintly sweet scent too. Honey. Cinnamon. The brief tang of an envelope before it is sealed.

'It's here,' he says. 'Just park where you can.'

She slows down and reverses in between two cars.

'You know,' says Joe, 'actually I'm not entirely sure about this.' He glances back at Dog. 'I mean, have you got a lead for him or anything?'

'A lead. I told you, he's a stray.'

'It's just, you know what people are like about dogs.'

'He's fine. He's not going to hurt anyone. Anyway, we're only stopping long enough for him to stretch his legs, and then ...' Then what? What will she do? How is she going to find Ziad now?

She gets out and opens the back door. Dog jumps down and shakes himself, head through to tail. He sniffs the back tyre of the car, then cocks his leg and pees on it.

'Baba's going to love that. Right, you stay close to me, okay?'

They follow Joe into a small green space hedged in by mid-rise buildings. Well, "park" is certainly rather generous, she thinks, but at least there's grass. There are shrubs and trees, benches too. She can even see a litter bin. A sign says 'Jardin des Jesuites.' She never knew this existed. She really might as well be a tourist.

Dog lollops past them as Joe points at two large buildings on either side of the gardens. 'Look. One, two hospitals. Just in case he does try to eat me.'

He's only trying to lighten her mood, but she still doesn't feel like smiling.

There are a dozen or so people in the park, which includes a small children's play area. She can barely believe it, it's such a rarity. Lebanese children don't have the luxury of parks and playgrounds. It was a shock to see so many parks in London; to see children running and people jogging after work.

Dog leaps onto some low stone tiers, wanders across the tufts of grass and cocks his leg against a palm tree. Then he jumps down and trots towards an elderly woman on a bench beneath a cypress tree. She's reading a newspaper and eating a sandwich half wrapped in foil. When she looks up, her face widens in terror. She scrambles up and retreats behind the bench.

'*Ya Allah*, now they're bringing giant dogs in here to gobble up old ladies!' She waves her newspaper at Dog as if it were a flaming torch. 'Get away!' But Dog remains put, his nose raised to catch a whiff of her food. 'I don't taste good. I'm nothing but a bunch of aching bones!'

'It's all right, he's friendly,' calls Layla. Hurrying over, she strokes him. 'He won't hurt you. See?'

'Won't hurt me! Another minute and I'd have been tomorrow's headline.'

'Oh for God's sake!' It's all too aggravating. 'Look, he really wasn't going to hurt you, okay?' And Layla steers him away back towards Joe, who has settled himself on a bench in the sun. 'Something funny?'

'No, no, nothing.'

'What are you smiling about then?' Although it's more that he is trying *not* to smile.

'Oh, it's just that you – you and the dog – you both go around gobbling up old ladies.'

'What do you mean?'

'Do you always speak your mind?'

'Why? Shouldn't I?'

He tries to shrug it off.

'Well accept my most sincere apologies for having thoughts in my head!'

He slides along the bench away from Dog. 'Sit down?'

'No thanks.'

Dog rubs his face in the dust, first one side then the other, and flops down with a whiny yawn. He stretches out, twitches a hind leg and closes his eyes against the sun.

A woman, her two children and a South Asian maid come into the park and head towards the playground.

'I've got a joke about maids.' Joe thinks a for moment. 'Yes. A Saudi man falls in love with a Sri Lankan woman and takes her back home. She steps off the plane and what does she see? All around her, there's nothing but desert. So she looks at the man. "If you think I'm sweeping all of that up, you've got another think coming!"' Joe waits. 'Okay, it's not the greatest joke.'

She squats down to pet Dog. She can't be bothered to have a conversation about political correctness. Anyway, he's just trying to be nice. 'You don't have to make me laugh.'

'I'm not trying to make you laugh. I'm just trying to make you slightly less pissed off.'

'Well how am I not meant to feel when I hear how your brother and his stupid friends have behaved?' Anger bubbles up fresh inside her, and she wants to drive back to the flat, grab Jacques and shake him till his curls fall off.

'I'm sorry.' Joe looks sorry, he really does, but it doesn't make her feel any better.

She straightens up. 'How could they be so thoughtless?

He was already upset. Couldn't they see that he needed his friends to actually be friends? God, I've got to find him.'

'Why was he already upset?' asks Joe.

'What?' She'd forgotten that he doesn't know. 'Oh. He had a quarrel with my dad.'

'Right.'

'It's not Baba's fault or anything.'

'I wasn't thinking that.' Joe's inky hair is unbelievably shiny in the sun. Does he use gel on it, she wonders, and spend ages in front of the mirror getting it just right? Or is this just the way it is?

'Jacques' an idiot sometimes,' he says.

She is not going to deny this evident truth. 'Ziad doesn't usually mind – you know, when people look at his leg. He's got used to it. Although … maybe that's changed.' She thinks about what Mama said, that Ziad would give anything to prevent just one child from having to limp their whole life. So maybe he does mind about it more than he used to. 'Still,' she says, 'looking at his leg is one thing, but saying stuff and acting on it – that's different. And when it's someone close to you …' She remembers fighting over a toy; pushing Ziad, and him, freshly landed on his bottom, unable to get to his feet again.

'Are your parents worried?'

'My mum always worries. Baba's more pragmatic.' Should she call Mama and tell her what's happened? No, better actually finds Ziad first.

'What about you? I mean, you seem really ... do you think you're worrying too much about him?'

Finally, she sits down. Across the way, the old lady Dog bothered earlier has gone. Only the scrunched-up aluminium foil from her sandwich is left, a spiny silver ball tossed to the ground. 'You don't understand.'

'What don't I understand?'

'The quarrel. Baba really lost it with Ziad.' Briefly, she explains about the money and the watch. 'And also ... well, there are things that happened a long time ago.'

'What things?'

Traffic rumbles in the roads around them. In the hedge at their backs, a sparrow is twittering. She doesn't need to see it. The sound it makes identifies it; is more particular even than its appearance. 'There was another time when Ziad was lost.'

She tells Joe about that sun-bleached day at the end of summer, August tipping into September, when the shutters were closed to keep out the heat, and she and Ziad were outside playing hide and seek. She searched and searched for him that day, then finally gave up and went inside where it was cooler. She waited for what seemed like ages but he didn't appear, so she went out again.

Beneath the fig tree, he is standing surrounded by three other boys. He is crying. His T-shirt is stained with pink juice. There are clumps of wet fig in his hair.

His trousers are gathered around his ankles, and the boys are clutching and pulling at his underwear. His bad leg, bent in at the knee and more wasted than the other, twists and buckles as he tries to get himself free.

When they see her, the boys stop. Still laughing, they run off, and she is left facing her brother. Ziad, his pants torn and his face streaked with dust and tears, is horror-struck. Tugging at his trousers, he scowls at Layla with an expression she has never seen in his eyes before: intense hostility.

She doesn't know what to say. She goes over and helps him fasten his trousers.

'Why didn't you come?' Fresh tears start. 'Why didn't you find me sooner? I was waiting, but you didn't come!'

'I did search, but it was so hot.' She looks down the road. 'Those boys. What did they … what did they do?'

Ziad wipes his nose along his forearm. 'They must have seen where I hid. They … they pelted me with figs. Pinched me. Pushed me. They said things about my leg. Called me names, and …' His voice wobbles like heat. 'They pulled down my trousers.' More tears. 'They said they needed to check if … if other bits of me were crooked too.'

Guilt floods black through her. Guilt that she is able-bodied; that she has been luckier than him.

A piece of squashed fig slides off his hair. She wants

to hug him, but something about him holds her at a distance.

'I'll go and find them!' She'll hit them, bash them, hurl them to the ground and stamp them out.

'No. No, I don't want you to.'

'Why not?' She can still hear their laughter slipping around Ziad like oil.

'Because they'll hate me even more.'

After that day, Ziad had nightmares for a long time, except that in his nightmares the boys weren't boys any longer. From what she could gather, they were wolves, all red mouths, sharp-toothed grins and dirty paws.

'Nothing like that had ever happened before,' she tells Joe. 'And he changed. Almost overnight, he grew up.'

Joe is watching her, his face full of pity.

'So you see? Back then I wasn't there when he needed me. I found him too late. But now ... well, this time I don't want to let him down.' The anger she felt – for then, and now – has dissipated. Her mouth starts to shake and she has to tighten her face in order not to cry.

She bends down to stroke Dog, but it's too late: Joe has seen her moment of weakness.

Dog gets up and heads off towards the playground, loping from tree to tree and stone to stone, sniffing, joyous. At the edge of the playground, he stops in front of a pink ball, then begins to nose it around in the sand.

'Oh no,' groans Layla, getting to her feet and hurrying towards Dog. He's trying to stretch his jaws around the ball now.

The mother they saw earlier shouts to her maid to get the children. The maid corrals the children together and shields them with her body while the mother edges her way towards them.

Layla reaches Dog. 'Leave that alone.' But Dog lowers his front legs, sticks his bottom in the air and wags his tail.

'I'm not playing, alright?'

Joe comes up, and Dog bounces away, tail still wagging.

With his arms spread out, Joe tries to herd Dog out of the play area.

'You are allowed to touch him, you know,' says Layla, but Joe keeps his distance. 'Oh for pity's sake!' Finally Layla catches Dog and makes him drop the ball. It lies in the sand, wet with spittle, but when she turns around the mother, her maid and the children are already halfway out of the park.

'Sorry!' she calls after them. 'So sorry!' She turns back to Joe. 'Perhaps we'd better go.'

'Where to?' asks Joe. 'Have you got any ideas where Ziad might have gone?'

She kicks at the sand. 'No. I'll drop you off back home.'

But Joe doesn't move. Instead he reaches into his

jeans pocket and pulls out his mobile. A moment later he is speaking to his mother, then to Jacques. He's asking him about where Ziad likes to hang out.

'Starbucks,' he repeats. 'The museum. And *Malak Shawarma*.'

Layla bites her lip, hurt that Jacques should know this when she doesn't.

'Okay, bye.' Joe hangs up and smiles at her. 'Let's go.'

Is he just feeling sorry for her? She takes out her keys. Right now she doesn't care. She's just glad he's coming with her.

Chapter Six

The door swings closed, and Layla squints in the sun. Behind her is the air-conditioned coolness of Starbucks – the huge windows, the low-hanging ceiling lamps, the familiar menu of coffees – that for a few minutes took her straight back to London.

A heat-haze shimmers on the bonnet and roof of Baba's car.

'Well?' asks Joe when she gets back in.

She shakes her head. There were a few teenagers in there, a couple of well-dressed women, a young family, but that was all. She had described Ziad to the girl behind the counter. 'She knew who I was talking about, but said she hasn't seen him lately. Which I suppose is hardly a surprise: Ziad wouldn't have enough money to come here very often. I left my phone number in case he turns up though. She promised to tell the others who work there, and leave my number taped up behind the counter when she finishes her shift.'

Her phone beeps. It's a text from her friend Chrissy,

violinist extraordinaire. *Hi Layl. How's your hol going? Lying roasting on a beach, pretending I'm not with my parents. So much bare flesh you wouldn't believe! Miss you loads. C x.*

She replies briefly: :-) *Having a good time. Will txt you later. xx.*

Chrissy knows hardly anything about Lebanon. Layla didn't talk about it. Her favourite professor, who used words like 'niminy piminy' and 'obstreperous' and had hands like hams, asked her once what living in Lebanon was like and waited, his little blue eyes fixed on her. But she didn't know what to say. Musically, he knew a lot about her – how strong her left hand was, her struggles with fingering – but the rest of who she was remained invisible. Her home, her family, her country, he knew nothing of those; and she didn't want him to either. Because when people heard 'Lebanon', they thought of a time before she was born: of war and blown-out buildings, of Terry Waite and John McCarthy. But she doesn't remember the war. Nor, with Ziad's birth, the start of peace.

She puts down her mobile and drapes both arms over the steering wheel, trying to get some cool air to flow into her armpits. She can see the attraction of the malls that have sprung up in Beirut, with their air-conditioning and designer shops. 'God,' she groans, 'it's baking.' Has it always been this hot here in summer? Or has she adapted to the UK climate?

In the back, Dog is panting, but Joe, who has been waiting for her in the hot car too, looks as if he has his own internal cooling system. His T-shirt is still fresh, and there's no sign of sweat anywhere on him.

'Next.' He points. 'That way.'

Malak Shawarma, the shop sign says, in English on the left and Arabic on the right. Joe gets out of the car this time and holds the door open for her.

Inside, fans whirr in two corners, circulating the heat around the small restaurant. It's coming up to four o'clock, but a few tables are still occupied. A customer waits at the counter for his takeaway order. But Ziad, she can see from a single glance, is not here.

She and Joe look at each other. 'He might have been in earlier,' says Joe.

The counter is free now. The middle-aged man serving wears a blue and white coat and a small, circular white hat. He stares at the blonde and pink streaks in Layla's hair. 'Meat or chicken?' When she hesitates: 'There are *falafel* if you prefer.'

'Actually,' says Layla, 'I'm looking for my brother.'

'We don't sell those.' The man snorts at his own joke.

Layla smiles. 'He comes in here sometimes.'

The man wipes his forehead on his sleeve. 'Is he here now?'

'No.'

'Aha.' He looks fed up, and briefly, she wonders if something has happened today to upset him or whether it's the constant heat of the grill and the incessant rotation of the meat that he dislikes. 'What about you?' He jerks his chin at Joe. 'Are you after something to eat, or have you lost a relative as well?'

'No,' smiles Joe, 'no lost relatives. I'll have a meat *shawarma*.'

Layla throws him a look.

'Well?' he says. 'Aren't you hungry?'

Thinking about it, she is. She hardly ate any lunch earlier, and the smell of this place is making her mouth water. But that's not what she has come for.

'My brother's sixteen. His name's Ziad. He's slim. He's got brown hair and—'

'Let me guess, brown eyes. Look around, my girl.' The man waves the bread in his hand towards the tables. 'You could be describing anyone.'

'Maybe, but he's *not* anyone.'

The man's face is shiny with sweat. 'No, of course he's not just anyone. And neither are you. And neither am I. And neither's my grandmother's cousin twice removed.'

Layla stares. Does he think he's being funny? He doesn't look like the humorous sort.

The man dabs his forehead against his sleeve again. 'Look, do you expect me to remember every customer who walks in here? Half the time I've got my back to

89

them and the heat in my eyes.' He turns and, with a long knife, begins to shave meat off the spit straight into the round of bread. He adds *tahini*, pickles and salad, folds the bread, wraps it in paper and hands it to Joe.

'He has a limp,' says Layla. It sounds ordinary – as ordinary as the colour of Ziad's eyes or what he might have been wearing. It does not define the smaller limb, the awkward angle, the way Ziad has to lift up his right hip and swing his leg round with each step, or the jolting gait this gives him. 'A bad one.'

The man stops. 'Why didn't you say so then? I think I know who you mean. Yes, he was in here earlier today.'

'Really?' She looks around as if she might have missed him. 'Did he say anything?'

'He ordered a sandwich,' says the man, as if she's simple.

'Right.'

'Do you want to wait a while?' Joe asks her. 'He might come back, you never know.'

He's right, so Layla orders a chicken *shawarma*. She can just see her the look of horror on her father's face – what about salmonella, E. coli, obligate aerobes? – but, as she tells Baba in her head, if Ziad comes to this place regularly then it must be hygienic enough, because he hasn't contracted gastroenteritis, has he?

They get some water too, pay the man and sit near

the window. Layla puts her mobile on the table and unwraps her *shawarma*. She can imagine Ziad sitting here slurping a Coke and picking at chips, watching the TV attached to the wall high in the corner. It's on now; there's some sort of game-show, although the volume is too low to hear any of it.

She takes a bite of *shawarma*. It tastes so good. The food at Maria's wedding comes back to her – the smoked salmon and gnocchi, the *petit fours* and tiny roses made of sugar. All that fuss and bother, yet this tastes better.

From Baba's car, Dog is watching her every mouthful.

'Poor Dog,' she murmurs.

Joe swallows and wipes a paper napkin across his mouth. 'Has Ziad ever gone missing before?'

'No, never. Although I haven't actually been living at home.'

'Yes, Ziad mentioned you were in London.'

'Right. Sorry, I keep forgetting you've met him.' So Ziad told Joe she was in London. The city comes back to her in sounds. The roar of rush hour traffic down the Cromwell Road and the thick engines of the London buses. Commuters' heels clicking as they surge towards tube stations. And inside the stations, the clack of barriers opening and shutting, the drone of escalators, a tube train screeching and grinding into the station. The slackening of all this on a Sunday as the city takes a slower breath.

'Do you like it over there?'

'Yes.' Although that wasn't always the case. At first, she was unhappy and missed home. Whenever she opened her mouth to speak, Arabic came out. She heard her voice and it sounded different. Even her sneeze, they said, sounded Arabic. But slowly, things changed. She changed. 'I love it there. I feel freer in London.' Free to study and get a job, to go jogging and have sex with boyfriends.

'You mean it's more liberal.'

'Maybe.' It was one thing she loved about London. You could look like anything and nobody would bat an eyelid. One time she had seen a middle-aged man in a wheelchair, bearded and scraggy, with tattooed arms, and enormous breasts. 'People see things differently there. Like Ziad's limp, for example. Here it's apparently a big deal. And other things are too. What you look like, what race or sexual orientation you are, whether you're a man or a woman.'

'*That* one matters no matter where you are.'

'All right, but …' she struggles to explain. 'As soon as I step off the plane here, I have to rearrange my values. Adjust my ideas of what's acceptable and not acceptable.' But it's even more fundamental than that. She feels split between two landscapes and climates, two languages, two ways of behaving. Belongs to both and neither. 'I mean, Ziad's leg caused a family rift.'

She tells Joe about her grandparents. How when her parents were first married, and Baba's mother came across a two-centimetre stalk of parsley in Mama's *tabbouleh*, she wrote her off as slovenly. A woman who rushed parsley-picking wasn't good enough for her son, she said. Later, when Ziad was born and it became clear that his leg would never function properly, Baba's parents laid the blame squarely at Mama's door. She was a woman who couldn't even produce a healthy boy to carry on her husband's name. There was a row and Baba ordered them to leave his house and never come back. She remembers him shouting, and Mama holding Ziad, cradling his feet in her hand. Since that day, neither Mama nor Baba have spoken to Baba's parents.

Layla feels strange telling all this to Joe, but she wants to prove a point.

'So you don't like it here,' he says.

'It's not that. I couldn't wait to come back, but ... I don't know, it's almost as if the place I remember no longer exists.'

'Or you've changed.' He thinks for a moment. 'Well, there are loads of things happening this summer. Cultural stuff, I mean. Exhibitions, concerts, plays, that sort of thing. Even more than usual. There are going to be lots of tourists, and lots to do.'

They sit quietly eating for a minute. Outside in the car, Dog is still watching them intently, as if he's at the

93

cinema. She feels bad that he has to stay in the car, even if it is parked in the shade with the windows half open. What she'd love is to see him running in the open. Hampstead Heath, Wimbledon Common, Richmond Park. A proper legs-pumping, jowls-flapping gallop. But there are some things, she realizes, that will never happen.

Joe clears his throat. 'I didn't ask what you're studying in London.'

'Music.'

'Wow.' He looks at her with an expression of wonder. 'That's great!'

She's surprised and pleased at his reaction.

'What does that involve day to day?'

'You sit in a room and practise scales and arpeggios till your hands ache. You go over and over passages you're bad at. You try to make something that is meticulously structured sound natural; something that's difficult sound effortless.'

'How long do you have to practise every day?'

'Oh, somewhere between two and five hours.' Two when she's waitressing, five when she's not.

He whistles softly. 'You must really love it, then.'

She shrugs. 'There are other things I could have loved doing too.' She pictures herself standing behind the pharmacy counter serving a customer. Not having to put in piano practice hours. Perhaps not even knowing how to play the piano at all. Even as she thinks it, though, panic bursts inside her chest, sheer terror that the polished Yamaha back home might no longer exist; that all that is left is a tall block of wall paler than it should be, and a rectangle of burgundy rug several shades darker than the rest.

'Anyway,' she says, 'what about you? What are you studying?'

'Medical Imaging Sciences.'

'Oh. Like taking X-rays?'

He nods. 'And ultrasound, mammography, that sort of thing.'

'How did you decide on that?'

'You mean did I always know, like you? Did I always want to be a radiographer?' He laughs. 'No. It had to be something with a secure job at the end of it. It was either medical imaging or medicine, and I don't think I'd like to be a doctor. A surgeon perhaps, but not a doctor.'

A surgeon. Yes, she can see him cutting and slicing, carefully stitching. He would be meticulous, exact, a good surgeon.

He finishes eating his sandwich, balls up the paper in his fist and waits for her to finish.

She glances at the door as someone comes in. 'He's not coming back here, is he?'

'Maybe he just needs some time to sort things out.'

'I don't want him to be by himself. I know him: he's sensitive, he gets overwrought.' Just like Mama. A quick downward spiral. With a sigh, she stuffs the last bit of *shawarma* into her mouth. When she puts out her tongue to lick a drip of *tahini*, she catches Joe watching. When he sees she has noticed, he blushes and starts to tug at his earlobe.

Behind him, on television, the game-show is over. There are pictures of devastation now: crying women, chanting youths, coffins. A rolling news headline at the bottom of the screen says that the Israeli Defence Force has dropped a 550 lb bomb on a building in Gaza City, killing a family of nine.

Layla can't bear to look any longer. Will it never get better over there? Then she wonders about closer to home: the two Israeli soldiers who were abducted this morning into her own country. There have to be repercussions from that, don't there?

Joe pushes back his chair. 'Shall we go?'

'Yes. I'll just leave my number here too, just in case.'

The man behind the counter doesn't mind, and pushes a grease-spotted notepad towards her. She jots down her mobile number, then asks for another *shawarma*. 'Meat this time.'

He picks up another round of bread. 'You've got a good appetite.'

'Actually, it's for my dog.'

The man freezes, his knife halfway to the meat. 'You're giving my *shawarma* to a dog?' He looks at Joe, as if in search of an explanation to this insanity.

Joe rubs his right earlobe between thumb and forefinger. Layla has noticed him doing this a couple of times today. It must be a habit when he's uncomfortable.

'So what?' says Layla. 'The poor animal's starving.'

Joe lets go of his earlobe and laughs placatingly. 'He's a king among dogs,' he tells the man. 'He enjoys the finest things in life; like your *shawarma* for example. Believe me, there's no higher praise.'

The man grins and turns to the spit. 'Alright. Meat. Gherkins. And extra juices.' He holds the sandwich beneath the dripping meat for a moment. 'There, fit for a king, even if he is only a dog.' Layla pulls out her purse to pay, marvelling at Joe's easy charm.

As soon as she opens the car door, Dog leaps out, then rises up on his hind legs to sniff what she's carrying.

'You're one lucky dog.' She unwraps the *shawarma* and puts it down on the pavement.

Almost before she has straightened up again, it's gone, and Dog is sniffing for crumbs and licking the pavement.

'Here.' She hands her water-bottle to Joe. 'Pour some into my hands.'

'What?'

'Go on.' She cups her hands and Joe fills them with water.

Dog laps noisily. People stop to stare.

'We could have asked for a bowl,' hisses Joe.

'What for?' She wipes her hands on her jeans. 'There. Done.'

Joe's lets out a burst of laughter.

'What?'

'Nothing.'

'No, something. What are you looking at me like that for?'

He shakes his head. 'I've just never met anyone like you before.'

'Meaning?'

'Meaning just what I said. Girls here aren't ... well, they aren't like this.'

Should she be pleased or offended? She's not sure. 'We're not potatoes in a supermarket, you know. You can't lump us all together that way.'

'Potatoes! No, you're not a potato. And as for lumping you together with the rest ...' He laughs again.

'Fine.' She turns away, smiling. 'I'm going to the museum now.'

This is what Layla learns from Joe while they are stuck in traffic. That during the civil war, the National Museum of Beirut lay smack on the Green Line that separated Muslim West Beirut and Christian East Beirut, the heart of the battle zone. The checkpoints along the line were at various times controlled by

Lebanese militia, Syrians and Israelis, and the museum became a barracks. The curator and his wife would rush there during lulls in the fighting and try to protect the artefacts. They had concrete poured over the mosaics, and piled sandbags against the sarcophagi. The smaller treasures were carried into the basement, where the entrance was sealed with steel-reinforced concrete. But even then, the artefacts had to withstand fifteen years of bombing, fire and flood, not to mention fighters who used the sarcophagi in the gardens as bunkers to shoot from. In the end, the museum walls were pocked with bullet- and rocket-holes, while inside, every surface was covered in graffiti.

Layla learns all this firstly because Joe knows such things, and secondly because the drive that should have taken five minutes takes so long that they never actually get to the museum at all.

Joe looks at his watch. 'It'll be closed by now.'

Layla bangs the steering wheel. 'Shit, shit, shit!' In frustration, she honks her horn at the unmoving traffic.

Joe looks a bit shocked. Through her open window, she hears the man in the car in front proclaim loudly about women nowadays.

She honks again. 'We should have walked.'

'Sorry,' says Joe, 'I should have thought about the traffic at this time of day.'

'Why should you? You can't know everything.'

They inch along Rue Pierre Gemayel in a blur of

heat. A little boy walks down the middle of the road between the two lines of traffic, selling candy floss and sweets. Layla waves her hand in front of her face, trying to create a breeze. Her back is sticking to the seat. She lets her hair down, shakes her head to allow some air near her scalp, then reties her pony-tail. Surely, she thinks, it's hot enough for a hair or a flake of skin to erupt into flames at any instant. In the back, Dog gets up, circles and sits back down again, panting hard. Even Joe is looking a touch warm.

In England, there is Weather. There is no Weather here. No days of grey and gold. No bellying clouds cut through with slices of sunlight, or east wind to blow the hair off your head. Nor are there avenues of cherry blossom, fluttering bridesmaids in pink, or red brick houses. Here, everything is more fundamental. Stone, rock, gravel, dust. A sun that comes crashing down to burn through layers.

She drums out some finger exercises on the steering wheel – double thirds, fourth and fifth finger trills – more out of habit than anything.

'What shall we do?' asks Joe.

'I don't know. I guess I drop you off and go back home.'

'Let me call and check if Jacques knows any other place where we could look.'

He calls and speaks to his brother, but Jacques doesn't know of anywhere else that Ziad likes to go.

Joe hangs up. The traffic moves forward another inch. Layla switches on the radio. It's just after five and the news is on; the station Baba likes to listen to. They're reporting on the two captured Israeli soldiers on Lebanon's border.

In the south, locals are celebrating the soldiers' capture by setting off fireworks and handing out sweets. Hizballah's leader, Sheikh Hassan Nasrallah, has said that no military operation on Israel's part will result in the soldiers' release. They will only be returned through a trade. Israel has agreed prisoner exchanges with Hizballah before, and this again looks likely. Other news now. With the crisis deepening in Gaza—

Joe turns the dial. The crackle turns into more news. 'There's got to be some music on.'

'Should we be worried?' asks Layla uncertainly.

'No. They'll do a prisoner swap. They always do prisoner swaps.'

In the rear-view mirror, she watches saliva drip off Dog's tongue. She ought to know more about what's been going on politically in her own country, and the region. Only, there's always so bloody much of it going on.

Joe can't find any music he likes, and turns off the radio. 'Let's go for a swim.'

'What?'

'A swim. You know, moving in water.'

'I'm meant to be finding my brother. I can't go swimming!'

'Well, if you have any other ideas of where we can search for him …'

But no, she can't think of a single thing they can do for the moment to find him.

'Someone from Starbucks or the *shawarma* shop might call,' says Joe. 'Or even Ziad himself.'

That's true. Perhaps Ziad has calmed down and will find a phone and call soon. And it's so hot.

'Don't you like swimming?'

'I do.' Occasionally she will go to the London Students' Union pool and trawl up and down doing breast-stroke or front crawl. 'But I haven't got a swimsuit.'

'Oh, we'll have to drive through Bourj Hammoud past a dozen shops where you can pick one up. So?' He smiles. One of his top teeth slightly overlaps the other. It's a pleasing imperfection. 'Do you want to?'

Chapter Seven

She turns off the main road and drives down a bumpy track, making the blue bead and Saint Maron hanging from the rear-view mirror jolt about wildly, and stops near a little hut, as close to the beach as she can get. Here, where a wide boundary of tall, purple-flowering plants separates the road from the shore, the brushing of the sea replaces the snarl of traffic.

Layla has only been to the seaside in Lebanon once before, on a bright summer morning with Baba driving and Mama sunlit in the passenger seat. On the way, they stopped for *mana'eesh* fresh from the baker's oven, and as soon as they got to the beach, she and Ziad stripped off and splashed in the waves.

Baba sat on the beach away from the water. 'Because it's not clean,' he said when they asked him why he wasn't swimming. Of course there were bits of rubbish that people had left, but that's not what he meant. 'There are things you can't see. Industrial waste. Bacteria from sewage.' Which made Layla wonder how on earth Mama had persuaded him to come.

She and Ziad sprawled on the sand with their legs stretched out into the water. What did industrial waste matter when warm water was curling up your legs? What did bacteria matter in the face of pure happiness?

After a while, Mama waded in and Layla followed her. They swam out until Layla got tired; then she clung onto Mama's neck and Mama carried on swimming out. The water grew cold but still Mama swam. Layla felt the steady kick of her legs and watched the water drip from her hair and ears. 'I didn't even know you could swim, Mama,' she said, and it struck her then that there was a lot about her mother that she didn't know.

At last Mama stopped. Treading water, they turned and looked back towards the shore. Ziad and Baba were still there, tiny on the beach.

'This is what it feels like,' said Mama.

'What what feels like?'

Mama's lips touched the water. Her arms and legs swirled and kicked. 'Not to be over there.'

Layla clung on tighter. 'I'm cold.'

'We'll head back then,' said Mama, but she stayed where she was, treading water, allowing the salty sea to flow into her mouth.

Suddenly Layla was filled with a dread certainty that her mother would never take them back. But then Mama struck out again, and slowly, inevitably, they returned to their lives.

Layla turns off the engine. When Dog sees they have stopped, he circles restlessly, eager for release.

'Well, this is it,' says Joe.

'It's nice.'

They get out. Dog runs left and right, investigating, his nose ploughing the sand, as they make their way down to the beach. Under her clothes, Layla has on the cheap swimsuit she bought in Bourj Hammoud. Joe bought some trunks too, and changed in the curtained-off cubicle in the corner of the shop.

A large outcrop of rock curves across the light blue water, shielding it from the open sea. On the sand is a row of five plastic sunbeds that seem to belong to no one. It's a beautiful spot.

Dog charges towards the water, spraying sand up behind him. When he reaches the sea, it surges towards him and he leaps back, barks, then jumps into a wave. For an instant he vanishes, then reappears, swimming.

They drape the two garish towels they bought over sun loungers, and Layla strips down to her navy two-piece, trying to hold in her stomach. Joe looks, but gives nothing away. He unfastens his watch, leaving a pale strap-mark across his wrist. Layla studies his hand: the tanned skin and slender fingers; the neat, slightly flat nails; two tiny moles close together at the base of the thumb. There are twenty seven bones in that hand. Its wrist is crammed with tendons and muscles that control every movement.

Already Joe is down to his green trunks. He has a nice chest, with a thin wash of dark hair across it, and tiny nipples. Decent shoulders, not-too-thin legs, a port wine stain on one shoulder-blade. And that absolutely straight posture, as if he's standing in a military parade.

Dog is still bouncing in the waves. He barks at a big one, forcing it to retreat, then races along the shoreline with his ears flat against his skull.

'It's strange hearing his voice,' says Layla. 'His sound, I mean. I never heard him bark before.' She has never seen him behave like this either. This isn't the Dog who was sitting next to the garbage drums across the road from her house. It isn't even the Dog from the back seat of Baba's car.

'He's happy.' And Joe beams, as if the feeling has infected him too.

'He's never seen the sea, I'm sure he hasn't, but he loves it.'

She eases her sandals off, cheap yellow ones she bought in a shop on Carnaby Street. A rainy grey day that had precluded all possibility of summer ever coming again. A day on which it was necessary to buy yellow sandals. Yet even as she slips them off she feels guilty about the prospect of enjoying herself when Ziad is almost certainly feeling miserable.

Joe is already in the water. She hops quickly across the burning sand and steps into the sea, the coldness a shock on her hot skin. Wet sand oozes up between her toes, interrupted here and there by the clarity of a piece of grit, or a pebble, dislodged from its cradle of sand. Water pulses higher and higher around her until she is enveloped in coldness.

Dog is following, nose raised, floppy ears skimming the water, his tail stretched out like a rudder. As he swims, he laps, then snuffles at the salty surprise.

'Don't follow us,' she tells him. 'Go back and wait on the beach.'

He takes no notice.

She tries to sound commanding. 'Go. Back.'

He still doesn't obey, but after a while seems scared to follow them out any further and stops of his own accord. As they swim on, Layla hears him whining, but when she turns to look, he's swimming back to the shore.

Joe dives under. A few moments later his head emerges near her, gleaming like a black egg in the sun. He smiles and wipes his face. 'Sometimes you can see turtles here.'

'Really?' She scans round as if one might pop up to prove him right.

'That's what I've heard. They're mainly further south, near Soor – they nest along the shore over there – but they say you can see them here sometimes too.' He rubs the water from his eyes.

'Does it sting?' It's so long since she swam in the sea that she can't remember.

'No. It's salt water, like tears.'

So she dips her face into the sea. It is dim and green down there. She sinks further into the coolness. Water slips into her ears, muffling the rest of the world, and closes over her head. In the stillness of the sea, she hangs, listening to silence. There are rocks and weeds and flecks floating in the water, but no turtles. Not even a fish.

She pushes back up.

Joe is nearer than he was. A lot nearer. 'See anything?'

'No.' But now she can see everything: his shining wet hair, the soot-black eyebrows that almost meet in the middle, his brown eyes, his mouth. The two gentle waves of his top lip. And beyond him, the sea.

The moment opens up. Bodies close and legs moving beneath them, they bob in the water, and all around them is blue. Here with Joe and the sea and the wide open sky is a resting place, a bright gap that has materialized in the middle of Layla's life; as she and Joe gaze at each other, she again feels an alignment between them.

He will kiss her. Here in the hot sunshine, with the cold water swirling around their bodies, he will kiss her. And from nowhere, overwhelming, comes the knowledge that she wants him to. In fact, she is shocked at how much she wants this boy she's only known for half a day to kiss her.

She moves closer. Smiles the tiniest smile. Everything is right. He will kiss her now, and when he does, she will find out something about herself as well as about him.

In the distance, Dog barks, and her eyes unlock from Joe's. On the beach, Dog is pacing like a caged animal. Can he see them, she wonders? Can he feel even from where he is the tingling between them?

But when she looks back, Joe is wiping a drip of water from his eyebrow, and the moment has slipped away. He is busy studying the water in front of his face.

'What is it?' She is alarmed. Memories of Baba's talk of pollution and raw sewage come back to her. 'Shouldn't we be swimming here? Is it dirty?'

'No, it's clean enough. I was just ... look. Look at the waterline.'

'What?' It's water. The sea. Just like it was a minute ago when they should have kissed but didn't.

'It's amazing. You know, the line that separates the sea from the air.'

She treads water. Maybe the sun has got to him. Or is he trying to deflect attention from what just happened and didn't happen, talking for the sake of something to say? 'Do you mean the surface tension?'

'I mean the thing that stops the sea from spilling out into everything else.'

Okay, so the sun has got to him. But this doesn't even sound like Joe. She thought she had him figured

out – fussy, charming, and concerned with raw facts –
but perhaps she was wrong.

'There's always an inward force at the surface of
water wherever it meets air.' Should she explain? 'It's
because water molecules are more attracted to each
other than to molecules in the air. That makes it look
as if there's some sort of skin there, but there isn't.'
Magic doesn't exist. Liquid flowing up between the
hairs of a paint-brush, a plant drawing water into its
stems, blood moving against gravity towards the heart.
None of it is magic, just surface tension and capillarity.

'Right.' Joe looks amused. 'That's exactly what I
meant.'

She grins. 'All courtesy of my dad.'

'Come on, I want to show you something,' and he
strikes out towards the rocky outcrop. She follows.

When they get to the rock, the lower part of it is
slimy from the slap and rise of the water.

'Look down there,' says Joe. 'There's a hole in the
rock right under here.' He ducks under for a moment.

Layla goes under too. Four metres or so beneath
them, shafts of sunlight shimmer through a hole in the
rock.

'You can swim through there,' says Joe when she
comes up. 'Me and Jacques have done it before.'

Jacques. The very thought of him makes her feel
pissed off.

'Do you want to do it?' asks Joe.

'I don't know.'

'I'm going to, but ... well, you don't have to, okay?'

He takes a deep breath and goes under, head first, curving into the water like a porpoise. Briefly his feet appear, and then she is floating alone in the middle of the sea, a child again, with no one's neck to cling to.

'Shit!' She wishes he hadn't done that. She also wishes he hadn't said that she didn't have to. Because now it's like some sort of test. 'I can do it. I can do it.' Three deep breaths, the final one the deepest, and the sky vanishes.

A few tiny fish flicker away. Below her, Joe has reached the hole in the rock and is obstructing the fingers of aquamarine light streaming through it. With one hand, he pushes himself through. Arms and head vanish; torso, legs and feet; then the shafts of light are restored to what they were.

Layla battles against her own buoyancy, pushing water upwards with her arms. It doesn't matter that she doesn't want to be doing this; it's too late to back out now. If only swimming downwards wasn't so slow. She kicks harder. Light wobbles beneath her, fanning out bright through darker water. The hole is smaller than she thought it would be. Around it, seaweed sways like long hair. She reaches it and looks through to the sunny side of the rock formation. Joe is probably at the surface by now, catching his breath. Beneath her hand, the rock is surprisingly jagged. She starts to swim through, head then shoulders, but somehow she's in the wrong position or at the wrong angle. Or perhaps it's just that she's too fat. Whatever the reason, she finds her back arched against one side of the hole and one knee jammed against the other. She tries to twist round, but she's stuck like a pickle in a jar. Water sings in her ears. She hears her heart beating. The sunlight fades a little, leaving hard grains of fear. For an endless moment all is still, and she is curled inside rock and sea, stranded between two places, neither here nor there.

She wants to breathe.

Up above, Joe's legs are moving in great, slow kicks. He is putting his head under to see what has become of her. He sees her – oh God, like this! – and dives down.

When he reaches her, he takes hold of her shoulders and pulls.

She squirms. Rotates. Pushes.

One more pull, and rock rasps against her leg. A scrape of pain across her belly, and she is out. She pushes off from the rock, flapping and kicking to get up faster. There's a humming in her ears, faint but insistent, and growing louder.

Joe is gliding beside her.

A last push towards the sunlight, then her head breaks through the surface, jumbling up that line between sea and air. She gasps deep, urgent breaths. Around her, the air is booming. Like the flick of a switch, the underwater humming has turned into a roar, loud and strung out in the air.

She's still gasping and coughing. She hangs onto Joe's shoulder so that all she has to concentrate on is breathing, but he isn't even looking at her. He's staring up at the plane that's passing over, a faint frown tightening his silver-glistening face. A haze of cloud has covered the sun, and the sea has turned a shade darker and colder.

The plane is gone but the air is still shaking. Underwater, the humming will have faded away too, like a bee moving on to a different garden.

'Are you okay?'

Abruptly, she lets go of his shoulder. 'I'm fine.'

'Sure?'

She nods. 'I didn't need rescuing, you know.' After all, it's always been her role to be the strong one. Hasn't she had to be there for Ziad her whole life? Even in London, before he grew silent? Even now? And she knows – has always known – that as long as she lives, she will always have to be there for her little brother. 'I'm going back.'

As she breast-strokes through the water, Joe follows, slow and silent, and her thoughts rearrange themselves. God, what must he think of her? He goes out of his way to help her find her brother, brings her to this lovely place to have a break, rescues her when she gets into trouble underwater, and this is the way she reacts.

She stops and treads water until he catches up. 'I'm sorry. I didn't mean that.'

'That's okay.'

'No really, I'm sorry. Thank you for … you know, for saving me.'

'It's okay, don't worry.'

They carry on towards shore.

'That plane …' says Joe.

'What about it?'

'It didn't look like one of ours.'

'What do you mean? Whose was it then?'

'Maybe Israeli.'

'What? Are you sure?'

'Not a hundred percent.'

That means he's pretty sure. Down there in the blue-green water, as she hung trapped between two worlds, the country changed its mood. The sun crept away. An Israeli jet cut across the sky, and she became the sort of girl who needs rescuing.

Ahead of them is Beirut, backed by blue mountains, and on the beach Dog is still waiting. The sight of him sends a surge of warmth through Layla, but there are two people on the beach now, other swimmers perhaps, she can't quite tell.

As she gets closer, she sees that they are two men, fully clothed. One of them, squat and thick-set, is watching Joe and Layla swim in. The other, smaller and wiry, is waving his arms at Dog. He bends and picks up a stone, aims, then throws it with a shout.

'Hey!' screams Layla, trying to right herself in the shallow water. 'What do you think you're doing?'

The thick-set man smiles and gives a little bow of the head, and she realizes now from the cheap black jacket and tie that that he's a waiter.

Finding her footing, she scrambles up the beach. 'Stop it! That's my dog!'

The wiry man pauses with another stone in his hand, then drops it. As she approaches, he glances down at her breasts, her bare stomach and legs.

She stops in her tracks and throws her arms wide. 'Shall I take off my swimsuit so you can get a better look?'

The older man frowns disapprovingly at her and turns to his charge: 'Go get a table and chairs. Hurry up.' The little wiry one scampers up the beach like a puppet towards the hut-like building she parked Baba's car next to.

As soon as the man is gone, Dog rushes over, tail wagging, nails scratching her feet. She laughs and grimaces at the same time. 'Calm down!' It's as if he hasn't seen her for weeks. He sniffs her and starts to lick her stomach. Looking down, she sees watery trickles of pink flowing from her scraped stomach and thigh. Picking up her towel, she dabs at her wounds, then wraps the towel tightly around herself.

Joe is slow-walking out of the shallow water. The

head waiter greets him, and as Joe dries himself, they chat a little about his swim, and make some comments about the beauty of the spot. During this exchange, the man eyes Dog suspiciously, as if he might still maul them all. 'Now how about a nice lunch? We have anything the gentleman would like: *Sultan Braheem*, sea bass, octopus, *sayadeeyeh*.' He talks to Joe in the assumption that he is the sole decision-maker.

The little waiter returns weighed down with a small plastic table under one arm and two plastic chairs under the other. Following his boss's brusque stream of orders, he sets them so they stand just a couple of inches deep in the line of foamy water at the sea's edge.

'Fine, fine,' says the older waiter as the younger one steps back with wet shoes. 'Now go away.' He turns back to Joe. 'Or if you prefer something light, perhaps a plate of *hoummous* and a few olives. I have some sardines that I swear have just jumped fresh from the sea into the frying pan. Whatever you like, sir.'

'What do you fancy?' Joe asks Layla.

She considers. Swimming has made her hungry.

'If the lady's on a diet, we could grill the fish instead of frying it. With some salad perhaps.'

Anger flickers in her. Christ, is there anyone around here who *doesn't* feel that it's their God-given duty to point out that she ought to lose weight? 'Actually I'm not hungry.'

The waiter leans back, as if she has taken a swipe at

him. 'Are you sure, *Mademoiselle?* Not even something small?'

She shakes her head. 'We already ate.'

Joe thanks the waiter, compliments the setting again, and the arrangement of the table in the surf. Another time, he's sure. Layla says nothing. How in hell can he manage to be so courteous all the time? Has he got a book of the right thing to say in every situation? Or is this a skill she would have learned too if she'd stayed in Lebanon?

'In this country, you should enjoy yourself wherever you can,' says the waiter, 'before things change. You see what's happening in the south.'

'What's happening?' asks Joe.

'You haven't heard? Israel has sent tanks and troops into Lebanon. They're bombing the south near the border.'

'What?'

'Yes. Like I say, you never know around here. One minute everything's as good as it can be, and the next thing you know, your country's been invaded. That's why I'm saying, have a nice meal. But ...' he shrugs and turns to bellow towards the building: 'Jiryes!'

At a trot, the little waiter returns.

His boss jerks a thumb at the table and chairs. 'Back they go.'

The little man sags. Then he stacks the chairs one on top of the other again and, loaded like a donkey with saddle-bags, totters away, followed by the head waiter.

Dog noses Layla's shin, and she reaches down and strokes his head, more to comfort herself than anything else. An invasion. Bombing.

The sea sparkles, hurling minuscule spears of light into her eyes. It bulges and dips in a thousand crests, as if it really is being held in by an elastic membrane that's being stretched this way and that. Somewhere out there, beneath that uneven surface, away from waiters and food, tanks and bombs, turtles are swimming. She wishes to God she had seen one.

It pops into her head – the silliest thought – that if only she and Joe had kissed, everything would have followed on differently: she would have glided smoothly through the hole in the rock; the young waiter wouldn't have shouted at Dog, nor the older one commented on her weight; and there would be no invasion. Instead, she and Joe would be sitting face to face at the table, feet dabbling in warm water, crunching on whitebait and leaning in close to scoop *hoummous* with pieces of flat-bread.

But the sea's surface tension seems to have failed, and the membrane has split. Layla blinks. A wave curls over the sand and slides up the sand, frothing white, then retreats, pulling a stone that goes rolling along with it.

Chapter Eight

'There's a message,' says Layla.

'Is it Ziad?'

'No. It's that girl in Starbucks.' She listens. 'She says he's there! But—' she checks. 'That was half an hour ago.' When they were out there in the sea, perhaps when she was underwater, her phone rang but was not picked up. 'She hasn't left a number.' Layla looks back at the list of incoming calls, but the phone number the girl was calling from is withheld. 'Shit!' She grabs her trousers.

Joe is already pulling on his T-shirt.

'He might still be there,' she says.

On the way, they switch on the car radio to get the news. The waiter was right: Israeli artillery and aircraft are hammering not only Hizballah posts, but bridges, roads and power stations all over the south, effectively cutting it off from the rest of the country. This, Israel claims, is in order to prevent the kidnapped soldiers from being transported.

'God,' says Layla. 'God.'

She pushes open the door and scans round the room: at one table, a group of four young men; at another, a couple talking intently, the woman hanging onto her cup as if it is nailed to the table. There is no one else.

They go up to the counter. 'Hi,' says Layla.

The girl turns round, a coffee filter holder in her hand. 'Oh, hi.' Layla can tell from the girl's face that with her damp, unbrushed hair and creased clothes, she looks even scruffier than before. The girl looks across at Joe and smiles, showing little teeth. He, of course, shows no signs of creasing, and his hair is as neat as it was before he went into the sea.

'I called you,' says the girl to Layla. 'Did you get the message?'

'Yes, thanks. I came right away, but ...'

The girl shakes her head, her bobbed hair brushing her shoulders. 'He already left. I thought maybe he'd gone to meet you.' She gives Joe a sugary smile, and glances from him to Layla, as if she's trying to work out what they are to one another.

'Can you tell us what happened?' asks Joe.

'Well, he sat over there and had a coffee.' She points to a table near the window. 'I asked if he wanted a biscuit too, for free, but' – she shrugs – 'he said no.'

Layla bristles. The girl felt sorry for him. Ziad would have hated that.

'Then I called you. He seemed upset,' she adds. 'As

if, I don't know, maybe he'd been crying.'

'Did he say anything to you?'

'He asked me twice what time it was. That's why I thought he was meeting you here. But then he left.'

'When was that?' asks Joe.

The girl checks her watch. 'Must have been just before six.'

Behind them, the young men burst into laughter.

'Did you notice if he was on a scooter?' says Layla.

'Yes, the red one. He parked it right outside.'

Layla doesn't know what more to ask. Ziad was here. He was upset, and keeping an eye on the time. Then he left. 'Thanks.'

Joe thanks the girl too, and receives another rare smile. Does he even realize that this girl fancies him? Is he tuned in to such things?

They move away from the counter.

'Maybe he was meeting someone at six o'clock,' says Joe. 'Although not here, obviously.'

Layla wanders over to the table Ziad was at. Here, reflected in the window, he sat drinking coffee. What did his reflection show? What colour T-shirt was he wearing? Was his hair standing up on top the way it always used to? Who would he be meeting? Did his reflection give away that he had just been shunned by his friends? She stares at a coffee ring on the white surface of the table and her insides contract. Ziad took a sip of coffee – she can almost smell it on his breath –

121

and put down his cup right there.

'Come on.' Joe touches her elbow gently. 'Let's go.'

In the back of the car, Dog is busy scratching. 'Great,' thinks Layla as she gets in, and wonders vaguely where on earth one gets flea medicine from around here.

'Are you okay?'

'I'm fine.' She takes out her phone and dials home.

Mama picks up. 'Oh, hi, *hayati*. I've been wondering where you'd got to. I was about to call.'

'Has Ziad phoned, Mama?'

'No. Why, has something happened?'

'No, no.' She can't tell Mama what happened last night, not yet anyway. It would cut her to the bone.

'But you don't know where he is.'

'I know that he's fine. I was just speaking to someone who saw him a little while ago.'

'Oh thank God.'

'I'll try to find out where he went.'

'Right.' A brief pause. 'Have you heard what's going on in the south?'

'Yes, I heard.'

'*Ya Allah*, I wish Ziad would stop being so touchy and come home now.' The bombing in the south has made Mama even more afraid for him. 'Sweetheart, I don't want to crowd you – I know you're not used to having to account for your comings and goings – but what time do you think you'll be getting back? With what's going on ... I think you should come home as soon as possible.'

'The trouble's only in the south, Mama.' She tries to sound light-hearted. 'I'm not going to leave Beirut and head south, am I?' Although what if Ziad has headed southwards for some reason?

'I know you're not going to do anything stupid, darling, but I worry. You never know what's going to happen in this country. Things can move so fast here.'

This idea unsettles Layla. 'Well, I'll give you a call when I'm on my way, okay?'

After she hangs up, she and Joe sit in silence. Behind them, Dog sighs and collapses into a lying position.

'The invasion,' she says. 'Do you think it'll spread further north?' The question acknowledges that he knows more about these things than she does. She has been absent from class on that count; exiled from events.

'No,' says Joe. 'They want to get their soldiers back, and that's where the soldiers will be, somewhere in the south.' But he sounds uncertain.

If only she could see Ziad, have him in her sight and know that he is safe. But he's okay, she tells herself. He was sitting in Starbucks less than an hour ago, so he's got to be okay. Only now she's at an impasse, and all she can do is sit and wait for the next phone call.

'Look,' says Joe, 'why don't we go to my halls?'

'What? Why?'

'We can't sit in the car just waiting. And that way if Ziad calls, you won't be too far away.'

'What makes you think he'll get in touch?'

'I don't know. Maybe he'll want to talk things through with you before heading home.'

She is silent.

'Well, we can't just sit here forever.' Joe sucks his lip thoughtfully. 'You know, there's a piano on campus.'

Her heart startles.

He smiles. 'You could practise there if you like.'

The American University of Beirut is in a lovely residential district. Layla parks the car on Bliss Street. Opposite the university campus, the road is lined with eateries and other shops. They get out. The early evening air is warm and thick as a layer of wool; the metal of the car is warm too, and dusty.

'It's this way.'

'Wait,' she says. 'Can't we take Dog?'

'It's against the rules.'

'Right.'

Dog puts his paws up against the window. The pads press on the glass, and long nails scrape as his paws slide down again. He is whining.

'I know,' she soothes. 'I know you want to come and it's not fair, but … well, I won't be long.' She checks that all the windows are open a couple of inches. 'You'll just have to wait, okay?'

She and Joe follow the campus wall.

'Wow, a real pavement!'

'I know,' says Joe. 'Good, isn't it.'

On the other side of the road outside a cafe stands a ragged man with a mess of grey hair and a long beard.

'Hi, Ali,' calls Joe.

The man raises a thin arm in response.

'Who's that?'

'Everyone around here calls him Ali. He lives here.'

'What, on the street?'

'Yes. We have a chat sometimes. I buy him a coffee or something to eat. Lots of people do.'

Layla looks back. Ali is standing motionless in the middle of the pavement, staring into the traffic. In London, she has seen people step over a homeless man, or veer around, avoiding eye contact, but she has never seen them buy food for one. Nor, she thinks, feeling embarrassed, has she ever bought food or a drink for a homeless person.

They go through the campus gate, passing beneath two plaques, one in Arabic, the other in English, that read: 'That they may have life and have it more abundantly.'

The bustle and traffic of Bliss Street fade away. Down a wide set of steps, and she and Joe are walking along a wide pale path bordered with rocks. Old stone buildings with columns and arched windows glow gold in the evening sun. To their right, a sea view opens up, and all around is a profusion of greenery that takes Layla's breath away.

The campus is holiday-quiet. Joe says hello to two boys, one tall with a goatee, the other wearing glasses, who pass them.

'Finished that project yet, Joe?'

'Nearly. You?'

'Another week should do it.'

Joe introduces Layla, then they walk on.

She hadn't been expecting this. In here, behind those high walls, everything is different. Calm and pristine. Another country. She recognises some of the trees – citrus, olive, cypress, carob, pistachio – but has to glance at the plaques on a couple of others that she doesn't know. *Albizia lebbeck. Jacaranda mimosifolia.*

'You like trees?' asks Joe.

She has never thought about it before. 'I don't know. I suppose so.'

'That eucalyptus was brought here from Jerusalem a hundred years ago in a biscuit tin.'

She laughs. 'Is there a thought in your head that isn't a fact?'

'I doubt it. But come, you've got to see this. It's just down here.' And they follow the path a little further.

Near the chapel, it looks like it has landed from outer space.

'It's a banyan tree,' says Joe.

Two cats, a black and a ginger, look down majestically at them from the crook of its branches. The branches themselves are nothing out of the ordinary. It's the network of aerial roots cascading down from them that is so bizarre.

'It looks as if it's melting,' she says, then takes in her surroundings again. 'It's like Old Beirut in here.' Before the civil war, years before either of them was born.

Joe nods. They know it from photographs, and the odd street or district that has remained untouched. Old Beirut: civilised, orderly, beautiful. And not for the first time, she gets a sensation of discrepancy between time and place, that feeling of belonging nowhere, her own roots floating in mid-air.

'Well?' Joe is smiling. 'Aren't you going to try it?'

They have come into a small building, gone past one room full of stacked chairs, and another with three kettles in a corner. This room, at the back of the building, is empty save for an electric keyboard standing beside a window, and a wooden chair with a woven twine seat in front of it.

Layla lets out a long, disappointed breath. She has played on electric keyboards before, of course, but not ones as basic as this. This is too small. Too light. Too unlike a piano. There are sixty-one keys, twenty-seven fewer than there ought to be. But Joe has been nice and brought her all the way here, and he is waiting.

She sits down. Tries to ignore the way the whole thing sways slightly on its spindly old-man legs. The keyboard is already plugged into a socket, and she flicks the on-off switch. A small red light comes on. Well, at least there's electricity.

She balances her forefinger on middle C. The key is the same width as a real piano's key, but plastic-smooth to the touch, and not as warm as it ought to be. She presses the key. The movement connects a circuit and a tone is generated. It is middle C, but no steel string has been struck by a padded hammer; no resonance has been produced by the vibration of that particular string. The sound she hears is a computer-generated noise. It imitates a piano, but it is still not right, like someone speaking in a voice that doesn't belong to them. She hits the same note harder. The key is weighted and touch-sensitive, which is something: she has hit the key harder, and the noise generated is louder.

The Royal College, with its twenty-six practice rooms, and another twenty-two sound-proof practice rooms, a sum total of one hundred and fifty-six pianos, has vanished like a stone into water. She looks up at the window, through which she can see part of an awning, branches of pine tree, a piece of evening sky. So, five octaves instead of seven. That means almost nothing after Mozart. She needs something compact and precise, a Baroque cut jewel.

But perhaps an early Beethoven.

She begins the first piano sonata. Once, a finger hits the plastic surround where the missing key should be.

At the end of the first movement, she stops.

Joe is still standing in the doorway. He is looking at her in a new way. Admiring. 'That was amazing.'

'Thanks.' She feels flattered, and for some reason nervous. She didn't expect him to like classical music.

'Do you want to stay and practise a while? There are some books I've got to drop back at the library. It's on the other side of campus, but I shouldn't be more than half an hour.'

She nods.

He smiles. She likes his smile – the white teeth, the way it transforms his face. Then he pulls the door to behind him, and she is alone. Layla, the keyboard, and a fragment of pink sky.

She plays. Each piece's unique combination of notes expresses the composer's mood and intent at a specific moment in time; the mood long evaporated, the composer dust, yet both utterly present, here in this room in Beirut.

She doesn't know how long she sits there playing. The instrument is less than a metre length of plastic, but still it is as though she has risen up through water and can breathe again. And she is in that place she has inhabited for hundreds upon hundreds of hours, for days and weeks; the place she enters not when she is only practising, but when she is playing. It is a parallel universe where there is only music, and everything else, including herself, ceases to exist. It is no longer her brain that generates sound, but little engines in her fingers, tiny brains that already know the shape of the music. She does not have to think, and there is a feeling in her mind like light.

She is in the middle of the Variation 1 of the Goldberg Variations when a noise disturbs her.

The notes fly away into the walls, scurry behind the blinds, vanish into corners. She turns and stands up, still half trapped inside the music. The wooden chair tips over behind her. 'What are you doing?'

Joe starts.

The breath is hot in her nostrils. 'What did you sneak in for? Why didn't you say something to let me know you were here?'

'What?' He starts to laugh. 'What are you so angry about?'

He was there, watching her while her mind was somewhere else. It feels as though he has watched her sleeping, dreaming, but she cannot put this into words. 'I didn't know you were here.'

'Sorry. I just … I didn't want to interrupt you.'

She swallows. It has all come back. Beirut. Ziad still missing. The bombing in the south.

'I didn't mean to upset you, okay?' Joe smiles uncertainly.

'Sorry. I don't know what's wrong with me. I'm not usually like this.'

Back in London, there are mirrors in the college's practice rooms. She has seen herself in them, assessed her posture and position, but she has never been able to see her own face as she plays. Now, with her feelings falling over each other, she wonders what Joe has seen: whether it was the face she knows, or another Layla – happy, sad, floating, dreaming. Her yet not her. And whether he liked it.

She sits down and starts on the fourth of Chopin's Opus 33 mazurkas, slowly, with the main melody, and as she plays, what is left of her upset crumbles and blows away, easy as C major.

Standing between the keyboard and the window, Joe leans his back against the wall and slides down so he is sitting. She can't ignore him, but a minute later it doesn't matter any longer. Her hands cross, catching every grace note and trill, enabling each of the eight re-emergences of the melody. She feels the music, and Joe – the warmth of him, like a little sun, turning the side of her face pink.

Light glints off the white plastic keys as her fingers press them, and music glints off the walls. She is completely, entirely happy.

Then it is over.

Joe is still there. Neither of them moves.

'Well,' she says at last, to break the silence, 'thanks

for bringing me here.'

Joe stretches his legs out on the floor. 'Now I understand why you left.'

'Left?'

'Why you went to London. I may not know much about piano playing, but even I can tell that you're too good not to make something of it.'

Her mouth feels dry, but her head is clear. Because while she was playing for Joe, something crystallized. Here in this room, on this instrument, two thousand-odd miles away from the Royal College, she realized that making music is the one thing she loves above all else.

They are standing beneath the banyan tree again. The cats are gone and the light has begun to fade. A middle-aged woman, a lecturer probably, walks by with books and a folder tucked under her arm. She greets Joe, nods to Layla, and walks on.

'Well,' says Layla, 'it doesn't look as if Ziad's going to call.'

Joe is chewing his lip.

'Do you want me to drop you back off at your mum's?'

He doesn't reply.

'Well, I'd better go.'

At last he moves, takes a breath. 'Or you could stay here. You could stay tonight.'

She blushes. Is he asking her what she thinks he's asking her?

'I mean, in case your brother calls. It's not too late, and … and you don't want to be half-way home and have to come all the way back if he does.'

'That's a point,' she says slowly.

'Hopefully he'll go home tonight, but if he doesn't, we could carry on looking for him. Go to those places again. And the museum.' He is speaking quickly, nervously. 'It would be easier, wouldn't it? I mean, we could be at the museum first thing when it opens.'

Above them, the tree is a mass of twists and knots. Roots fall down from over their heads. Everything is upside down. Is he asking her to spend the night with him? Or is he being the perfect gentleman? She doesn't know.

'I'll sleep on the floor,' he says.

Oh.

'And I'll get Dog too. We can't leave him in the car all night.'

'But I thought it wasn't allowed.'

'Don't worry, no one will know.'

Even though she has only known Joe for half a day, she is utterly amazed by this. Because within a few minutes of first meeting him, she recognised that he is the sort of person who doesn't break rules.

'It would be easier, wouldn't it?' Joe frowns. 'To stay here?'

Easier than driving the hour back home to where Baba and Mama are still at odds with each other, and having to wade through the tension of Ziad not being there. On top of which, she knows full well that they will not want her to return to Beirut tomorrow. 'Yes, it would be easier.'

'So you'll stay?'

'I'll stay.'

Chapter Nine

'Are you the only one here?' Layla asks as they enter the dorm building.

'No. Those two guys we passed, they're staying on for a while too. Their rooms are upstairs. And there are a few students in other dorms, but most people have gone home for the holidays.'

Inside the main door is a noticeboard with details of a karaoke night that has already passed, and a poster advertising the World Cup in Germany, 9 June – 9 July, with the results of all the games pencilled in. It makes her think of Maria, and the wedding reception that already seems such a long time ago. Further along on the noticeboard is a doctored picture of Einstein as a rapper, and next to that, a list of students who live in this hall.

Layla scans down the list of surnames. *Ghandour, Habeeb, Haddad.* That's Joe. But—

'Hang on.' She points. 'That should be you. There's only one Haddad here.'

'It is me.'

'But it says Yusef.'

'Yep. That's me.'

'But you're … you're not Joe?'

'Yusef, Joseph, it's the same thing,' he laughs. 'Or have you been in England too long to remember?'

She lets out a laugh, at the same time trying to work out what the joke is. 'But it's not the same thing. They're two different names.'

'The name on my birth certificate is Yusef, like my grandfather – you know, stick to tradition – but my parents have always called me Joe. Some of the lecturers call me Yusef, but so long as no one calls me Zouzou, it doesn't bother me.'

Everything wavers. In the blink of an eye, the new name has entirely deconstructed the person she thought was Joe. It's just like Mama said on the phone. Everything's changing. Nothing stays the same for long.

'Women do it every day, you know,' he says, 'get married and change their name.'

'Their family name.'

'And that's less important?'

'Maybe.' Your first name is the one that is knit most closely to you, from the moment when, still a baby, your mother breathes it onto your face. That's what Layla would like to say. Instead she shakes her head. 'Oh, I don't know. Forget it.'

'Well, I'm still Joe, alright? Come on, let's go and

see what's going on with the news, then I'll go and get Dog.'

They go into a common room with light-blue sofas arranged around a low table, and a large, blurry picture of cornflowers hanging on the wall. In one corner are two computers. Joe turns one on and sits down. Layla takes the chair next to his and watches as the screen flickers into life and Joe searches for the latest news about the fighting in the south.

'There, there, stop.'

He scrolls down and they read the first few lines. *Israeli Prime Minister Ehud Olmert has said that his country holds Lebanon responsible for the Hezballah raid, and promises a 'painful and far-reaching response.' He is calling this morning's attack 'an act of war.'*

'War!' says Layla.

'They've invaded. That's war.'

'Is that what he means? Or is he suggesting that it'll get worse?'

Joe clicks on a link, and they watch footage of Lebanese civilians in the south stranded by the bombing. They are carrying bags, trying to find their way home down back roads as ambulances blare past them. Other footage shows two young men standing amid rubble and tangled metal rods. They're used to this, they say. This is what it has been like their whole lives. Then one of them breaks out into a big smile. But the capturing of the Israeli soldiers, he says, that was like Italy winning the World Cup.

Joe turns off the computer. 'My room's down this way.'

They go down a corridor and he unlocks a door. The room has a tiled floor and white walls. There is a small free-standing wardrobe, and in the far right corner, a desk with two shelves above it. Beneath the window is an old-fashioned radiator set into a niche in the wall. There are some football pictures on the wall, and a poster of an astronaut floating in space, the Earth a little blue ball in the distance.

Joe grabs a big bag of crisps off a shelf and pulls it open. He tilts the bag towards Layla. 'Want some?'

She leans over the bag to peer inside, and takes a few. When she looks up, her face is close to his. 'Thanks.' She steps back, her cheeks warm.

The puffy, orange-coloured crisps taste tangy. She brushes the crumbs off against her trousers and wishes she had something to do with her hands.

'You can sit down,' says Joe. 'You are allowed.'

She pulls out the chair from under his desk and sits, wondering what would be a good thing to say right now. There's a pile of blank paper on the desk, and she takes a sheet and begins to fold it. Should she comment on the news, or the swim, or make an observation about the room perhaps?

'Is that ...?' Joe snaps his fingers a couple of times.

'That Japanese thing. What do they call it?'

She presses and turns, folds and tucks. 'Origami.'

'That's it. Is that what you're doing?'

She nods.

'I didn't know you could do that.' He gives a short laugh. 'But I guess I wouldn't know, would I.'

'I didn't even know your name until a few minutes ago,' she says.

He munches another crisp. 'Help yourself.' He puts the bag on the desk. 'I'll go and get Dog.'

Yes, Dog. Dog who at least has no name to lose. Layla puts down what she's doing and gets up. 'I'll come too.'

'No, better not. I'm going to sneak him in a back way.'

She hands over the keys. 'What'll happen if someone sees you?'

'So long as it's no one who works here, or anyone who'll tell …'

'But what if the university finds out? Then what?'

He shrugs, trying to be flippant. 'No one'll see. It'll be fine.' He turns to go.

'No, wait. If you get caught, you'll get suspended, won't you? I can't let you do this.'

'But you already said yes. You're already here.'

'I know, I know. But … I just didn't think it through.' She had other things on her mind, like music, and invasions, and not knowing where Ziad is, or why she is spending the night here. 'Look, I'll just go home, and if I need to, I can come back to Beirut in the morning.' Assuming Baba will let her have the car again, and assuming Mama doesn't throw a major fit. 'You've got studying to do, and you shouldn't be running such a big risk just because ... well, because you feel guilty about what Jacques did.' She traces some scratches on the surface of the desk.

'It's not because of that, okay?'

'It's not?'

Joe tugs his earlobe, pressing it between finger and thumb. It seems to make him feel better, and his frown clears. She imagines him as a toddler, soothing himself to sleep. 'I just want to, that's all.'

'But what if—'

'Look, when you don't agree with the rules, you have to decide for yourself what's right or wrong. And there's nothing wrong in this.' He opens the door and, before she has a chance to say anything else, he's gone.

Layla stands at the window and watches him come out of the building and vanish into the darkness. When she turns back again, the room looks even more spare. Her own room in London has a fitted carpet and fitted wardrobe, a desk and bookcase, a sink with a mirror, light and a sign warning that this isn't drinking water. It has a towel rail, a padded chair, overhead storage, a fire alarm on the ceiling.

She calls home. As the phone rings in her parents'

house, she hikes up her voice to sound cheerful.

'Hello?'

'Hi, Baba.'

'Layla. Are you on your way home?'

'Well, no, not exactly.'

'Did you find Ziad?'

'No, not yet.'

A disappointed silence. Then: 'Is everything okay?'

'Yes, everything's fine.' With one hand over her eyes, she tells Baba that she is going to stay at Rima's tonight. 'You remember Rima. She was at the wedding reception.' The lie slips out easily in the dark, where she can't see Baba and Baba can't see her.

'It's flared up in the south,' says Baba. 'It's better to come home now, *habibti*, without delaying.'

'It's late, Baba, and I'm tired. A few hours either way isn't going to make a difference.'

'But darling—'

'Look, I'm not a child any more,' she says softly.

He sighs. 'I know that. But you're still my daughter.'

Through the half-open window, she hears the whirr and hum of night insects. 'I love you, Baba,' she says.

A beat passes as Baba takes in what she does not often say. 'I love you too.'

With the phone wedged between her ear and shoulder, she picks up the half-finished piece of origami and continues folding.

'There's still no word from Ziad,' says Baba, stating

the obvious. 'Your mother's going to ring round all his friends. I mean, I know we argued, but to be out for a second night …'

Mixed up in her are concern for her brother, especially given the violence that has erupted, and annoyance at his moodiness. Why doesn't he get a grip and at least call home? She doesn't say anything to Baba about Jacques or the night club. After all, what good would it do to tell him that Ziad had something more to be upset about than their argument? 'I'm sure he's fine, Baba.'

'But we don't *know* that. Your mother's beside herself. You know how she panics.'

'Yes, I know.' Layla remembers when, still a little boy, Ziad had got a fish-bone stuck in his throat, and while he was coughing and retching, Mama had gone half crazy. Of course the bone had come out, but from then on it only took the slightest thing to set Mama off: a temperature or rash, a fall, a bump on the head. It was as though Death were stalking them, waiting for a misjudged step. 'Life turns on moments like these,' Mama said.

'Layla?'

She puts the origami bird on the windowsill. 'Yes, I'm here. Look, I'll see you tomorrow. But call me right away if Ziad gets in touch, even if it's late.'

Footsteps are coming down the corridor, accompanied by the patter of nailed paws. The door opens.

'I've got to go,' says Layla. 'Rima's just come in.' She says goodbye and hangs up.

Dog bounds towards her. He's on a lead that is actually Joe's belt, but he pulls it out of Joe's hand and jumps up at Layla, tail wagging. His nose leaves cold, wet spots on her bare arms.

'I know,' she laughs. 'I missed you too'

He drops to all fours and gives a shake.

'I realize you got confused about my name earlier,' smiles Joe, 'but am I called Rima now?'

'That was my dad.' She flushes, then rubs her forehead hard, suddenly angry with herself. 'I didn't tell him what happened with Jacques. And I didn't tell him where I am either.'

'Don't beat yourself up about it. You only kept it back so he wouldn't worry.'

'It's still a lie.'

'Yes, but ... well, we all say things like that, because their generation has worried enough. They've had decades of living on the edge.'

'Do you tell those sorts of lies too?'

Joe's eye snags on the paper bird on the windowsill. He goes and picks it up. She can tell by the look on his face that he likes it. 'Well, I did call my mum when I was walking back to the car, and she asked about you.'

'And?' What he told his mother about her feels important. 'What did you say?'

'I told her ...' He runs his fingers lightly over the

bird's wing and tests the tip with his forefinger, gently so it doesn't bend. He touches the bird's beak and caresses its head; then his fingertips travel slowly over the white back until they are exploring the pleated tail. 'I told her you were spending the night with a friend.'

Layla is so busy watching his hand that she misses his answer. 'Sorry?'

He repeats what he said, and looks up at her, a piercing look.

She needs to say something. Anything. 'It's a sparrow, you know.'

His eyebrows rise slightly; then he returns the bird to the windowsill. 'Can you make other animals?'

'Yes, but it's birds I like best.' The sparrow sits on the windowsill facing out. Something about it reminds Layla of Mama and Ziad. Blank, unknowable, pinioned yet yearning to fly.

Dog is sniffing his way around the room, trailing Joe's belt. She reaches down, unloops it from around his neck and hands it back to Joe. 'I hope he doesn't … you know, do it in here.'

'He did it already.'

'In the car?'

'No.'

'Thank God!'

Dog flops down in the middle of the floor, head between his paws, and heaves a sigh.

'On the lawn.'

'Oh no.' The clipped lawn, grass the likes of which you hardly ever find in this country. Grass that must be tended and loved by someone. 'I'll go clean it up.' She starts for the door. 'Where exactly is it?'

Joe laughs. 'You'll never find it. You don't even know the campus. I'll do it.'

'Really?' A Lebanese man picking up dog mess? That's got to be a world first.

He opens the wardrobe and empties laundry out of a plastic carrier bag. She can tell he isn't relishing the prospect. He will find it disgusting. But he's going to do it anyway, and confound her expectations of him again.

While he is gone, she eats some crisps, throwing one every now and then to Dog. 'Maybe he's not just a typical Lebanese guy, then. Or maybe such a thing doesn't even exist.' She throws Dog another crisp. 'Did you have to go and crap on the lawn?' But Dog just thumps his tail on the floor.

When Joe gets back, he goes straight to the sink and turns on the tap.

'Sorry,' she says. 'That you had to deal with that, I mean.'

'Well' – Joe is washing his hands meticulously, with a nail-brush – 'I guess he's got to do it somewhere.'

'Have you have something he could drink out of?' She feels bad even asking. 'He's panting. I think he could use some water.'

Joe dries his hands, then goes and takes a bowl down from the shelf. He tips paper-clips and staples out, fills it with water from the tap and puts it down on the floor. Dog scrambles to his feet and slurps noisily, following the bowl along the floor, and Layla wonders where stray dogs find water in this dry country. No wonder he charged into the sea.

When he's finished drinking, she leans over and gives him a pat, then scratches behind his ear. 'Look, he likes that.'

Joe smiles.

Dog rolls onto his back, paws in the air, and she strokes the lines of his sticking-out ribs, following the steep decline from breastbone to belly. With his mouth open and his tongue flopping out sideways, she can see his canines, and the row of small, doll-dainty teeth between them. She touches the pads of his feet, rough and warm, that make her think of long journeys.

Suddenly Dog swivels over, sits up and begins to scratch, his hind claws raking his body.

She glances nervously at Joe. He says nothing, but his lips are pursed tight. 'I really must get him some flea medicine,' she murmurs.

Chapter Ten

Layla is lying in Joe's bed. She has showered and borrowed a clean T-shirt, and now, under the covers, she slips off her trousers. Propped up on one elbow, she adjusts the bed-cover. A scent of soap lingers on Joe's pillow, along with something warmer and mustier: the smell of him sleeping. She wonders how long ago the bedding was changed; how many times he has been cocooned in these sheets. Lying here makes her consider what Joe might have done in this bed, and who he might have done it with. It makes her think of her own bed in halls, and Anders, and Ben. The initial guilt that sex carried, and how quickly that had cleared.

The door opens. Joe has three large cushions he has stolen them from the common room tucked under his arms, and he drops them on the floor. He too has changed into night T-shirt and shorts.

'Are you sure you don't want me to sleep in the common room?' he says.

'No. This is your room.'

Beneath the window, he arranges the cushions in a line and floats a sheet down over them. She examines his legs as he moves about: the movement of his calf muscles, the hair on his shins, the square kneecaps and nice feet. She likes his toes. But she is beginning to suspect that, even though she is lying half-naked in his bed, nothing will happen, because either Joe doesn't fancy her, or is too moral to do anything about it if he does. He is so moral they ought to canonize him.

Dog examines the bedding arrangement on the floor, then steps onto it.

'Hey.' Joe pushes him off with his leg. 'This isn't for you.'

Dog retreats, circles on the spot a few times, then collapses on the floor beside Layla.

Joe gets into his makeshift bed. 'It's funny. I've never seen the room from this angle before. It looks different.'

'Does it?'

He nods. 'Well ...' Is it her imagination, or does he look a bit nervous and self-conscious; a little hot and bothered? Is he thinking about sex, but persuading himself that they mustn't? Maybe he is considering the shame that would be heaped upon her – her, not him – if anyone found out. The immediate plummeting of her reputation. Or perhaps he's thinking that plenty of people here have premarital sex, just please don't talk about it. 'Well,' he says, 'good night.' As he reaches up to turn off the desk-lamp, his T-shirt parts with his body, and Layla glimpses the circular wash of dark hair around his navel. Then they are in darkness.

Slowly, her eyes adjust. In the dim light coming through the blinds and the gap beneath the door, she can make out the shape of things in the room.

'Thanks for the bed.' Beneath her damp hair, her scalp and neck are warm. Her body too, right down to her feet.

'No problem.'

Her thoughts sift and settle. Disappointment. Uncertainty. Confusion

'Things'll turn out okay,' says Joe. In the darkness, his voice has a huskiness to it. Not the harsh rasp of gravel, but finer, like salt or sand, or the movement of a skirt against tights. 'Your brother, I mean. Things'll work out.'

'Will they?'

'Of course. Why wouldn't they?'

She doesn't know exactly. It's just there on the outer edges of the day. Battles breaking out in the south. Mama and Baba chafing against each other. Ziad's silence. 'I think ...' It hurts even to say it. 'I think Ziad would have preferred it if I hadn't come back.'

For a moment, Joe says nothing. Then: 'I can't believe that.'

'He feels that he'll never be a source of pride to our parents.'

149

'Unlike you, you mean?'

'No! That's not what I mean.' The darkness clarifies her emotions. 'What I'm trying to say is, he thinks I'm the special one, but that's not true. It's him. It's always been him. From the beginning, they've cosseted and adored and protected him. Especially Baba. The first-born son!' Nothing so special to a Lebanese man. Passing on his name, his lineage. A daughter couldn't possibly compete. 'And then there's his leg. Because of his leg, he got more sweets than me, more toys, more hugs. He got to choose what games we were going to play, and what we watched on telly.'

Joe shifts. 'But maybe that's not the way he sees it.'

It slams into her how at odds her and Ziad's experiences of home life and parental love are. How they both believe it's the other one who holds first place in their parents' hearts.

'After all,' says Joe, 'it was you who got the chance to go and study abroad.'

'Yes, but it was what my parents wanted. At first my mother, then both of them. They pinned that on me and sent me off. God, the pressure!' Why is it so much easier to talk in the dark? But it is. 'They made the sacrifice of letting me go, yes, and had to find the money for me to live in London. But I never asked for any of that! I never asked to be talented. That's just the way it turned out. I couldn't help it.'

'It's okay,' says Joe softly. 'No one's blaming you.'

She listens to Dog breathing: the in-breath and quieter out-breath. 'Sometimes having a disabled brother is crappy.'

Silence.

She wishes she could see Joe's face. 'Are you shocked?'

'No.'

'Well it is. Because ... well, it's always there. Always. Even when you're not on the same continent.' Often, she has stopped in the middle of laughing, or had her mood dented by a swift guilt when she was having fun. 'Occasionally, just occasionally, I've wanted him to be the same as everyone else. Does that make me a terrible person?'

'No. It makes you normal.'

Her muscles relax. She hadn't realized her body was so tense.

'Has Ziad always limped?'

She nods, realizing at the same time that he can't see her. 'Yes. At least, when he was born no one knew, but a year or so later, when he began to toddle, then to try to walk, it became clear something wasn't right. Then everything changed.' The smiles were wiped off Baba and Mama's faces. There were arguments and tears, and doctors and more tears. 'After a while it didn't seem to matter so much to Mama, but Baba couldn't accept it, not for years. The doctors said that it would be permanent – that no surgery was possible – but Baba got a second and third and fourth opinion; kept going until he finally understood that no one could fix Ziad's leg. It's just the way he is. And that's just the way Baba is too. He wants everything for Ziad. That's why Baba's always pushed him.'

These are things she has never told anyone.

'Pushed him, how?'

'To do better. To compensate for what people see when they look at him.'

'That's sad.'

Again, she nods in the darkness. How did they even get started talking about Ziad? 'Does your father push you to do better?'

'He's not around long enough for that,' says Joe. 'He travels abroad a lot for work. Like now. It's always been that way.'

'Don't you mind?'

'I've never had anything to compare it with.' She hears him turn over. 'My mum depends on me instead, which I don't mind really; but I like being here and only having myself to look after.'

'Is that why you stay on into the holidays?'

'Partly.'

Joe. Yusef. Big brother, stand-in father.

They lie quietly for a time, until it seems wrong to start another conversation.

'Goodnight,' she says.

'Goodnight.'

She wriggles down into a more comfortable

position. She can just see the outline of Joe's shoulder, the silhouette of an ear.

He falls asleep first, his breathing growing slower and deeper.

Layla pulls the bed-cover up to her chin, hoping to God that Ziad has found a bed somewhere. For a second night, no one knows where he is. For that matter, no one knows where she is either. They are beyond home. Like Dog and Ali. Outsiders. Vagrants.

Something, she is not sure what, has woken her. Her phone says it's nearly four o'clock. Her legs are hot, and when she tries to move, a warm, solid weight is pinning down the bed-cover. Dog is on the bed, pressed up against her and curled up smaller than she would have imagined possible.

She tries to get back to sleep but can't.

Dog gives a couple of little yips in his sleep. On the floor, Joe who is also Yusef is asleep too, his breathing steady and deep. He lies stretched out on his cushions, the sheet drifting off him. And as she looks at the whole of him lying there half covered, she understands in a heartbeat what a marvel of engineering a body is. How expertly the two hundred and six bones are strung together with sinew and ligament, and sealed beneath skin.

She sits up and, wriggling around Dog, swings her legs to the floor. Stands, takes the two steps to where

Joe is sleeping, and kneels down. She touches his shoulder but he doesn't stir. She touches his cheek. It is warmer than she expected. With her index finger, she follows the line of his jaw. This time he stirs and opens his eyes. Blinks. Starts awake. He half sits up, leaning on one elbow, his eyes registering surprise.

She is surprised too. But then, in the last twenty-four hours, the foundations of her life – her family, her country, herself – have been twisted into unfamiliar shapes. If everything is constantly changing, then why not try to be happy while she can? Surely that's the only point of life. Life, which may decide to stop tomorrow, or next week or next year. So change it, she thinks. Live it. Do the things that, years from now, you'll wish you had done.

All this passes through her mind in a second, as Joe, completely awake now, looks at her, his dark brows knitted together. He is searching her face for clues about what is going on. And she, in turn, is trying to read him. Is he shocked? Outraged? Or does he want this too? It hangs so delicately, the whole thing, suspended on a thread of spider's silk. One wrong move, a wrong word, and everything will fall apart.

She takes his hand and touches the pads of his fingers, which are imprinted with a pattern no one else in the world shares with him. 'I want to know,' she whispers, and leans towards him to find out the answer.

Their mouths meet. She senses his surprise in the changed pattern of his breath and the tenseness of his body. But he does not push her away. So she kisses him again. Already it's clear to her that she is the more experienced of the two. But Joe is kissing her back now. She is kissing him and he is kissing her; with each small movement, a fall into empty air, stomach left behind. Then they are in the sea again. His skin tastes salty, his mouth an iridescent blue. This didn't happen with Anders or Ben. They didn't taste of colours. But now ... Azure, cerulean, navy, teal.

Joe sits up. His left hand holds onto her shoulder. The fingers of his right hand slide through her hair to the back of her head, then down her neck. She touches his face, reading his features as though she were blind. Here is her answer, and she has moved a step closer to belonging.

She kisses him harder. Indigo, turquoise, cobalt. Moves his hand from her waist and puts it on her breast. Feels the change again in his breathing. What is he thinking? A girl he met only this afternoon. Is he thinking that she's easy? That she would do this with anyone?

His arm hooks behind her and pulls her closer.

She explores the bumps of vertebrae that form his spine, back-strokes the bristly hair on the back of his head.

He is kissing her fast now – her mouth, her throat,

her jaw, her mouth again. He pushes up her T-shirt. She detaches her mouth from his and pulls her T-shirt over her head.

The risk of what she is doing strikes her afresh. She knows full well what people would think of her – this is not the way for a nice Lebanese girl to behave. From being a good, clean girl, she will become one who is seen as promiscuous and unmarriageable. Still, she won't have to put up with these attitudes first hand, because she'll be back in London, where such things don't matter. But then there's her family to consider too: not only will what she's doing affect her, but it will blacken her family's name. They will be shamed, disgraced, talked about, ridiculed. If Mama and Baba find out, what will they say? How will they look at her? Will she be shunned?

She knows all this, but the door has closed, the latch fallen. The decision is made: there is no going back now. And she will not, cannot, be a hypocrite.

Joe's hands are hot on her bare back. His T-shirt is off, and she brings his head into the crook of her shoulder. Next to her ear, his breathing sounds like the sea. She thinks she hears her name. Layla. Night.

'Why didn't you ... earlier, in the sea ... why didn't you kiss me?'

'I didn't want to jump the gun.' He kisses her throat. 'Scare you away.' Kiss. 'Make you leave.'

The words to make sense of all this are curled up

somewhere in the various corners of her head, but to tease out the correct ones, then string them into just the order that will express it, is impossible. If she tried, it would not come out right. It would explain something altogether different. So she does not try. She simply lets what is happening carry her onwards.

Chapter Eleven

They are lying side by side on the floor, falling into sleep, when there is a thunderous boom. The shock of it makes Joe's hand clamp around hers so hard it hurts. He sits up, his eyes wide. The air is shaking, and Dog springs down off the bed. A plane roars over, sawing the sky in two. Then there's the thud and shake of a second explosion.

Layla's heart is hammering. Dog circles the room, whining, his tail tucked deep between his legs. Joe kicks the crumpled sheet to one side and gets to his feet.

'What is it? What's going on?'

Dog climbs onto her, his nails digging into her legs, but she pushes him off, too scared to deal with his fear as well as her own. He goes and crawls under the bed.

Joe grabs his T-shirt and heads for the door.

'Wait!' She scrambles to her feet. 'Where are you going?'

'It's okay, I'm only going to the common room.' The door closes behind him.

Yes, the common room, with its T.V. and

computers. Quickly, she pulls her T-shirt on. Dog is shivering under the bed, but when she opens the door, he crawls out and follows close beside her, his breath hot on her fingers.

In the common room, one of the computers is humming into life, but Joe is standing in front of the T.V. On the screen, the footage is shaky, a hand-held camera probably, but there are images of fire and planes.

'The airport,' says Joe blankly. 'They're bombing the airport.'

On television, a distraught man is repeating that the airport is under attack by Israeli gunship helicopters. A minute later he says that the runways are being destroyed. As he speaks, fuel tanks are hit and turn into fireballs.

Layla is breathing hard, as if she has just run a race. The airport – God, the airport where she arrived only two nights ago, and from where, until this moment, she was intending to leave. How in hell will she get back to London now? The door has closed, the latch fallen.

Joe goes to the window and stands there with his arms limp at his sides. When Layla joins him, she sees it too. From the building's position on raised ground, the southern side of the city is visible, a skyline on fire, ghastly and beautiful. The thud and flare of explosions continues. And through it comes the faint sound of morning prayers.

There's a thump-thump-thump of footsteps on the stairs, and two young men burst into the common room. Layla recognises them from earlier, when she and Joe were walking around campus. They're dishevelled now, barely dressed, their hair tousled from sleep.

The one with the goatee, Tony, sees Joe first. 'What the fuck's going on?' Then he sees Layla. 'Oh. Hi. You're ... you're still here.'

She refuses to be embarrassed. 'That's right.'

'Well, sorry about the language, but—'

'Israel's bombed the airport,' she says.

Kamal, the curly-haired one with glasses, looks terrified. Then Dog comes out from behind the sofa and he looks even more terrified. 'Jesus! What in hell is this?' He looks from Joe to Layla.

'He's mine,' says Layla.

'Does he bite?' asks Kamal, getting the sofa between him and Dog.

'No, he's fine.'

Kamal inches closer to the T.V., trying to hear to what the reporter is saying.

'Christ, Joe, a girl *and* a dog!' says Tony. 'If Mr Ayoub finds out, you'll be packing your bags.'

'Shut up, will you?' says Kamal over his shoulder. 'I can't hear a thing.'

They stand watching; taking it in.

'I don't understand.' Kamal tugs nervously at his T-shirt. 'What has the airport got to do with Hizballah?'

'It's got as much to do with them as bridges and power stations do,' says Joe.

One plane then another pass overhead. They carry on watching in silence. Then more news: Israeli warplanes have hit the television station Al-Manar, which has links with Hizballah. A broadcast tower has been destroyed.

With Dog at her heels, Layla hurries to Joe's room to fetch her mobile. When she comes back into the common room, the other three are still glued to the television. Going to the window, she dials home.

From Baba's voice, she can tell that she's woken him up. But she wants to spare them even a minute of worry. As she talks, she hears him turn on the television.

'But I'm fine,' she says, trying to sound fine, 'that's what I wanted to let you know. I'm in Ras Beirut, nowhere near the south side.'

She hears Mama's voice, scratchy with sleep: 'What is it, Fadi? Is it one of the children?'

Baba hands Layla over.

'Layla? Darling?' The television is on in the background, the reporter's voice speaking rapidly. 'Oh God. Oh God.'

Quickly, Layla explains.

'Look, stay where you are, *habibti*. Don't go out anywhere, not anywhere, till morning.'

'No, of course not.' Here on campus, where *Jacaranda mimosifolia* grows and cats laze in trees, nothing bad can happen, can it?

'Tell her to come home,' instructs Baba in the background. 'Tell her.'

'Baba says—'

'I heard,' says Layla. 'Look, Mama, the battery's getting low on my phone. I'll call you in the morning.'

'God help us. It's just like before.'

'No,' says Layla, 'it's not.' This is not like the civil war she has heard so much about from her parents. This is sudden and fast-moving. An assault, not a war, because there is no sign of the Lebanese military. 'It's not like what happened before.'

There's a brief silence, as if Mama is digesting this. 'But this might not be the end of it. This is ... God, I don't know what this is!' Mama's words come out *staccato* with dread. 'Please, Layla, come home as soon as you can. First thing. If anything were to happen ... to you, or Ziad ... God, Ziad. Where is he? Where can he be?' There are tears in her voice.

Layla tries to sound calm, but her heart is sprinting with fear for Ziad. 'He's got no reason to go to south Beirut, Mama. He doesn't know anyone there. And he'll be in touch now, I'm sure he will.'

'Be careful, *habati*.'

'I'll see you in the morning, okay? And tell Baba not to worry.'

162

After hanging up, she looks back through all the texts that she's received from Ziad over the last few months. She assesses each one, lifting out words and phrases like organs in an autopsy; but there are no clues as to where he might be right now. 'Christ, Ziad!' she whispers. 'Where the fuck are you?'

Joe is on the phone to his mother. He speaks reassuringly, calmly. 'Jacques' there, right? Good.'

Half an hour later, the bombing stops. The others make calls home too, and the T.V. stays on. Tony remains standing, Kamal sits in the armchair, and Layla and Joe take the sofa. Layla wants to put her hand on Joe's, hold onto his arm, anything that will make her feel safe. But now the tension is coming off Joe in waves, and here, with Tony and Kamal in the room, and the world outside going insane, touching Joe seems like a big thing. So she bends down and strokes Dog instead: touches the wet nose and loose jowls, strokes the hard flatness of his skull, and the soft ears. Affection for this animal surges through her, and guilt that she has dragged him into all of this.

When she straightens back up, Kamal is staring at her.

'Do you think they're done?' asks Layla. 'The planes are gone.'

'Who knows?' says Tony, but he turns down the volume on the television. 'It's all on the south side of the city, though. God, I should have gone home when term ended.'

'Stop moaning, you're here now,' says Kamal. He rubs his hair, which is standing up on one side anyway from where he's been sleeping on it. 'I still don't get it. I mean, stuff's been going on in the border region for years. Hizballah fires missiles into Israel, and the IDF comes back at them with heavy artillery and aerial bombing.'

'True,' says Joe. 'Except that when IDF shot those Palestinian demonstrators a few years back, and Hizballah kidnapped three of their soldiers in retaliation, the soldiers were sent back home dead.'

'But even that didn't cause anything like this,' says Layla. 'They've exchanged prisoners before, haven't they? Isn't that what they do?'

'Hizballah wanted to do that this time too,' says Joe.

'It's not what they got, though, is it?' says Tony, pacing up and down.

'Not what *we* got, you mean,' says Joe.

'Yes yes yes,' says Kamal, 'but what I'm saying is, there have been attacks from both sides a hundred times these last years, so what makes this different? Israel could just swap prisoners and get their soldiers back.'

Tony comes to a standstill. 'Who cares about the whys? It's already happened. Our country's being blasted to pieces, and it's all down to Hizballah! What in hell gives them the right to sit on our border and poke and prod Israel?'

'Isn't that their agenda?' says Layla. 'They're hijackers and murderers.'

'Yes, says Joe, 'but they're also a social services provider for the Shia. They fund schools and hospitals, they have social development programmes ...'

'Really?' Layla didn't know this. 'But that doesn't change the fact that they're terrorists.'

'No, of course it doesn't, no one's disputing that.' Joe sounds impatient. 'The Arabs kill Jews just because they're Jews, and the Jews kill Arabs just because they're Arabs. Where's the solution? I'm only saying that Hizballah is embedded into society here. They're too powerful for the government to do anything about.'

Layla can see that this much is well-known to the other three. While she has been away, they have had time to become familiar with the political landscape here, and keep up with its changes.

Tony starts pacing again, his eyes on the television. 'Fuck the lot of them! They're destroying our country!'

Layla and Joe stand in his room. Dawn is breaking, and Tony and Kamal have gone back to bed. It's quiet outside.

'I'm scared,' says Layla.

What is there to say to that? If he told her everything was okay, it would be a lie.

'It's all right to be scared.' He turns and puts his

arms around her. But it is a conscious movement, with an awkwardness to it.

They come apart again.

'Where do you want to sleep?' she asks, feeling uncomfortable.

He looks at the bed, studying it as if it is entirely unfamiliar. 'If we put all the bedding down on the floor …'

'Okay.' She smiles weakly. The heat and fizz of a couple of hours ago has vanished, but perhaps they will lie close and manage to comfort each other that way.

It feels strange to be on the floor again. Layla wants to snuggle into Joe and find the right place between his arm and chest where her head will fit; but with daylight coming through the blinds, and the images and words from the television fresh in her mind, and worry for Ziad twisting her gut, she finds that she can't get that close to him. Perhaps he feels the same way, because they just lie side by side not touching.

Back under the bed, Dog is already asleep.

Layla closes her eyes.

Chapter Twelve

When she wakes, the stillness of early morning has shifted into the settled feel of the middle of the day. She checks her phone: twelve thirty-three. No messages. And the battery's still low.

Joe is not there, and neither is Dog. She finds them in the common room, where Joe is seated at a computer reading the news. There is an intensity about the way he is sitting – the tight shoulders, the hunch of his back – that scares her.

Dog scrambles up to greet her. Joe turns, but there is no smile today, no glimpse of those wonderfully overlapping teeth. 'Hi.'

'Good morning.'

'Did you sleep okay?'

She nods, and he turns back to the screen.

'Anything new?'

'Here.' He moves to one side. 'Read for yourself. If I told you, you wouldn't believe it.'

Hizballah has fired more than one hundred and twenty rockets into Israel, one of which has hit the port town of Haifa, killing two. The list of towns in the south of Lebanon that have been hit by Israel goes on for half a page. Two small military airports have been attacked, and the main road between Beirut and Damascus has been cut off. The attacks have left at least fifty Lebanese dead. Israeli warships are lining up along the coastline, and have blockaded the ports, while Israel has declared Lebanese airspace closed to everything but its own jets. On the border, Israeli tanks are gathering.

Even in the heat of mid-day, she feels chill with fear. She reads on. Lebanon's call for a ceasefire has been rejected. Evidence is surfacing that the capture of the soldiers was only an excuse, a starting pistol for a long-planned attack to devastate Lebanon to such a degree that its people will turn against Hizballah. Layla bites down on her thumb. In Gaza, more bombs have been dropped. The Israeli prime minister has said that these are difficult days for Israel. If there were any humour left in her, she would laugh.

For a long time, they sit in silence. Then Layla pulls out her phone and calls home, but there's no answer. Baba will be at work, and Mama will have gone out to buy bread or tomatoes or olive oil.

'Let's go outside and see what's going on. And maybe get something to eat.'

'Okay,' says Joe.

'Can we take Dog?'

They sneak out of a back gate. Bliss Street is quiet, a strange, shocked sort of silence. A holding in of breath. Yet there are still some normalities, like the smell of roasting coffee, a pale blue sky, and a trickle of traffic. The few people who are about give Layla a wide berth, and she knows why. Before they came out, she knotted one of Joe's socks around Dog's neck and threaded a belt through it, and now Dog is panting on the end of his makeshift lead, looking as strange as this strange day will allow. But she doesn't care what it looks like: better this than having him run away. Even though he has never walked on a lead before, the belt is slack in her hand, and Dog close by her leg.

She and Joe walk side by side. She is aware of the occasional brush of their arms, but they don't hold hands. It makes her think about last night, before the planes and the bombs. Them kissing, his hands on her body, and hers on his. Him pulling her close. The short, soft hairs at the back of his head. Them lying, skin against skin. Is Joe thinking about it too? Will they, at some point before she heads back home, kiss again?

But her thoughts keep straying back to Ziad, wondering whether he is on his way home, or if he could have been caught up in the trouble. And then there's the bigger picture. She tries to imagine Heathrow Airport being bombed, British motorways and bridges being destroyed. Whole swathes of towns and villages. She imagines warships peppering the

British coast. A blockade, with nothing – no goods or fuel or food or people – allowed in or out. She tries to imagine this, but can't.

'There's a coffee shop and bakery just down here,' says Joe.

They pass a grocery store scuttling with customers. They are grabbing what they can, unfussy. Even though she has never seen this before, it is still familiar. Many times, Baba has spoken of having to rush out between bouts of shelling during the civil war to get food or water. She and Ziad have listened to tales of taps running dry, of their parents huddled in a basement with no telephone lines or electricity, no food or water.

Outside the coffee shop, she hands Joe his belt. 'What do you fancy?'

'Oh, I don't know, a croissant. And some water.'

He looks beautiful standing there. Not the person she interpreted outside his flat yesterday, but someone more. She wants to kiss him, right here and now, but out here in the open and in daylight, it is too bold a step. 'I'll just be a minute.'

At the back of the shop, the owner has the radio on. In spite of herself, Layla listens for the announcement of a dead teenager, but none comes.

She comes out with two bottles of water and a paper bag of *za'atar* croissants. They eat one each as they wander back, Layla tearing bits off and dropping them to Dog. The bits vanish instantly, but Dog still stares up at her as if he has eaten nothing.

Her phone beeps. She pulls it out of her pocket.

'Is it Ziad?' asks Joe.

'No, just a friend.' Her friend Sophie, who plays bassoon. *Jesus. Just saw the news. Are you okay???*

That world of letting Sophie do her hair while they discuss boys and music and clothes seems like a story in some book. She texts back: *I'm fine, don't worry. X*

Joe stops outside a small DVD store. The door is propped open, and he waves at a young man in a baseball cap serving behind the counter. 'Hey, Bashir.'

The man raises a hand in greeting. 'Hi.' He is only one in a whole network of friends and acquaintances that, Layla realizes, has nothing to do with her.

'Business is good, I see,' says Joe, and he's right: the shop is crammed with people chatting and choosing films. It looks more like a social club than a DVD store.

'If people are going to be trapped indoors, they need something to do,' says Bashir. 'So long as the electricity lasts, anyway.' Turning to serve a man and his daughter, he taps a finger on one of the films they have chosen. 'Are you sure you want this one? It's heavy. Upsetting.'

'Oh,' says the man. 'Then no.' It is extracted from the pile. 'Can you give us something funny instead?'

'Yeah, sure.' Bashir selects a couple of films from the shelves behind him and adds them to the pile on the counter. When he has finished serving, he smiles at Layla. 'Come in, please. You can tie up your dog just there.'

She knows he is only being polite.

The father and daughter come out of the shop. 'Who knows how long this madness is going to last?' the man is saying. 'So we'll watch films, play *shesh besh*, eat … it'll be all right.'

As the pair walk away, Layla imagines how in various towns and villages in Lebanon, the routine of lives has been interrupted. The grandmother stirring *sneyniyeh* in celebration of her grandchild's first tooth, the IT man mending the same ancient computer for the ninth time, a boy and girl falling asleep side by side in halls in Ras Beirut.

'Come on,' says Joe.

'The radio was on in the coffee shop,' she tells him as they walk. 'They were saying that Israeli planes dropped leaflets over Dahiye this morning.'

Joe slows down.

'That means there's going to be more bombing, doesn't it?'

He swallows his mouthful. 'Fuck.'

Layla starts. It's the first time she has heard Joe swear.

'Do you … do you still want to go to the museum?' he asks.

That's what they had agreed yesterday, when the

world was an entirely different place. 'I'm going to go, but you don't have to come with me. Actually ... actually I don't think you *should* come with me. Not with everything that's going on.'

Will he mention what happened last night now? Or maybe acknowledge it by touching her arm or face?

He considers. 'I'm not sure the museum'll even be open.'

She shrugs, hurt by the distance that has sprung up between them. 'I'm going to go anyway.' Even if it is open, she's almost certain Ziad won't be there. Who in their right mind would visit a museum on a day like this? But she will go anyway and at least leave her phone number. 'It's the only thing left that I can do. Then I'll have to go back home.'

In silence, they cross the road and head towards Baba's car. Just past the main gate, Ali is sitting against the campus wall. A cigarette is pinched between his thumb and forefinger, as if it were a bee held by its sting. His white beard and moustache are stained brown from smoking, and his hair hangs in dirty clumps.

'How's it going, Ali?' asks Joe sombrely. 'Have you had your coffee today?'

Ali looks up with enormous, sad eyes. 'Yes, yes.' His jeans are torn at the knee, and the trainers on his feet are certainly not his size. Bunched up on the ground beside him is a jumper that he must use for a pillow.

He takes in Layla and Dog but makes no comment about either. Dog sniffs his feet and legs, and when Ali doesn't so much as blink, Layla warms to him.

'Would you like something to eat?' she asks, holding out the bag.

'Thank you, thank you.'

She hands him the bag with the rest of the food in it. She's still hungry, and Joe probably is too, but she can see he doesn't mind.

Ali takes the bag and, not even bothering to look inside, puts it down beside him. 'Where did you find such a sweet girl?' he asks Joe. 'Face as lovely as the moon.'

Layla smiles at the compliment. She is surprised at how well-spoken Ali is.

'Did you hear the bombing this morning?' says Joe. 'They were—'

'No.' Ali shakes his head vigorously. 'I didn't hear anything. Not anything.'

Dog pulls on the lead to get closer and sniff Ali's beard.

Layla pulls him back.

'I don't mind,' says Ali. 'We understand each other, don't we?' He is eye to eye with Dog. 'Does he belong to you?'

'He's a stray, but for now ... yes, he's mine.'

'Ah, what luck!' says Ali to Dog. 'We live, don't we, my friend, by these little acts of kindness. May they remain forthcoming.' He squints up at Layla, the bags heavy beneath his eyes. 'Abundance,' he says. 'Have you had your abundance of life yet?'

It takes her a moment to realize what he is referring to. The plaque on the campus gates: *That they may have life and have it more abundantly.* She doesn't know what to say.

Ali takes a drag on his cigarette. 'You can calculate the critical temperatures that determine the hydrogen-helium abundance with the assumption that they are driven by the internal energy of the expanding universe.'

Joe lets out a short laugh. 'Are you playing with us, Ali? You know I'm not a physics major. And neither is Layla.'

'Ah, Layla. "I pass by these walls, the walls of Layla, And I kiss this wall and that wall." ' He takes another drag on his cigarette. '*Une telle abondance.* It flows over.' He presses his hand against his head, then starts to talk in numbers and letters, as if calculating something. Whether it is sense or nonsense, Layla can't tell.

'See you later, Ali,' says Joe.

'Bye,' says Layla, but Ali is already somewhere else, lost in his calculations.

'He quotes poetry,' she says as they walk away, 'and speaks French.'

'You could have talked to him in English too if you

wanted. He's well educated. Sometimes the professors give him scientific articles to read.'

'But how did he get to be living like this?'

'Because he goes crazy. Sometimes like he did just now, sometimes worse. They say it was the civil war that did it. The things he saw. The things that were done to him.'

'You mean he was tortured?'

'Maybe. No one knows for sure. Either way, he never recovered.'

It was years ago, September beginning to cool the air, and she was the only one home when Ziad came in. He looked tired but pleased, the expression of someone who has accomplished something. He was rumpled and untidy, streaks of dirt on his arms and across his face, as if he had been in a scuffle. And in his hand, a knife.

He does not see her. And she, in turn, does not know what to think. But that look on his face, together with the knife, fills her with horror.

Perhaps she makes a noise, because he looks over. When he sees her, he freezes.

'What have you been doing?' she asks in a small voice.

His face hardens, then he shrugs, nonchalant. 'Nothing.'

'The knife.' It is sturdy, short-bladed. One that

Mama uses to cut tough meat or stringy vegetables. From where she is standing, Layla can't make out if the metal is stained with anything. 'What … what did you need the knife for?' She glances at the floor, looking for drips.

Ziad shifts from one foot to the other, his face dark.

It is hot in here, suffocating. Sweat prickles at her temples.

'I didn't do anything.' He marches towards her. 'So you can just leave me alone.' He pushes past, and she follows him down the hall.

'What have you done?' The possible answers hang suspended around her like paintings and she hesitates. 'You didn't hurt anyone, did you?'

Ziad stops. Slowly, he turns around and gives her a look that says she never has and never will understand him.

'Well?' She is not so sure now. 'Did you?'

He breathes in and out, hot, angry breaths. 'I was at the bottom of the hill. Alone. Are you happy now?' He turns and goes into his bedroom, pushing the door shut behind him.

She stands staring at the door for a few moments, then leaves the house.

She doesn't know what she is looking for at the bottom of the slope, but whatever else she expected, it is not the thing that she finds.

Something catches in her chest when she sees it and

realizes what he has done. Not long ago, Baba explained to them how the vascular system in humans worked, and as a comparison, he talked about plants. And trees.

'Poor thing,' she whispers. 'Poor thing.'

Weeks later it begins. A tinge of yellow to the leaves. Then yellow turns to brown and, months before their time, the leaves drop to the ground. Instead of ripening in the sun and splitting to reveal their tightly packed seeds, the remaining figs shrivel on their branches.

She watches it, week by week, and hates her brother, because she cannot do a thing to prevent this slow starvation. With Mama's knife, Ziad cut into the bark of the fig tree and stripped off a ring of it all the way around the trunk. On the ground were a couple of sharp stones that he probably used as well. It must have taken him ages. When Baba finds out, he shouts at him. Mama covers her mouth in shock. But Ziad remains doggedly silent.

On the steps, lit bright by the sun, Layla tilts her head back to take in the museum. It's a handsomely restored pale-stone fortress of a building, fronted with four massive pillars.

The museum is not closed, but it is not exactly open either. Inside, there is nobody at the ticket office. She and Joe, who insisted on coming with her, pass through. The hum of an electricity generator comes from somewhere. In the entrance hall, Layla stops to take in the newness of the polished stone floors and white pillars. Laid into the floor directly in front of her is a mosaic. To left and right, intricately carved sarcophagi. Straight ahead, two female sculptures on either side of the wide staircase. Each object is ringed with a pool of light. But there are no visitors here. Not a soul. The place is a capsule of cool stillness.

Inexplicably, it settles on her like dust: the feeling that Ziad is hiding in here somewhere. That he is pressed up behind a statue or crouched smiling behind a sarcophagus, waiting for her to find him, just as he waited that bone-dry day in August when the heat had sent everyone else, even her, indoors. She walks up to a sarcophagus – she can't help herself – and looks behind it. Nothing but gleaming floor.

Joe's trainers squeak as he comes up behind her.

'What's upstairs?' she asks.

'Smaller antiquities. Spearheads, coins, jewellery, figurines, bowls.'

She imagines Joe's brain must be full of lists like these. Still, the objects he has mentioned are all too small to hide behind.

She stops in front of a case with a small marble figure of a toddler inside it. Something about the little boy reminds her of Ziad. Perhaps it's the ungainly way he is sprawled on the ground, as if struggling to stand up. The Phoenician inscription to the god Eshmun gives thanks from the parents for healing their child.

She swings round.

'What is it?' asks Joe.

A sudden urgency tightens her chest. 'I've got to find him.' The course of her life is tied up with having to look out for Ziad, and now, more keenly than ever, she feels foreboding. 'I've got to know he's okay.'

A door slams. Two men appear, walking in a hurry, followed by an elderly woman in a cleaner's uniform. The men are talking to each other and gesticulating. The woman carries a bucket. One of the men, short and fat with rimless glasses, stops in his tracks when he sees Joe and Layla, then hurries over. 'Sorry, but you cannot be here. The museum is not open. It's not open.'

The other man stays back. He takes a packet of medication from his pocket, pops out two tablets and throws them into his mouth.

Layla starts to explain: her brother, he's missing, but she knows he comes here often. He has a severe limp. Perhaps someone has seen him?

'We're closed,' repeats the man in front of her. His face and bald head are sweating. 'There's no one here. Haven't you been watching the news?'

'But you don't understand, I've got to find my brother.'

The cleaning lady unlocks a cupboard and puts her bucket inside. Layla catches a glimpse of bottles of cleaning fluids, a mop and broom.

Joe starts to speak, but the man cuts him off. '*Mademoiselle*,' he says to Layla. 'You will both have to go now.' Stress virtually oozes out of his every pore.

'Can I leave my phone number then? If my brother does come, then—'

'Please, this is a museum, not a detective agency!'

The cleaning lady, who is watching now, flinches at the raised voices.

'*What?*' Layla frowns.

Joe touches her elbow – 'Let's calm down' – but she shakes him off. How can he stay so cool? Even now, there is an annoying correctness in every line of him: his smooth hair, his ironed clothes, even his straight nose. She wants to rumple him up, scuff and mess his clothes a little so he can look and feel the way she does.

The museum man wipes a hand across his glistening forehead. 'Look, we have work to do. Don't you know what they did the last time around?'

She knows. The Green Line. This, right here, was the demarcation line between the armies and ideologies of the civil war, a place so uninhabited that plants took over and turned it green. But she is also at a junction.

'Don't you understand?' says the man.

A lump rises in her throat. 'I understand that you care more about objects than people!' Because after all, wasn't it people who hewed these objects from their previous incarnations of stone and metal and wood?

Without them, none of this would exist.

She turns and makes for the door. At her back, she hears Joe speaking to the man, his voice measured and calm, soothing things in her wake.

Outside, at the top of the steps, she stops to take deep breaths. Around her, Beirut glares beneath the unrelenting sun. Ziad walked up these steps, she knows that; haltingly, his bad leg refusing to bend as much as it should, so that he had to half haul it up. Even now, the ghost of him reaches the top step and limps past her, the displaced air wafting against her cheek. At her back, the heavy door opens and closes again.

'Your brother.' The voice is not Joe's. It is a woman's.

Layla looks round. The cleaner is squinting in the sun. She is in her sixties perhaps, with wispy brown hair tied back in a bun. Through the glass doors behind the woman, she can see Joe coming towards them.

'Is his name Ziad?' asks the cleaner.

Stunned, Layla nods.

'He's at my house.'

Chapter Thirteen

Layla shifts into third gear. There are three people and a dog in Baba's car now, driving to the south of the city, towards two spirals of smoke that are still rising from the airport. In the rear-view mirror half of Joe's face is visible, while in the passenger seat next to her, Najat, the cleaning lady, sits holding onto the door as if the old Renault were moving at the speed of sound.

'Are you going to leave your house?' Joe asks Najat.

'Leave?'

'Yes. Didn't you see the leaflets they dropped?'

'I can't read, but a neighbour read one to me. They want to hit Hizballah's headquarters. People who live close by should leave, that's what it said.'

'You know what that means, though, don't you?' says Joe.

'Their offices aren't near my house.'

'Israel doesn't cares where your house is,' says Joe. 'They mean Dahiye, that whole area.'

Najat shakes her head. 'That's not what the leaflet said.'

In the rear-view mirror, Layla sees Joe look out of the window and mouth silent words, as if to the buildings moving past them. Then he leans forward and addresses Najat again. 'You can't take that chance.'

They drive past a petrol station with queues of cars in both directions, and Layla silently thanks Baba for keeping a full tank. *Just in case*, Baba always says. *You never know*. A war mentality.

While they waited outside the museum for Najat to get her things, Layla had called home and told Mama that she'd found out where Ziad was, and was going to go and speak to him. Then, while Mama was midway through asking her where exactly that was, the phone battery ran out and the conversation was cut off.

'My brother,' Layla says. 'Tell me how he is.'

'Well, he's all right now,' says Najat. 'But he didn't look so good yesterday morning. I was going about my work at the museum and there he was wandering around looking as though someone had yanked the joy out of him.'

'And then?' prompts Layla.

'He said he had nowhere to stay, so I said he could come home with me when I finished work.'

'Do you finish at six o'clock?'

Najat looks surprised. 'That's right.'

Which was why Ziad kept checking the time when he was in Starbucks. Why he left just before six. 'That was really kind of you.' Layla is no longer used to the natural hospitality of people here. But even by Lebanese standards, offering a stranger a place to stay is a big thing. She glances across at Najat, trying to judge what sort of person she is. She takes in the slightly rotund middle in its blue uniform, tattered patent beige shoes, the crepe-paper skin and thickening joints of her hands. 'Had you met him before?'

'Oh yes. He'd been in before. Once we got talking about something – that army of little stick-men they've got in the museum, I think it was. Anyway, we talked.'

Layla doesn't know anything about an army of stick-men. Another thing her brother never thought to mention to her. 'But yesterday, what did he say yesterday?'

'Well, I asked him why he'd been walking around for so long, and he said that he didn't want to go back home. That he was never going back. He was angry – you know how young men are. He mentioned his parents, but … ' Najat gives Layla an apologetic look, 'he didn't say anything about a sister.'

'Oh.'

'He said he'd spent the night wandering about the city by himself, and he was planning on doing the same that night. So what could I do? I couldn't let a boy like him spend the night on the streets.'

'Thank you,' says Layla.

Najat shushes the thanks. 'I live alone now. My

husband passed away, God bless him. My son too. So there's room. And your brother … well, he needed the rest. When I left this morning, he was still asleep.'

'He's not ill, is he?'

'No, no, he's fine.'

Relax again. 'Good. Thank you,' repeats Layla, 'for letting him stay.'

'But you'll take him home now, poor boy, won't you?'

'Yes, I'll take him home.' She will talk sense to him, and hope to God he listens.

She glances in the rear-view mirror. Joe is tense and silent. The sight of his face brings mixed emotions. Now that Ziad has been located, there will be no need for Joe to help her search any longer. So will that be it? Game over? When they get to Najat's house, he'll go home. Then she and Ziad will go home.

They're moving slowly through the densely populated district of Dahiye now: a mess of high-rise buildings, vertical living where people are packed as tightly together as possible. Almost all the traffic is moving in the opposite direction, heading out of this area. Cars have cases tied onto their roof-racks, and bulging boots. Layla's stomach turns to water.

Almost every woman they see is covered, either in a *'abayah* or a *hijab*. A moped, but not a red one, speeds past them with two boys on it, the one on the back barely holding on. They swerve around a corner. On the pavement, a man squats beside crates of fruit and vegetables, calling to the drivers to buy food to take with them. They drive past a butcher's shop, an internet cafe, a barber's advertising 'Hizballah beards' and, following Najat's directions, turn into a narrow street dimmed by tall buildings on either side.

'Everywhere's shut.' Joe is frowning. 'People are leaving.'

That is what he wants to do too, she knows that. She can see it. And part of her wishes he hadn't insisted on coming, because it is evidently against his better judgement. He is either just too chivalrous, or else he feels that, having slept with her, he now owes her something.

They pass a church. 'Mar Yusef,' Najat tells them, crossing herself. St Joseph's. Joseph, Yusef, Joe. Things that are themselves and not themselves. And not only is this true of Joe, but also of her. Because while she is Lebanese, in this unfamiliar part of Beirut she feels more than ever like a foreigner. Yet here, in this place that is emptying fast, she will have to confront Ziad. Afloat in her unease, she will have to be sympathetic and persuasive, tactful and smooth like Joe. And they will have to be gone before nightfall.

At the far end of the street is a line of small shops. One of them, a grocery store, is still open. A poster of Hizballah's leader in the window smiles out at them from between boxes of Ariel and Persil. Outside, three young men sit on plastic chairs. One of them is smoking a *nargeel*, setting it bubbling with each inhalation. Music plays from a radio set on the pavement.

'Here, here,' says Najat a minute later, and Layla pulls up beside a two-storey square stone building.

'His scooter!' Suddenly short of breath, Layla points to a red moped parked across the road. She recognises it from the pictures Ziad e-mailed to her.

Dog is trying to get out of the car with Joe, but gently, she pushes him back in, and gives him some water to drink. 'It's alright.' She fondles the floppy, warm ears, hairy on the outside, waxy-smooth on the inside. 'I'll leave the window open. We won't be long, and then ...' Then, with any luck, she, Ziad and Dog will go home together.

What will Dog do when he sees Ziad, she wonders? Will he surge out of the car and jump up on him, tail going, whining with desperate happiness? Or will he hardly care? And what about her? What will she feel when Ziad is standing in front of her? The prospect of seeing him has been changing colour every ten seconds. Joy, exasperation, elation, annoyance.

Leaving Dog protesting in the car, she follows Joe and Najat up an exterior stone staircase. Her heart quickens, and she can't stop chewing her lip. The stairs curve round a corner. As they near the top, Najat's legs land more slowly and heavily.

'He won't mind,' Najat says. 'You're family.'

They reach a terrace shaded by a grapevine that throws dapples of light across a concrete floor. Potted plants stand in rows along the edge of the surrounding wall. There's a little table, and chairs that have seen better days. A line of washing is hanging out to dry. Two doors, both closed, lead from the terrace into Najat's flat. Up here, it feels as if they ought to be looking down on the houses of a little village, but all the buildings around are taller than this one.

Najat opens double doors that lead into a living-room. 'I'll tell him you're here.'

Standing next to Layla in the shade of the vine, Joe checks his watch and grimaces. Ripples of panic wash over Layla, like the loosening of water around an ice-cube. A black and white cat stalks along the wall, dainty on ballerina-toes, and Layla sees a slice of Najat's life with inexplicable clarity: the daily quiet of the museum, the scent of detergents and shimmer of wet floors, the shapes of ancient objects silhouetted in the dim light; then here in the evening, where cats stalk through the gloom, she sits swatting mosquitoes and listening to the neighbourhood noises.

A sound comes from inside. Joe gives Layla a quick smile, his face open and glad. Her breath catches as she watches the doorway. A smile is fixed to her face, tight and uncomfortable, but one she can't help. As Najat appears, she takes a step towards the door.

Layla looks down into the street. The rounded gladness inside her has shrivelled. 'But his scooter's still there.' And there it is, the red paintwork and triangular seat gleaming in the afternoon sun. 'He wouldn't leave his scooter behind. He loves that scooter.'

'I don't know about that,' says Najat. 'He's gone to buy something to eat, maybe.'

Layla stands watching the corner of the road. She can see Baba's car too, and Dog sitting inside it. A little way down the street, a family is getting into a car, a boy trailing a toy gun from a strap on his shoulder, a girl with scraggly pigtails crying as her mother herds her into the back seat.

Joe heads for the stairs. 'I'll go and take a look around.'

'Okay.' Layla turns to Najat. 'Are Ziad's things still in the room?'

Najat's crescent-thin eyebrows rise up in bewilderment. 'I ... I'm not sure.'

'Can I take a look? Do you mind?'

'No, no, of course not. It's in here, on the right.' She shows Layla down a dim hall.

The room is plain, with old, dark furniture. A cross hangs above the bed. The bed itself is rumpled, the cover pulled loosely up to the pillow. Against one wall is an old chair with a threadbare seat, and on the bedside table is Baba's father's watch.

How strange to see it here. Layla goes and picks it

up. It is cool, the gold strap sinuous, the crystal curved like a beetle's carapace. The golden hands are still.

'It's not mine,' says Najat. 'It must be your brother's. You see? Don't fret, my girl, don't fret. He'll be back any minute.'

'Yes.' She laughs, relieved, and slips the watch into her pocket. Although Ziad himself, she knows, will have to give it back to Baba. 'You're right.'

Outside on the terrace, Joe has returned, but he hasn't seen anyone who looks like Ziad.

'It's okay,' says Layla, and explains about the watch.

'Sit down now, sit down,' says Najat.

Layla takes a seat. This terrace feels somehow familiar. Perhaps it's the way the vine leaves frame the sky, or the tiny movements of the laundry on the line and the corresponding shift of shadows on the wall. Or it might be the crack in the mortar beside the door, or the rusting tin cans filled with marigolds and geraniums, a sun-faded picture of a saint propped up among them. And the cleanness of all of this. The woman who cleans the museum comes home and carries on cleaning. In any case, now that Layla is assured about Ziad, she drinks in the quietness that has fallen, and accepts these moments as an opportunity to breathe.

'Now what can I offer you? Tea? Coffee? Or there's cordial.'

'Thank you,' says Layla. 'Some cordial would be lovely.'

Najat goes in at the other door.

'Can I help?' calls Layla, but Najat says no. Joe is sitting with his chair angled so he can see the stairs. 'Look, don't feel as if you have to stay. You didn't really have to come with me at all.' She tries to sound composed, even casual.

'Was I supposed to let you drive off with a stranger?' he says in a low voice.

'Well, yesterday I drove off with you.'

He sits back. 'That's different. Your family knows my family.'

'Why does everyone around here think they have to protect me? I'm an adult!'

Joe shrugs. 'Life's different here, that's all. Anyway, maybe I wanted to come. Has that occurred to you?'

'But looks at you: you don't want to be here. So if it's because of … you know, because of last night – if that's why you came here and why you're waiting with me, then there's absolutely no need.'

The slightest of furrows appears between his eyebrows, and he has that searching look, the one that she imagines can see right into her. 'What happened last night; it's not the sort of thing … that is, I wouldn't normally … not with someone I just met.'

'I see.' She feels herself turn prickly. 'You mean you wouldn't usually have a one-night stand.'

He tenses. The sound of clattering plates comes from the kitchen.

'Oh, it's fine,' she says. Although if he thinks that last night was a one-night stand, then it is not fine. It is anything but fine. 'You think I sleep with people all the time, is that it?' All the anxieties she ignored last night bubble to the surface. 'You think I'm a slut.'

He starts to laugh. 'No! No! Why would I—'

'Because I know what a lot of people would say.'

Quickly, the smile drops off his face and he is all seriousness again. 'Well I'm not a lot of people.' He leans towards her, intent. 'It wasn't that way for me, Layla.'

Has he said her name out loud before? She can't remember. The sound of it from his lips brings the closeness of last night hurtling back. It is more intimate even than a touch.

'What was it then? You said you don't do things like that. Does that mean it was a mistake?'

He doesn't blink, or hesitate. 'It wasn't a mistake.' His hand covers hers. 'Okay?'

She struggles childishly between embarrassment and joy. 'Sorry, I didn't mean to push.'

Najat steps out of the kitchen, and Joe withdraws his hand. She is carrying a jug of red cordial and some glasses on a tray, which she sets down on the table. 'I made these *ma'caron* the other day.' She points to a plate of fried dough-balls with their bumpy latticed surface. 'I know it's not Epiphany, but I have a sweet tooth, so once a week I make myself something nice. A treat. One needs a treat. Help yourself, help yourselves.'

Layla takes a *ma'caron*. It's been years since she tasted one. 'Mm, that's really good.'

'Delicious,' says Joe. 'But you know, we really shouldn't be sitting here eating when—'

'Here, have another.' Najat pushes the plate towards Joe. It's clear she likes him. But then, everyone seems to like him.

Layla wipes the syrup off her fingers with a paper napkin. The black and white cat is gone now, but a tortoiseshell one appears from somewhere.

'Oh, it's you,' says Najat. 'I haven't seen you for a few days. Now where have you been?' She leans down to stroke the cat that's curling itself around the legs of her chair.

'Is it yours?' asks Joe.

'No, they're all strays. They come now and then to be fed. This one, now this one's the boss. She sees the others off if she's in a bad mood and doesn't want to share me. Don't you now?' The cat's back arches and bends beneath Najat's hand. Layla can hear the thrum of a purr. 'The neighbours downstairs, may God destroy their house, give the cats a kicking whenever they get the chance, but it still doesn't stop them from coming up.'

Joe glances towards the stairs again and checks his watch.

'To touch a living thing, that's important.' Najat falls silent for a while. 'When my son was little and ill in bed, he would reach out to make sure I was still there next to him. In the darkness, he would touch my arm, my stomach, my hair. Yes, she's still here, he'd think, and then he could sleep. Even when he became a young man, he'd squeeze my arm after an argument to soothe things between us. Except for the last time we argued, before he went to fight with the militia.'

The cordial is overly sweet in Layla's mouth. 'I'm sorry,' she says, sensing that the son must have died in one of the many battles of the civil war. The sun is low now, its light needling out between two high-rises. 'Ziad ought to be back by now.'

Joe gets to his feet and goes to look down at the street. He doesn't sit down again, but remains near the low wall, pacing up and down. 'Everyone's leaving.'

'Not everyone,' says Najat. She talks some more: about the cats, about the museum and how she gets there (a crowded mini-bus driven by a man in a dirty vest), about what this neighbourhood was like when she first moved here, before Israel drove the Shia up from the south. Layla wishes she would stop.

'It's gone six o'clock,' says Joe. 'We can't just sit here and wait.' He points down into the street. 'There goes another family. Look, they're scribbling their name on their water tank.'

'What for?' asks Layla.

'It's what people used to do in the war. So they'd know which house was theirs when they came back.'

Layla hears a car start up and drive away. 'He's got to come back. He left his scooter, and Baba's watch.'

Joe strides towards her and leans his hands on the table. 'It's been over an hour. Well over.' Beads of sweat dot his forehead, tiny things that sit there like dew.

Wiping her palms on her trousers, Layla pushes her chair back and goes to look down at the street for herself. She doesn't know what on earth to do. Down there in Baba's car, Dog seems to be asleep. Right now, she envies him.

Joe turns her around, holds her by both shoulders. Even through her T-shirt, his hands are hot. 'Don't you realize what might happen to us if we stay?' Then, slowly, so as to emphasise each word: 'They're going to bomb this whole area.'

For a moment, nothing but his eyes, and her thoughts.

'No.' Najat gets up. 'Here, you can see for yourself.' She goes inside and returns with a piece of paper, which she hands to Joe.

Joe reads it out loud. 'To the Inhabitants of Lebanon. Due to the terrorist activities carried out by Hizballah which destroys the effort to find a brighter future for Lebanon, the Israeli Army will continue its work within Lebanon for as long as it deems fit to protect the citizens of the State of Israel. For your own safety and because we do not wish to cause any more civilian deaths, you are advised to avoid all places frequented by Hizballah. You should know that the continuation of terrorist activities against the State of Israel will be considered a double-edged sword for you and Lebanon. The State of Israel.' He carries on looking at the leaflet in silence, as if trying to extract more meaning from it.

'Hizballah don't frequent my house! The Israelis can target a single building if they want to, the way they do in Gaza. That's what they'll do.'

Joe drags a hand down his face. It comes away wet. 'And if they don't? If they decide to flatten this whole place?'

Najat frowns and picks at her fingers.

He flaps the piece of paper. 'Dahiye is Hizballah territory, that's what this leaflet is saying.'

'Najat!' A woman a little younger than Najat is hurrying up the last few steps of the staircase. 'Turn on your television.' The woman doesn't even stop to greet Joe and Layla, but carries straight on into the kitchen.

'My neighbour,' explains Najat as they follow her in. 'The nice one,' she adds.

In the kitchen, the woman snaps on a little television on top of the fridge.

'Has the government sorted it out?' asks Najat as the picture flickers into life.

The woman doesn't answer. They stand and watch in silence.

There is no way in or out of the country. At the height of the tourist season, tourists and Lebanese from abroad are stranded, milling in hotels. In the south, civilian casualties are escalating. The dead include a family of twelve, including eight children, and another of seven, in the same village. All bridges and main roads in the south have been destroyed. Footage shows people running, women screaming, cars thick with dust. The remains of houses and blocks of flats. Entire villages flattened. Smoke, rubble, dead bodies, and others, still living, walking away from their homes, northwards towards Beirut, on foot because there are no longer roads for cars to drive on. The European Union is criticizing Israel for disproportionate use of force, but President Bush has said that Israel has the right to defend itself. Now, Israel's military chief of staff is warning that Beirut will be a target. Leaflets have been dropped over Dahiye warning residents to stay away from Hizballah offices. In Gaza, there has been an escalation in the three weeks of ground and air strikes, and Israel says that it intends to make the current campaign painful for both sets of antagonists, Hamas and Hizballah.

Najat reaches up and turns off the television,

leaving a little well of silence in the kitchen.

Layla's breath feels hot in her dry mouth. She can scarcely process what is happening, and can only be grateful that her parents' house is in the mountains, where none of this horror has reached. At least, not yet. Her gaze drops. In front of her, the work surface is chipped and warped into curves. On a shelf below it is a basket filled with lemons. The yellow fruits are strikingly beautiful. They remind Layla of house makeover shows she's seen in the UK, where at the end, a bowl of citruses gives the new interior a stylish feel.

'We're just getting a few things into the car,' says the neighbour. 'Come with us.'

'No,' says Najat. 'I'm not going anywhere else today.'

The neighbour turns to Joe. 'Tell her, will you?'

'I've tried, believe me!'

'I won't be alone,' says Najat. 'Him downstairs – his grandfather's too ill to be moved. They're staying.'

'Yes, yes,' says her neighbour, 'there are some who won't leave, but those that know better—'

Someone is calling from the street.

'That's my husband. Come on, Najat.' The woman takes Najat's arm and starts to steer her out of the kitchen.

Najat holds on to the counter. 'Let go of me, will you?'

The man in the street calls again, louder now.

'He'll burst a vein if I keep him waiting any longer,' says the woman. 'Look, we've got to leave. Come on, there's room. And our relatives won't mind one extra person staying.'

'God go with you,' says Najat.

Ignoring the angry shouts from the street, the woman turns imploringly to Layla. 'Are you staying?'

Flummoxed, Layla shakes her head.

'Persuade her then, will you?' says the neighbour again. She gives Najat a tight hug then, muttering to herself, runs to the stairs.

As soon as the she's gone, Joe starts massaging his earlobe. 'Have you got family you can go to?'

Najat tips her head back and tuts: no.

'My parents' flat is in Ashrafieh. You can stay there; they won't mind a bit, I know they won't.'

'Or you could come home with me,' says Layla, imagining the look on Baba and Mama's faces if she walked in with Najat. 'There's plenty of room.'

Najat laughs. 'I'm too old to pack my bags and head off who-knows-where. I'm staying put.'

'You can't,' says Joe firmly. 'None of us can. It's already time we were gone.' The sun is no longer visible between the buildings. Out on the terrace, another cat, a white one this time, is curled up on one of the chairs.

Layla goes to the edge of the terrace and looks down into the darkening street yet again. It must be an hour and a half, perhaps even two, that they have been waiting here, and there's no denying now that Ziad is probably not coming back. At least not tonight. She tries to think through what might have happened. Did he go out for something and panic when he saw people leaving in droves? Maybe someone offered him a lift. Or he could have walked out of this district, rather than wasting time coming back for his things. Or perhaps he came back, but saw Baba's car and left again.

Behind her, Najat is tidying the plates back onto the tray. 'You know,' she says to Joe, 'this is where I stayed through all the years of civil war. And look, both me and my house are still standing.'

'This is different,' says Joe. 'They're going to target this particular area.' He is twitchy, his voice a pitch higher than usual. 'Come with us. We can take you wherever you like. Anywhere.'

Layla joins them. 'He's right. You can't stay here.'

Najat touches Layla's arm. Her palm is hard and dry. 'This is where my life has happened. This is where my memories are. I'm an old woman, and this is my home. It stays with me and I stay with it.'

'Why are you being stubborn?' says Joe. 'Listen to sense!'

Najat grows irritable. 'What do I know about what a bunch of old men somewhere are planning? All I know is, this is where my son took his first steps and where my husband took his last breath.' Her frown clears. 'Don't worry, my boy, I'll be alright. *Allah bi dabbir.*[1]

Joe closes his eyes and sighs. It's clear that Najat isn't going to budge.

Layla holds onto her forehead. Two days ago she was standing in the London drizzle, and now she is in Dahiye, waiting for the bomber planes to arrive.

'I have things I need to get on with now,' says Najat, picking up the tray. 'You two should be on your way.'

Joe looks at his watch again. Above their heads, the sky is grey, and getting darker. 'Isn't there anything we can say to change your mind?'

Najat shakes her head. 'God go with you.' And carrying the tray, she heads into the house.

For a few moments, they stand there in silence. Then Joe holds his hand out to Layla. 'Come on.'

But she doesn't move.

'Look, soon it's going to be too late, and we'll be stuck here to face God only knows what!' He tries to calm himself. 'I understand, Layla, I understand what it means to you to find your brother. But if something bad were to happen to *you,* then your parents— '

'My parents?' Even now, they must be sick with worry. And they have no way to get in touch with her.

'If something happened to you, where would they be then, without either of their children?'

---

[1] 'God will provide.'

The roughly-hewn stone scrapes her knuckles as she stumbles down the staircase. Joe has her by one hand, and is tugging her along like a child that's late for school.

In the street, it's darker than up on the terrace. Here, it is almost night.

She pulls the car keys out of her pocket. In Baba's car, Dog is asleep, a hind leg twitching as he dreams. She puts the key in the lock, but before she can open the door, the air reverberates, and a fighter jet booms overhead.

She hunkers down, as if lowering her body those few inches could save her. Inside the car, Dog springs to his feet. A second plane roars over. Through the window, she sees Dog's wild eyes. He dashes frantically from one end of the back seat to the other, then spills into the front.

'Get in!' yells Joe from the other side of the car. '*Yalla!*'

She finds the handle and opens the door, but as she starts to get in, Dog climbs over her, leaps onto the pavement and takes off.

'Hey!'

He doesn't stop.

She starts to run after him. 'Come back!'

'Layla! Wait! Stop!'

But she can't stop. 'Dog!'

Chapter Fourteen

Layla finds Dog trembling in a doorway, standing in a puddle of his own urine. Spray-painted on the wall above him is a picture of a trophy and the words 'France to win!'

She can barely breathe. The muscles in her legs are weak, and her T-shirt is sticking to her. Daylight has faded. She has no idea where she is. Around her, the tall residential buildings are so close together that there are hardly any gaps between them.

She crouches beside Dog and puts her arms around his neck. 'Where were you going, ha?'

Joe comes running around the corner. 'Christ!' he gasps. 'Are you completely insane?' Behind him, a car races across a junction. Apart from that, nothing else moves.

'Going after a dog, when ... ' Joe straightens up. 'He's just a *dog*!' His face is damp, his T-shirt patchy with sweat. 'We've got to go, Layla!'

She doesn't move. Because in that moment, Joe understands nothing. He doesn't get that Dog, apart from being himself, is all that she has of Ziad.

There is a screech, then an explosion that she feels in the cavity of her lungs. Instinctively, she grabs Dog by the scruff. Everything judders. Above the buildings, smoke rises from somewhere close by.

'Shit!' shouts Joe. 'Come on! Come *on*!'

Her legs don't want to move, but somehow she is running after Joe – Joe who must know how to get back to the car – and pulling Dog along with her.

Another screech, another explosion, and she sinks down onto her haunches, one arm over her head. Dog rakes at her leg. '*Aiy!*'

But Joe pulls her up roughly, and they are running again. Past a deflated football and a pair of trousers draped over a window-ledge to dry.

'But what about Najat?' she shouts. 'And Ziad?' But she can barely hear herself above the noise of her panting breath and running feet, the roar of another engine in the sky.

A third explosion. A fourth. So loud. She had expected that, if anything, it would be gradual. But it is not gradual. They are falling out of the sky. Not raindrops or autumn leaves, but bombs. There's a breaking, crumbling sound, and the smash of glass shattering. She is disoriented, like long ago when Baba used to hook his hands beneath her armpits and swing her round and round till she laughed and gasped and screamed for him to stop. Only now she is not laughing.

She still doesn't know where they are. They are just running. They turn a corner and there's a tree growing wedged between two walls; so… odd to see a tree in this greenless place. They stop a moment to catch their breath. One side of the tree is on fire and as she watches, a bird flutters out, ablaze, and disappears into the smoke.

God. Oh God.

Dog snaps at thin air as a plane passes overhead, and another blast rocks the ground. Joe looks left and right. They are standing in a narrow street with a line of shops. A tattered awning droops down over one of them. Outside, empty crates are piled up. There's a bin-bag with a watermelon rind sticking out of the top. She doesn't recognise this place, or know in which direction Najat's house might lie.

Joe runs from one door to the next, trying them all. 'Here!' One of them is opening, actually opening.

She stumbles over her own feet as she runs to it. Najat and Ziad might still be out here in danger somewhere, but all she wants right now is to close herself off from this bedlam of noise and terror.

'Get in!' shouts Joe. 'Get in!'

They're in a small shop. There are loofahs, melons, a stand of lollipops, bags of sesame seeds and of bread. Layla heads to the back: a doorway with a tied-up bead curtain. But then a man is there, short, moustached, his temples grey and his jaw dark with stubble. He's wearing a stained vest, and his eyes are terrified. His mouth moves but she doesn't hear anything. Her ears and body are filled with the noise of an explosion. It is like being caught inside a thunderbolt. The man gestures for her to hurry and go in past him.

A loud crash. 'Fuck!'

Even in this situation, the man looks shocked.

Another crash, and she reaches out and grabs his arm. Already the rules are upside down. She is touching somebody she would never ordinarily have touched. And even in the midst of her terror, she marvels at the heat of his skin.

He herds them down some stairs to a room with unpainted walls and a tiny barred window high up in one corner. By the light of a hurricane lamp, she makes out boxes of dried goods stacked at either end of the room, a meshed sack of potatoes, packets of toilet rolls, onions, cans of olive oil. It's a storage room, and in a clear space in the middle of the cellar, seated on low stools, are a young woman lighting a candle, an older woman wearing a headscarf, and a little girl on the floor between them. The older woman has a crying baby in her arms.

The women are startled to see Layla. When the younger one sees Joe, she quickly pulls a scarf up from around her shoulders and wraps it around her head. In the brief silence, there are quick introductions. The man is Aziz, his young wife is Kamila. The older woman is Kamila's mother – there's a thunderous crash and Layla doesn't catch her name. Copying Joe, she thanks them for letting her come down here.

'Don't thank us.' The mother-in-law has round cheeks and a purple patterned headscarf. 'This won't be the first time I've sheltered with strangers. In this country, nothing changes. Always trouble, always war.'

A stumbling, scraping noise, and Dog flounders down the stairs after them. At first there is alarm, and for a moment Layla sees Dog through the women's eyes: large, slavering, each rib outlined. When she explains that he is hers, the fear on the women's faces turns to wariness.

'That thing can't stay,' hisses the mother-in-law to Aziz. 'Not down here with the baby, and food.' She shakes her head and tuts.

The little girl grabs her father's vest. 'Don't make him go out there, Baba,' she says. 'Let him stay.' She turns to her grandmother. 'I want him to stay.'

Her grandmother stokes her hair.

'It'll be alright,' says Aziz. 'He'll stay for now, and we'll see.'

Kamila shoots him a disapproving look but says nothing.

The women and Aziz offer up their chairs, but Joe and Layla refuse. Another blast makes the grandmother cover her head with her arms, as if the ceiling will cave in. Opposite the staircase, Layla sinks to the floor with her back to the wall, knees bent to her chest. A few flat cushions are stacked nearby, perhaps meant for sleeping on, but she doesn't even want one of those. What does it matter where they sit? They will die in here, they will die. Like rats. Down here in the gloom with only that tiny window high up in the wall. Because outside, buildings must be falling, and the one they're in may crumble on top of them too, burying them in this ready-made grave.

She pushes her back into the wall, comforted by the solidity of it. On one side of her is pack upon pack of pink toilet rolls. On the other, Joe. Where their shoulders are touching, she can feel him shaking, as if something is going to give way.

The blasts continue, then there's a lull. She can hear the jangly tune of a child's toy that has been left on upstairs. Through the little window in the corner, all she can see is part of another building. But up in the night sky, she saw it earlier, the moon is full – what are the chances? – and further away are the constellations: Gemini, Orion, Perseus. Yes, far away in a place that cannot be reached, there is order.

She catches the little girl's eye. She must be four or five years old, thin and large-eyed, with long hair. Huddled in a little space between her mother and grandmother, her eyes watchful, she is clutching a small stuffed lion to her chest. Layla tries to smile at her but can't quite manage it.

It's hot in here, so hot, as if the day's heat has fallen and pooled in the cellar. Perhaps that is why Dog is trying to dig into the wall. When Kamila sees, she frowns and shakes her head. Layla orders him to 'come here' and leans over to pull him by the scruff, but he carries on regardless. Is he trying to get out, she wonders, or tunnel his way further into the earth?

She touches Joe's arm. 'Najat.'

'What can we do?' He presses his fingers into his temples. 'I don't even know where we are.'

Layla addresses Aziz. 'Do you know a woman called Najat?' She can't even tell him her last name. 'She's quite old, lives alone.'

But Aziz doesn't know her. Nor do the women.

Layla describes the building, the terrace, but there's still no recognition on the faces around her.

And what about Ziad? Please, please let him be home by now. Because the possibility that he is still in Dahiye with the bombs raining down is unthinkable.

The second round of bombing begins. 'This is crazy,' says Joe. 'This can't be happening.'

A bomb lands very close. Everyone tenses as the earth rumbles , and it feels to Layla that they are cut off not only from the rest of the world, but from Beirut itself. From anything, in fact, outside this cellar.

After what seems like an hour comes a second lull. Joe tries to call home on his mobile, but there's no connection.

'The masts must have been hit,' says Aziz. 'Curse their lives.'

'The land-lines are down too then,' says Kamila.

So there's no way to contact Baba and Mama; no way to let them know that she is safe, or find out if Ziad has been in touch.

Joe has contracted into his own bubble and is staring into space.

'Joe?'

He doesn't answer. Oh God, why did she ever get him mixed up in this? *Let's go back to your hall*, she wants to say. *We'll be safe there.* But she might as well offer to fly him to the moon. She takes hold of his hand.

In Kamila's arms, the baby is bawling. 'Make him be quiet, will you?' says Aziz, rubbing his head.

Kamila gives him a look.

'Pass me the water,' he says, extending his hand towards the plastic bottle at his wife's feet, but she does not even acknowledge him. And now Layla realizes: they must have argued. Kamila is not talking to her husband, and has not spoken to him since they have been here.

Aziz stares at his wife. 'I couldn't leave, *ya* Kamila,' he says at last. 'With a couple of hours' notice from someone I can't see, dropped down on a piece of paper,

I'm expected to abandon the only home I've got? How can I leave, to let looters break in and steal all my goods? This shop is all we have. It's our livelihood.'

'There'll be nothing left to steal, or anyone left to steal it!' snaps his wife. 'Would you rather we all died? Our neighbour has left.' She raises an arm to indicate which side the neighbour lives. 'Why is she good enough to leave and I'm not?'

'*Habibti*, we have nowhere to go.' The sweat marks on Aziz' vest have spread. 'We've no one here. Just where would you have us go? Do you want to walk north and sleep on the streets?'

Joe pulls his hand out of Layla's and holds his head as if the arguing is making it hurt. His jaw is darkening with the day's stubble. She is filled with an overwhelming pity for him, and guilt that this is all her fault.

Kamila falls silent, but the baby starts crying louder.

'Do *something*,' says Aziz. 'Can't you see he's not happy?'

Kamila bounces the baby up and down in her arms, whispers to him, strokes his cheek, but he doesn't stop crying, so she turns her chair round so her back is to the rest of them, and unfastens her dress to feed him.

It's still quiet outside. 'Maybe they've hit all the places they wanted to hit,' says Aziz. 'Maybe they've gone.' He looks up as if he might see through the ceiling to the sky.

The mother-in-law gives a snort of laughter. 'You lived through the last war just like I did, *ya* Aziz. Did Israel ever do anything by halves?' Her nostrils flare. 'They're going to raze this whole place to rubble, that's what they're going to do.'

Even through her fear, Layla feels sorry for Aziz. He is harassed, and it all seems too much for him: the crying baby, the onslaught by Israel, wife and mother-in-law.

'Well they've stopped,' he says. 'It's stopped.'

But right on cue, planes begin to whizz overhead, more and more of them, gathering like storm-clouds.

The family has prayed the *salat al-'isha*[2], facing the wall and touching their foreheads to the floor, and now Kamila has one arm tight around her daughter, flinching with each explosion. Sitting apart from them, Aziz gazes at the floor, sweat streaming down his face. The baby is in his grandmother's arms. He is crying again, and she is rocking him. Or perhaps she is only rocking to soothe herself, Layla's not sure. The heat has built up even more. Layla can barely breathe. Eight living bodies in the cellar, and only a one-foot square window to let in any air.

Baba often talked about how cheap life was in the days of the civil war. How a man even took a risk in

---

[2] Muslim 'night prayer'

owning a nice car, because, unknown to him, a buyer would be lined up, and the deal completed with his own murder. An easy way to make money. She recalls other things her parents said about the civil war: how Mama always kept her handbag ready by the door, packed with passports, money, documents and a miniature medical kit; how for months they lived without electricity or water; how the world broke down around their ears, and there was nowhere to run to. Even now, Mama can't stand fireworks.

If only she could go home, it could all be different. Better. Or if she could watch Dog lolloping through the waves, or feel Joe kissing her neck. She would give anything to be in those moments again.

The blasts are a fraction less loud now, a little further away. She leans into Joe, but he does not react. There's a dab of red on each cheek, as if someone has smeared blusher on him, and his forehead is slick.

'Why in hell did you have to go chasing that dog?'

She bites her tongue because he's right. Even those minutes could have had them out of Dahiye. But then, out of nowhere, comes anger. 'I didn't force you to come here! You decided to come!'

'I don't even know your brother,' Joe says.

'If you're going to blame anyone, blame Jacques and his stupid idiot friends!' Although right now she blames Ziad too for bringing them here of all places, and on this of all days.

'All right, all right,' says Aziz. 'There's no need for this.'

Joe ignores him. 'What was I doing getting involved? I should be with my family, that's where I should be.' He covers his face in his hands, and Layla's anger evaporates.

'You're right. You should never have spoken to me outside your flat. Never have asked me back in. Or had me stay the night in your room.'

Kamila and her mother are watching. The older woman leans forward to catch what Layla is saying.

'I'm sorry any of this happened, okay? I wish ...' She wishes she had left Joe in his mother's apartment, and Dog outside her house – poor Dog, who is whining and scraping at the wall again. 'I'm so sorry.'

But Joe doesn't even raise his head.

Outside, there's a crescendo in the barrage. In the planes up there are men. Real human men. When they look down, what do they see? Not people. She thinks of the way Dog pees, marking his territory: this is mine, or at least, it's not yours.

'Look.' Aziz has gone to the corner and is peering up out of the little window. Layla goes and joins him. She sees streaks of red, like fireworks, in the sky.

'What are they?'

'Anti-aircraft fire.' For a second she's surprised that he should know this. But then, he has lived through the civil war. Who knows what else he has seen, and done?

'Hizballah shooting them in retaliation.'

'Will it work?'

Aziz grunts. 'Hizballah's weapons are old and outdated, Russian leftovers from World War II. They're no match for what Israel has.'

'How long do you think it'll go on?'

'They'll most likely stop when daylight comes. That's how it always used to be.'

At some point Dog stops trying to dig into the wall and stands panting, his tail tucked high up between his legs. Layla tries to comfort him. Nearby, an empty bottle of bubble mixture lies on the floor, the wand loose next to it. Who, Layla wonders abstractly as she strokes Dog, has been blowing bubbles in the darkness of a cellar, where they cannot gleam and sparkle? Is this a place where the girl likes to play? Or does her mother come down alone sometimes, to pray perhaps, or reflect on the course her life has taken? Or perhaps it's a refuge for Aziz, where he can get away from the sound of crying children and nagging women.

Kamila sniffs the baby's bottom. 'He's done it.' She looks around but doesn't find what she's searching for. A particularly loud explosion makes her jump, and the walls shake.

'Didn't you bring any nappies down with you?' asks Aziz.

'No. I'm a bad mother. I don't operate well in war zones. What do you want from me?' Then, as if to herself: 'I should never had had this baby. Who would have babies here, to die before they're weaned?'

Her mother touches her arm. 'Don't, my love. Look, there are nappies over there.'

Aziz is already easing a bag of nappies out of a large cardboard box. He rips the bag open and hands a nappy to his wife.

'It's too big,' says Kamila, but takes it anyway. 'There, my poor darling,' she says as she unfastens the dirty nappy. She takes the baby's feet and holds them up while she slides the dirty nappy out and cleans her son's bottom with wet-wipes. Then she wraps the fresh, too-large nappy around him. 'It'll do, ha, *habibi*?' And she holds him close.

Hours pass. The bombing is sometimes on top of their heads and sometimes slightly further off. Layla loses count of how many rounds of shelling they endure, and how many lulls in between. During one of the lulls, they go to use the toilet at the top of the stairs. The mother-in-law, who is the last to go, pleads with Allah to hold off the shell-fire until she has finished, so she doesn't have to die on the toilet. Apart from that, they sit or lie down, rock and sweat and nod off. The little girl curls up on a cushion. The baby sleeps and cries and is fed, then sleeps and cries again. And all this time, Joe remains silent. Instead, Layla gets comfort from the feel of Dog's coat against her leg as he lies beside her.

As she sits there, the smallest details spring out of themselves: an end of thread hanging from Aziz's white vest, the shadow of a cobweb quivering where the wall meets the ceiling, the coastline pattern of sweat on Kamila's headscarf, the beautiful shape of Joe's thumb.

Noise slams against her ears and makes the ground shake. She twists round to lie down on the concrete floor and closes her eyes. She dreams that the little girl is smiling, and when she wakes, is surprised that this could not be further from the truth. Because the girl, startled from her sleep, is crying.

Layla is stiff, her side aching from the hard floor, but she crawls to the girl and puts an arm around her. 'It'll be alright,' she says, and the girl pushes her head into Layla's chest.

The world is still crashing but someone has put out food. There is a tub of *labneh*, a bag of bread and a dish of olives. Layla has no idea where it's come from. How long has she been asleep? One hour? Two? Joe is already eating, but she waits for the little girl to quieten. At last the crying stops and the girl pulls away. Looking up at Layla, she wipes her nose, leaving a glistening trail across one cheek, and gives the tiniest smile.

They sit side by side to eat. Layla accepts some bread from Kamila, and is surprised at how good it tastes when she dips it in the *labneh*; better than anything she has ever eaten before. It is the best, and perhaps the last thing she will ever eat.

She shares her bread with Dog and lets him lap water from her cupped hands. The girl strokes him, and the women don't even tut. Perhaps they have realized that he, in all of this, will not hurt them.

Afterwards Joe nods off, chin heavy on his chest, but she cannot sleep. She sits and takes in the olive stones in a dish on the floor, a half-eaten round of bread, a plastic bottle of water that trembles each time there's an impact. On her knee, her own hand, and at the wrist, her pulse jumping: *tick, tick, tick, tick*.

If only she had hugged Mama harder when they parted. And if only, when she last spoke to Ziad, she had told him never to do anything as bloody stupid as this.

Joe does not stay asleep for long. At four-thirty in the morning, missiles begin to hammer down, one after the other, with barely a pause. She didn't think anything could be this loud. They must be right on top of them, falling in the next street, and this one. She can feel each blast in the fibres of herself, and vaguely wonders how far a body, or parts of it, can be flung by the force of an explosion.

Dog is frantic. Whining, he circles in the corner of the cellar, then arches his body and defecates on the floor.

'I'm so sorry,' she says, mouthing it so Aziz and the

women will understand. She cleans the mess as best she can with tissues and wet-wipes, then puts the lot in a plastic bag. She apologises, and apologises again, but she can't be angry with Dog. She wants it to be yesterday again, and him to be the happy dog he was on the beach. She wants to be sitting with Joe, eating *shawarma* and believing that she's going to see her brother soon. What she doesn't want is for the world to be breaking apart.

The bombardment is horrific. The store-room shakes. The walls and ceiling will cave in. They must.

Her scalp prickles with sweat and her feet are slippery against the soles of her sandals. Beside her, Joe is breathing fast, kneading his earlobe till she thinks it will drive her mad.

In a moment of quiet, the mother-in-law starts talking nervously, quickly. 'Allah save us, they're going to do us in. We'll be buried down here like animals in a hole and nobody will find us. How could they find us, down here?'

'What?' The little girl gets to her feet. 'I don't want to be buried!'

'There, my love, there, it's only your silly grandmother talking nonsense. We'll all be fine.'

But the girl's face remains slack with shock, as though she has been slapped.

'Soon all this will be over and we can carry on like before.' The grandmother starts to rock backwards and forwards, tears glittering in her eyes. 'Just like before.'

No, thinks Layla. No. She has met these people on the day of their death. They will die and swiftly be forgotten. All that'll be found will be small markers of their lives: Kamila's headscarf, Aziz's water bottle, the girl's toy lion, Joe's trainers. And what will remain of her? A yellow sandal? A dog?

She wriggles her hands into her pockets. In one of them is Baba's precious watch, the gold warm from being against her thigh. Perhaps that is what they will find.

Her other pocket is empty, but she runs her fingers absently over the material, exploring the seams where the two sides of pocket are sewn together. And there, tucked into the stitched ends of cloth, is something small and hard. Pinching hold of it, she draws it out. A sunflower seed. Instantly, she is transported back to Terminal 3 at Heathrow airport, where she bought a packet of raisins and seeds. And where, when her flight was called, she shoved the unfinished packet into her pocket. This seed must have fallen out. Now it is in a cellar in Dahiye.

'Did you crack open the windows upstairs to stop them shattering?' Aziz asks his wife.

Kamila throws him a withering look. 'You think we have any windows left?' she whispers. 'I wouldn't be surprised if there's not a building left standing by morning.'

221

'Fine,' snaps Aziz angrily. 'Then you'll have the sea view you always wanted.'

It starts again. More enormous blasts. Dog paces close to the wall. The little girl, whose name she still doesn't know, is chewing the hem of her dress.

Joe has brought his legs up to his chest, wrapped his arms around them and sunk his head into his arms. His left hand is tapping the outside of his right knee. It's the only part of him that is moving.

Layla searches for something familiar in the room, but there is nothing, not even Joe's face, to grasp onto. She closes her eyes and tries to hear a piece of music – The Lark Ascending, Petrushka – but there is no music, only a cascade of earthquakes. She tries to remember Hampstead Heath, Richmond Park, Epping Forest, birdsong, the thrum of insect wings, but they are all out of reach. The only thing she can remember is that burning bird flying out of the tree.

Joe's face is still hidden in his arms. Is he thinking of his family? Is he asleep? Or crying? Is he telling himself jokes, or wishing he had never set eyes on her?

In the lamplight, she sees the gleam of wet mouths, dark eye-sockets, shadows cast across faces. Don't they know they already look like skeletons?

She scrambles to her feet.

'Where are you going?' asks the mother-in-law.

Layla heads for the stairs. She needs to breathe. She

needs air and space. To be higher up, where she won't be buried beneath rubble.

'Aziz!' cries Kamila. 'Where's she going?'

Out there somewhere is the sea. Perhaps it has solidified and she can sprint across it; run like a wild-eyed deer towards Cyprus or Turkey, away from all of this.

'Do you need the toilet?' shouts Aziz above the shelling. 'You can't go. Not now.'

She steps over the dishes. 'I'm leaving.' Her words are lost in the crashing outside.

'Sit down, girl!' shouts the mother-in-law. 'Do you want to be torn limb from limb?'

'I'm going,' she says. Her heart is pattering like a pigeon's. Dog understands: he's on his feet and ready to come with her.

A hand fastens onto Layla's trousers. Kamila's – only one, because the other is cradling the baby – but her grip is small and firm, like a bird clinging to a branch. But in a moment, any moment now, both branch and bird will be on fire.

Joe has lifted up his head. He's getting to his feet. But Aziz is faster. He holds onto her, weighting her down as if she is about to float off like a bubble into the sky. If only she could! She presses her eyes shut and sees it, a still-wobbling sphere slowly rising, shimmers of purple and white and blue and green. A thing so beautiful its existence seems impossible. Valueless, when it ought to be the costliest thing on earth.

'Here.' Kamila is talking to her. 'Hold him.'

Layla opens her eyes. Kamila is holding out her baby, nodding at Layla to take him from her. She notices Kamila's finely plucked eyebrows, a single deep frown-line between them.

Aziz moves aside. The baby feels odd and lumpy in her arms, and doesn't fit the way he seems to in the crook of his mother's elbow. She hasn't seen his face this close up before now. He's not the prettiest baby, his hairline a little too low, his chin a little too sunken for that. All he has on is the too-large nappy that rustles and twists around his chest. Yet he is the most wonderful thing Layla has ever seen.

His warm, impossibly smooth skin sticks to hers. He lets out a cry of complaint at being away from his mother.

'Shh,' she soothes. 'Shh.'

He waves an arm towards her and blows a little froth of spit-bubbles onto his lips.

Steadying herself, she holds him closer, and wonders if this curly-haired, wonderful thing will live. And if he does, what will become of him. Will he be an architect, a baker, a killer?

Gently, she lowers herself cross-legged onto the floor next to the little girl. This is not her world, yet it is also inescapably part of her. The civil war's long-reaching arms have always encircled her life, the cycle of battles that have taken place on this soil is knitted somehow into the very fabric of her. It is sunk into her cells and bones and hums across her synapses along with the usual electrical impulses. This county, and its people, inhabit her.

Aziz sits on his stool again. He picks up the water bottle, pours what is left into his hand and washes it over his face, then lifts up his vest to use as a towel, revealing a round, taut belly.

She strokes the baby's head. Will she ever be able to forget any of this? The close smell of bodies and sweat. Aziz's drum-like belly. The way the baby's silky-soft curls bounce up again once her hand has passed over them. The sense – at last, here in this cellar, with a stranger's baby in her arms – of belonging. She sighs, peculiarly contented. There's an enormous impact, and the baby squirms and begins to complain, so she hands him gently back to his mother.

Another explosion, almost on top of them. Layla's heart leaps, and the little girl huddles against her, still clutching her toy lion. Layla puts an arm around her. The girl feels even skinnier than she looks. There is a ladybird clip in her hair. She begins to cry. 'I want to go home,' she whimpers into Layla's side.

'It's all right,' says Layla. 'It'll be all right.' She begins to sing. '*Yalla tnam Reema, yalla yijeeha elnoum.'*[3] A lullaby Mama sang to her when she was this girl's age. '*Yalla tjiha el 'awafi kul youm byoum.*' One evening in London, after a jog, she stopped to catch her breath and, leaning into her legs, listened to a blackbird's song. And as she listened, the world temporarily faded away, everything distilled into that liquid sound of trills and chirrups. '*I will take you on a little trip, where plums lie beneath the apricot tree.*'

By the time the lullaby is finished, the girl has stopped crying. Her grandmother smiles and nods gratefully at Layla, then leans down to pull the girl onto her lap. And as she lifts her, Layla feels Mama's arms lifting her up, a child again. She smells laundry detergent, sees the curve of Mama's ear and hears her voice make soothing sounds.

Joe is not crying, but he has been. Now he's holding his face tense to stop it from quivering. With her heart banging in her chest, she slides close to him, puts her arm around his shoulders, and in the gaps between explosions, writes a whispered letter to the boy she swam with yesterday. 'I am back with you, floating in the Mediterranean. A good moment. Your hair is wet, black as a hole, and you are smiling back at me. Is it a good moment for you too?' She keeps her eyes fixed on Joe's dusty trainers. One of the laces is hanging loose. 'You tell me that you're fascinated by the line between

---

[3] A lullaby popularised by the Lebanese singer Fairuz.

air and water, remember? Then you dive down and swim through the gap in the rock as if it is nothing at all. The sea is bright and blue. The sun on the water. The taste of salt. Remember?' She kisses his shoulder.

For a while, neither of them moves. Then Joe turns, wet-eyed, and embraces her. The sea, forever shifting, glimmers around them, and she holds on tight. She will not let him slip away.

Chapter Fifteen

It is morning. They ease themselves up and walk stiffly up the stairs. She, Joe, and the family that, as far as she knows, is the only one left in this world. Half an hour ago, after what seemed like an endless night, the bombing slowed down, then stopped – actually stopped – altogether.

In the shop, Joe turns and grasps Aziz's hand in both of his. 'How can we thank you enough?' His voice cracks. All charm and smoothness have vanished. 'You've been ... so kind.'

'No, my brother, what did I do? I pointed the way down a set of stairs and let you sit in a corner. That's all.'

Layla turns to the two women. There ought to be proper words to say to people you have nearly died with, but she can't think what they could be. 'If it weren't for you ...'

The mother-in-law touches her arm and tuts. 'Stop, stop, that's enough. No more words. There's no need. No need at all.'

Kamila, with the baby finally asleep in her arms, nods agreement. Hanging onto her mother's skirt, the little girl yawns and rubs her eyes. Layla shakes Aziz's hand and mutters something equally banal, then turns to leave. After this day, she knows she will never see these people again.

Joe is waiting. He looks defeated, his clothes stained with sweat and dirt. Fleetingly, she wonders what will happen next. They have shared the zeniths and nadirs of what it means to be alive, but she doesn't yet know whether that will be a magnet that pulls them together or forces them apart.

At the door, she stops. The others come up behind her, their shoes crunching on broken glass. Her eyes see what has happened, but her mind cannot take it in.

It's a Friday. Lectures start late on Fridays, so Layla usually goes for a jog around Ravenscourt Park. She starts off near one of the tennis courts, heads past the children's play area, past the bowling green and cafe, then through the trees, silver birch, rowan, cherry, holly, elm; then she runs past long grass buzzing with grasshoppers, to the walled garden. Then along one side of the lake with its ducks and Canada geese, its swans and pochards, looping round the sports ground to the other side of the lake, then back the way she came, to finish near the paddling pool. Somewhere out there in space and time, all of that is still there. Here, however, the world has been undone; the jigsaw taken apart.

She closes her eyes. Opens them again. Yes, it is like some act of magic. The sun is hidden, and the sky. There is nothing but dust and powder and a wrongness deep in the world's bones. Acrid clouds of ash thicken the air. The earth swells and tilts around her like waves. Everything is jagged. It is Shostakovich's first cello concerto, Schoenberg's *Pierrot Lunaire*. It is Boulez' second piano sonata. Ten-storey buildings that stood across the road yesterday evening are gone. Instead, there are grey heaps and mounds of rubble. Beyond the rubble, a building flops limp, its floors hanging down like cloth from the central spine. To her right, a van lies on its side, crushed by a water tank. Electricity cables and phone lines trail hair-like into the debris. To her left, an aerial. Next to that, a bed.

The explosions have stopped, yet they are still present in the air, like the moments after an orchestra has played the final chord, when the sound is still held in the ear.

Layla steps out and stands there, simply looking. All that has been built up has simply fallen away, the contents of lives and homes tipped onto the street in heaps. Kamila's mother comes out too and sobbing, pulls her headscarf down over her eyes. Layla looks over her shoulder. Behind her, Aziz has turned several shades paler. And Joe. Joe is there too, stilled and silent.

Overhead, the morning sun glows beyond the haze

of dust, as if reluctant to shine. And then, the most unexpected of sounds. With morning, the Beirut finches are chirping.

Holding back a sob, Layla starts to crunch and scrabble her way forwards. Just like that day of hide and seek long ago, she has arrived too late.

'Wait,' says Joe.

Without stopping, she pushes her hair back off her face. Only one night ago, Joe's fingers had sifted easily through it. Now it feels greasy.

He catches up with her. 'Hey, where are you going?'

Beneath her feet, the rising mound of rubble is unsteady – rolling, settling, in places loose as sand. She wishes she was wearing something sturdier than sandals.

Joe takes her arm and turns her around. He looks haggard. In the hours they spent down in that cellar, the world has been peeled away from itself. What is left is a hard, alien place. In it, Joe is older, different. Perhaps he has become Yusef.

'I don't know what happened,' she says.

'But where are you going?'

'To find Najat's house. To know if she's okay, and … to see if Ziad is here someplace.' Pulling her arm free, she struggles onwards. She steps over a table lamp, finds a footing on broken stone. Ziad may still have been near Najat's house, and now he might be lying injured somewhere among these metal rods and pylons, beneath the corrugated metal, stone, cement. How can she walk away from this place if he might still be here? Down in the cellar, fear for herself was all of a piece with fear for him, but now that she is safe and can see what has been done, panic for Ziad expands like a hot air balloon preparing to launch.

Leaving Joe behind, she scrambles up a mound of rubble on four legs like Dog. Dog himself is close by, sniffing and following invisible trails, his body trembling. Apart from him, no other living thing is visible. There is nothing but man-made mess. It looks like something she might see advertised on a tube train in the London Underground, a picture of devastation with a phone number underneath for donations.

'Ziad!' she yells. There is no one here. 'Ziad!'

In the silence, he comes back to her clearly. Not the adult he is now, but the boy he was. A boy doing forward rolls on the floor. Leaping off his bed pretending to be Spiderman. His face screwed up in fascination as he leafs through a book about sharks. A jittery hand in hers on the first day of school. And that time in the swimming pool where the bottom shelved steeply away; where Ziad was splashing one moment and gone the next. Under the water, she saw him, sinking down with his arms lifted as if in flight. She took hold of him and pulled him up, sat him on the side and, without a second thought, carried on swimming. Only years later did it occur to her that, on that day, she might have become an only child. And there must have been a time – she knows this even though she can't remember it – when Mama and Baba were entirely hers. But that time cannot come round again. She must find him, she must, and raise him up again.

The air thickens with a mixture of dust, hot metal, chemicals and smoke that makes her eyes sting and her throat hurt. Ahead of her, through the smoky air, the buildings that are left are dim, as if they are only now coming into being. Out of the corner of her eye, she sees a movement and turns. A man is walking ghost-like towards her, covered in dust. She cannot tell his age. His hair is white, his face and clothes too. It makes her think of confections coated in icing sugar, a walking sweetmeat. He is entirely white except for a vivid spill of red on his left temple and cheek. 'Ruba!' he calls. 'Naji!'

Are they his siblings, she wonders, or his children?

As he disappears, she imagines him searching for them forever, not only in Beirut, but the world over, from Ghana to Chile, Korea to Alaska, searching on and on, because he has not yet seen them dead.

She goes on, past a purple boot, a refrigerator, a shock-haired doll with a sticking-plaster around its shoulder and its arm stuck out at a distressing angle. Coughing, she looks round for anything that will give her a clue which way to go, but all landmarks are gone.

Aziz's shop, wherever it was, is out of sight. Only Dog is still here, clambering awkwardly, front paws trying to find a purchase, hind legs occasionally falling away.

'Dog,' she calls.

He stops and looks up.

'Good dog.' He won't leave her. He won't abandon her, not even now.

She coughs and spits out the dust that is forming a silt on her tongue. Her mouth is so dry. If only there was water. Not just to drink but to plunge into: to bathe in and wash all of this horror away.

The rain in London was a revelation. The drizzle and mizzle. Rain blowing diagonally in the wind or pelting straight down. Sometimes, even without rain, it was damp, a moisture that hung in the air and dripped off leaves and lamp-posts. How many times did she arrive in halls soaking wet, with squeaky, leaking shoes? Then later stand in the kitchen with the smell of fish fingers coming from the grill and a pan of rice bubbling furiously on the hob; and more moisture, this time a steam of condensation that settled on the windows and slid down them again. The next day, the sky would be mirrored in a hundred puddles.

Jutting out of the rubble is a shrub, barely recognisable, looking as if it has forced its way up through all this, a remnant of what Beirut must once have been before people arrived: a paradise of olive groves and mulberry trees clustered around a river.

Away to her left, there is movement now, people standing around a crater and a few others muddling their way across debris. Layla carries on in what seems the right direction. A short while later she sees a woman sitting cross-legged beside the body of a little boy. She is not holding him, or even looking at him, just crying and sifting handfuls of dirt through her fingers.

This is not real. It's not. It's a film set, with fake damage, fake blood out of bags and a director, hidden from view, who at any moment now will shout 'Cut!'

Changing direction, she stumbles towards the woman, but before she gets there, a man in jeans and a dirty top reaches her, then a Red Cross paramedic who falls to his knees to examine the boy.

Layla doesn't go any closer, but carries on in the direction she was going before, searching for anything familiar that might tell her where Najat's house might be. Intermittently, she calls Ziad's name. And now hers is no longer the only voice. There are others calling out, or crying, beckoning.

'Layla?'

At the sound of Joe's voice, something inside her flutters up, like a bird rising from a dark well towards the light. She swings round, about to say something along the lines of 'I'm so glad you didn't leave,' but stops short when she sees the details of him. The normally glossy hair is dull with dust, and his eyes are red and tired with dark circles beneath them as if he has been punched. His soldier's bearing is gone too: his head has drooped, his shoulders bowed. His hands hang like dead weights on the ends of his arms.

'I thought you'd left.' Her voice sounds hoarse.

As if it's an effort, he shakes his head. His clothes and hands are covered in dirt, like hers. Dog goes and sniffs him, wagging his tail slowly in greeting.

Joe comes closer and touches her cheek. 'I wouldn't just leave like that, would I?' he says softly. 'Anyway' – he gestures around, his expression changing – 'there are still people in these buildings. Or underneath them.'

What has he seen? Who has he helped? Did it involve dead bodies?

She wants to put her arms around him, but she is too exhausted. In another time-line, where a handful of men didn't decide to blast Dahiye to hell, she and Joe might still be curled up behind a closed door, a drawn curtain. But the possibilities of that other life have been snipped clean off.

'Ambulances have come,' he says. 'There are others searching now.'

She nods, feeling numb.

'But there are still no phone signals,' he says, 'so … well, I'm going home.'

Ambulances. Phones. Home. Why is he talking

about normal things? Can't he see there's nothing normal left in the world?

'I can't get in touch with my family,' says Joe. 'For all I know they might be—' He clutches at his hair, but it's too short and his fingers close around nothing.

She doesn't know what to say. 'You're right. You should go.'

He frowns into her face, as if he's trying to read her. 'Haven't you had enough, Layla? Don't you want to go home?'

'Home?' He says it so easily, as if he knows exactly what it means. 'No, not yet.' She musters up a smile. 'Bye, Joe.'

But her words seem to have the opposite effect to what she intended. Joe puts a hand on her shoulder. 'Stop it, okay? Just stop it.' There's a mixture of resignation and pity in his face. An expression that says she will not find Ziad: that if he is here, she will probably never find him. She looks away. Dog must have cut himself on something because he is sitting and licking his hind leg, a sloppy, regular sound.

'Your family will be waiting,' she says.

Silence for a beat. 'I'll stay with you.' Honourable to the last.

But it's no good. He mustn't stay here. He should go and find his mother and brother. All right then, so she will make his decision easier. Roughly, she pushes his hand off her shoulder. 'I don't need you here, okay?'

'What?'

She wants to recant, to tell him that at some point during the last two days, between one breath and another, she fell in love with him. But she knows that he must go, just as she knows that she must stay. So fighting back the desire to keep him here, she says it. 'Just fuck off, will you?'

For a moment everything stops. Joe's eyes open a fraction wider, and retract again. Then he turns away.

Instinctively, she pushes off after him, but as she shifts her weight, a stone beneath her foot lurches, and she stands teetering like a child on a see-saw. On her shoulder is the damp warmth of his hand, the ghost of him still next to her. But half a minute later, Joe himself is gone.

It might be only half an hour, or as much as two hours later that she crosses what was once a street corner and sees Baba's car. It's spattered with rubble and plaster, the bonnet dented, a rear window smashed, its door still open as she left it. And nearby is Najat's house. No, Najat's staircase. Wrapped around the outside of the ground floor, it rises up, curves around, but then, nothing. The terrace is gone. Half of Najat's flat is gone too. The rest is tattered concrete.

'No.' Layla tries to run towards what is left of the house, but falls hard onto stone. 'No,' she groans and slowly, painfully, gets up again.

She picks her way through the devastation, moving as fast as she can. She sees a birthday card written in a child's hand, a candle, a dead cat. Is it one of Najat's? She can't tell. Her hands make out only ugliness – the flintiness of sharp-edged stone, the abrasive irregularity of broken concrete. She squirrels her fingers into gaps to gain purchase and pull herself through this unsteady landscape of grey hills. Stone jabs her ribs and scrapes her arms and legs. Just one more mound to negotiate and she will be at the staircase. Knowing this, she moves faster, but as she climbs, the rubble beneath her feet gives way. Crushed stone moves and rolls beneath her. Instinctively, as she slides, she grasps onto whatever she can.

Like a sunburst, pain opens in her left hand, and she cries out and falls to her knees. Her hand is stuck onto the sheared edge of a piece of metal protruding from the rubble, part of some larger object that is lodged beneath the mound. She breathes shallow, gasping breaths and lets out low moans. Then, teeth clenched, she works her hand this way and that, until millimetre by millimetre, her flesh is unhooked.

Oh God. Oh God. When she brings her hand in towards her body, it is streaming blood from a tear on the palm beneath the fourth and fifth fingers. The jewel-like brightness of the red is startling on her dust-caked hands. Moaning, she sits down heavily. Blood drips onto the rubble.

Dog has stopped. He is watching.

'It's all right,' she says, biting down on her lip. 'It's nothing.' But panic is turning her heart into butterflies' wings. What should she do now? What should she do? And what will happen? To her, her life, her hopes? If her hand stops working, if it is in any way compromised … but no. No, it can't become anything less than it was two minutes ago. Because her entire life's path lies here in her fingers. So it can't be as bad as the fire in her hand says it is.

She wraps the bottom of her T-shirt around her hand like a sort of hammock, and stifling a cry, gets to her feet.

She stands at the bottom of the stone staircase that, like something out of a dream, leads nowhere. Around her are heaps of masonry and a section of vine from Najat's terrace. There's no way she can see of getting to the top floor. Down here, the ground-floor flat has been blasted open, with two of the outer walls gone. Gasping, she clambers into somebody's living-room. There's a smell of burnt plastic, hot copper and plaster-dust. A sofa is half buried beneath cement and vine. A corner of rug is visible. On the wall, a clock is still ticking.

She picks her way across the room, eyes watering, hand throbbing, and searches among the wreckage. Looking up, she sees one of the chairs from Najat's terrace straddling the top of an internal wall, two legs in one room and two legs in another.

With Dog at her heels, she crosses a threshold into what must have been a bedroom. A framed photo of a young man and child lies smashed on the floor. In one corner, the ceiling has caved in, and sticking out of the rubble, grey as if it were also made out of stone, is an arm.

Layla presses her good hand to her mouth.

A minute later she moves closer, her eyes fixed on the only human thing she can see. But it is not Najat's arm, nor Ziad's. It is an old man's, veined and wrinkled, the knuckles swollen with arthritis. And she remembers what Najat said about a neighbour's invalid grandfather who could not be moved.

Feeling sick, she shuffles backwards. Is Najat lying somewhere down here too? Or up in the remains of her home? Is Ziad?

She looks down. Pain has radiated from the cut into the rest of her hand, and her T-shirt is red. At the sight, her heart begins to race, and her breathing turns fast and shallow. She wishes she believed in God so she could pray to Him.

Behind her comes the clump of footsteps. Dog barks. There is a hiss and crackle of something electrical. A voice says something, and another miniaturized voice replies. When she reaches the doorway, a man is standing next to the wrecked sofa.

He is bearded and dressed in orange overalls marked with the insignia of the Red Cross. The walkie-talkie fixed to his shoulder crackles.

He scans Layla. 'Are you alright?' He is looking at her blood-soaked T-shirt.

'There's someone.' She points behind her. 'In there.'

Quickly, he pushes past her. She doesn't look, but waits until he comes out again. There's no need to ask. The man in there is dead.

'And there's somebody – was somebody – upstairs. I need to look. To know if she's ... still there.'

She follows him outside, biting down on her lip to better bear the agony she is carrying wrapped up in her T-shirt. He goes halfway up the stone staircase, assesses the possibilities of reaching the upper level, then comes down again. 'I'll be back,' he says, and heads to a place where there is still road to park on, and two ambulances are squeezed at tight angles to one another.

A few minutes later he reappears with a second, clean-shaven man carrying a medical case. They go into the house again and search for a place where they might be able to climb up to the top level.

'There.' The bearded one points. 'This is the best place.' He takes hold of a dangling iron rod. 'Give me a leg up.'

The other man half squats and locks his hands together to make a footrest. He boosts his colleague

242

up, then turns and opens the first-aid box. 'Let me see your injury,' he says to Layla.

She comes closer and, gritting her teeth, peels back the blood-thickened cotton of her T-shirt. When she looks, she does not see a hand, but a poor bloodied thing, an animal mangled in a trap.

The paramedic reaches out, but she curls it protectively into her body like a foetus.

'I need to see it. Let me see it. Please.' Gently, he takes her hand.

Dog growls.

The wound is not bleeding as much as it was at first. The paramedic, a young man with acne scars and a sticking-out Adam's apple, cleans and dresses the wound, then begins to bandage it. It makes Layla think of Baba's pharmacy, and Mama treating her and Ziad's childhood cuts and scrapes. But most of all it makes her think of Joe. The way the paramedic is winding the bandage round and smoothing it against her skin, so careful, almost tender.

He pauses. 'Don't cry, it's not such a bad injury.'

But the tears keep on coming.

'You'll see,' he says. 'You'll see, it'll be okay.'

Chapter Sixteen

With her good hand, Layla eases off the block of stone that has crumpled the bonnet of Baba's car. Gravelly dust covers the windscreen, and has almost obscured the car's true colour, but still, the presence of this machine from another lifetime feels like a miracle. Dog is panting by her side. Overhead, the sun is finally breaking through, letting in the heat of the day. She doesn't know what time it is. A few minutes ago it felt early, but now it feels late and she is weak, her body wobbly as jelly.

People are out now examining the damage. Down the street, two men are shouting instructions to one another as they try to raise a slab of concrete. She doesn't want to know what they will find beneath it. There was no one in Najat's flat – no bodies, living or dead. She gets into the car. Dog too. For a while, she sits looking at the blue bead and medallion of Saint Maron hanging from the rear-view mirror.

When the paramedic had finished bandaging her hand, his emergency mobile phone rang. After he finished speaking, she asked if she could use it, and called home. Ziad was not there. Mama started to cry, at first with relief that Layla was alright, then with fear for what might have happened to Ziad. Layla didn't say anything about Ziad having been in Dahiye. She only told Mama that after what had happened last night it might her take some time to get home. Then the paramedic was needed elsewhere, so she had to hang up.

The car key is still in her pocket. She puts it in the ignition, expecting nothing, but – the most astonishing thing – the engine starts. It's just as well that the car is an automatic. Even so, she drives with her right hand, using her left thumb only when necessary to balance the steering wheel. Blood has seeped through the bandage and formed a small red flower on her palm.

It's hard work navigating through the streets. Some are blocked off entirely, and several times she has to reverse and find another route. Once she drives straight through the shelled-out ground floor of what was a block of flats yesterday, past a boy calmly spray-painting on a wall: 'HEAVEN', then beneath that 'HELL', and beneath that 'DAHIYE'. On one side, in large letters, he concludes with 'Death to Israel.'

'Where are we?' she asks Dog, who has his head stuck out of the broken window. 'Which way now?'

He doesn't know, but at last they are out of Dahiye. The highway north is a chaos of cars and trucks, scooters and buses. Vehicles are jammed close together, luggage hanging off their roofs and bursting out of their boots. People lean out of car windows and horns blare. The whine of an ambulance comes from somewhere, but the traffic does not move.

She reaches for the bottle of water on the passenger seat. Her lips are dry and cracked. She drinks half of what's left and pours the rest into the cup-holder behind the handbrake for Dog. 'I'm glad you didn't leave me,' she says as he laps. Hot tears well into her eyes, and with her good hand, she wipes them away. 'I'm glad you're still here.'

She stops the car on the beach, turns off the engine and pulls the handbrake. Daylight is beginning to seep out of the sky, and she is leaden with fatigue, the weight of sun-blazed hours heavy on her back. It has taken her hours to search the parks and car-parks the paramedic mentioned, where refugees from the south of the country are massing. There were some from Dahiye too, but Ziad was not among them.

Her head hurts with the things she has seen and heard today: a toddler lying asleep on a foam pallet, his face crawling with flies; crying babies and silent children; the stench of nappies and unwashed bodies; on a plastic crate, an old woman nursing her swollen feet. 'And when I looked back,' she said to the man next to her, 'my house was gone. Only the wardrobe was there, standing in a different place. So I walked, past burnt bodies on the roadside, all the way here.' A little girl ran past barefoot, her headscarf brushing Layla's arm. Two teenage girls clung to each other laughing, until she realized that they were not laughing but crying. A man accosted her, wanting to know if she had come with medicine for his diabetic son. 'They came, asked what we needed, wrote it down and left,' he said. 'Don't you know those people with the notepads?'

'No.' And this was the one thing she was certain of: that she did not know a thing.

She went to two hospitals as well, but couldn't get any further than the chaos of the lobbies.

She was three years old when Mama came back from hospital with Ziad in her arms. It is the first memory she possesses with a tingling clarity. It was a hot day, a splurge of burning heat smack in the middle of the year. The light taut, colours wild and bright, trills slicing across the still sky as if the birds were trapped in a blue cathedral. Plants were brown and dry, and the earth had begun to crack. With all this came Ziad, and something of that scorching day slipped inside him forever; it was him and he was it, sublimely bright and alive. Nothing like this day. She sees him hanging in water, waiting to be born. Waiting for his life to happen, a whisper of it already traced in the fluids around him.

In the back seat, Dog gets up and shakes himself. Then he turns his head and nibbles his thigh, viciously, urgently. Even now, the fleas are biting him, needing their minuscule feast of blood; the world is still rotating. She never did get round to finding him any flea medicine.

When he is done scratching, he starts to pace in tight circles.

'Okay, okay.' Groaning with pain, she leans back and pulls on the door handle. 'There.' After all, this is where he was happiest: in the sea, bouncing in the shallows. 'Go on.' Let him have a run and a swim before they head home, because that's the next stop. But first, she just needs a few minutes to rest and breathe; to gather strength enough to drive on.

Dog bounds down from the car. He stops to pee, then sets off at a gallop, large and pale in the gloom, towards the water. Part of her envies him. He will wash off the grime of the last two days, and rinse the smell of smoke from his nostrils.

She tries to swallow. Her mouth is still dry, and her hand no longer feels as if it has substance. It is nothing but pain. She brings it into her body and squeezes her arm muscles tight. As a distraction, she turns on the radio, but the information that comes out of it piles up in a sickening jumble in her head. Thousands upon thousands of people fleeing to Syria, even though the Beirut-Damascus road is being repeatedly targeted.

Since Wednesday, around three hundred rockets have been fired by Hizballah into northern Israel. Here, the Israelis have bombed food factories, milk factories, aid convoys, sewage plants, hospitals and countless schools. Joe was right. There is no solution.

Layla turns off the radio and slumps over the steering wheel. Joe must be home by now. She wonders where Aziz and his family are, and what they are doing. She hopes to God they have left Dahiye.

Her left hand throbs. The hand that carries the bass notes and harmonies, the foundation for melodies, sometimes even the melody itself. Please don't let it be anything irreversible. Please let it not be as bad as it feels right now. Even if she had the energy, there's no point in trying to get it seen to here. The doctors would probably laugh at her. *An injured hand? Can't you see what we have to deal with, girl?*

Fifty or so metres down the beach, Dog crashes into the waves, and for a moment she considers going in too. The air is thick and filled with a scent of burning. This day has branded her with its foul odour of sweat and rubble too, and left her smelling rank. She suspects this smell will always be with her too, ready to be called into being in an instant.

Dog rises on a wave, washing the mess and muck of people off himself.

She peers into the rear-view mirror. She looks pale and drawn, her eyes red and narrow with tiredness, her hair dusty, the pink and blonde streaks almost invisible.

A jet flies low overhead, making the air shudder. Oh God no, it's going to start again. The bombing. The crashing and thundering.

She flings the car door open and gets out. 'Dog!' In the fading light, she can just see him in the water. If only she could live that way: in the moment, with nothing existing beyond the here and now. She starts to head down the beach, then stops. Something is wrong. The colour of the sea further out, the sound of it too, and the smell that's blowing in off the water.

She starts walking again, faster now, her sandals sinking into the sand. As she nears the surf, a dark wave washes over Dog, and the waterline alters, as if it's being held down and is struggling to move. The invisible skin that holds the sea intact has turned glutinous black, a slick encasing everything it touches – the water, the sand, Dog. He is in there, struggling in oil that stinks of kerosene. She doesn't understand. How can the sea have turned to oil? But it has. Nature has gone mad.

Another black wave washes in, withdraws and leaves black, sticky sand. Out in the water, Dog has turned black and is no longer moving correctly.

Layla runs into the surf, calling him. He is only ten feet away, but he's floundering and struggling to stay afloat.

As she wades out into the water, he goes under; then his muzzle pokes up, a black bump in the black slick.

Oil washes further and further up her trousers. 'Dog!'

He turns his head, and she catches sight of the whites of his eyes and a flash of pink tongue.

'Come here!'

A crescent of white appears around one eye, a miniature moon in a night sky. He struggles towards her with a smacking sound as he licks his jowls, trying to get the oil off. He sinks in the water, then rolls closer, helped by the surf, as she wades towards him. And finally she's got him and they are staggering in the shallows. Dog falls down, gets up again, falls down again on the stuff that used to be sand.

Layla sinks to her knees, her hands sliding over his fur. He feels nothing like a dog. 'Get up. Please! Come on, get up.'

But he does not get up. He lies at her feet, coughing and snorting. She tries to clean out his mouth with her T-shirt, wiping oil off his tongue and teeth.

The sun has dipped below the horizon. It swells, large and red, its colour leaching into the sky. Its beauty mocks them. And it can afford to be beautiful; it is thousands of miles away from here.

Strange thoughts flash into her head, things she learned at school. That these waves were beating this shoreline when the Phoenicians set sail to colonize

Cadiz and Carthage. That they lapped as Alexander the Great built his causeway across the water to conquer Tyre. But now they swell black towards her, almost silent, then away again.

'All right then,' she whispers. 'All right.'

Somehow she manages to slide her arms underneath Dog, then hooks them around his belly. Her hand flares with pain but she ignores it. She braces one foot on the ground and heaves; gets her other foot on the ground and heaves again. It takes several attempts. They are both slimy with oil, and Dog is heavy, but at last he is in her arms and she is standing.

Several times between the sea and Baba's car, she has to stop. She isn't quite sure how she manages, but finally they are there and she is laying Dog on the back seat, pushing him in, almost falling on top of him.

Her good hand is oily on the steering wheel. Her other is black too. So are her clothes and her arms. And everything stinks of raw oil. She doesn't know what do. She only knows that she wants and needs to get home.

The traffic has eased. Now that night is falling, not many cars are on the road. So she drives, while in the back, Dog snuffles and wheezes and shivers.

'Where did it come from?' she cries, glancing back at him. 'Oh God. You'll be okay, Dog. You'll be okay.'

She turns onto the mountain road that will take her

home. Rising out of Beirut, the day's heat begins to let go, allowing a thin coolness to fall. In the back, Dog is straining to breathe. She keeps looking over her shoulder to check on him, talk to him. Again and again, she tells him that it is going to be all right.

When she and Ziad were children, Mama used to tell them fairy tales. Layla knew that each story would take a bad turn, but she also knew that just when things were at their worst, a miracle would happen. An elf would appear, or a geni, a prince or a fairy godmother, and evil would be banished. But not today. Today, all fairy tales have been cracked open and revealed themselves to be nothing but empty shells.

At some point along the road home, the sounds coming from the back seat of the car – the snuffling and wheezing and breathing – stop.

Chapter Seventeen

The kitchen door is unlocked. Layla goes in and stops on the threshold of the next room, idiotically unwilling, even now, to traipse oil further into the house. Baba jumps to his feet, and turns off the television. The pictures of Beirut vanish. Baba's words have vanished too. He remains frozen, staring. She can only imagine what she looks like – the dirt, the blood and oil.

The bathroom door opens and Mama is there, her hair still wet. The collar of her nightgown is sodden. When she sees Layla, she lets out a strange sound. Layla doesn't think she has ever seen her eyes open so wide. 'My god!' She rushes towards Layla. '*Habibit albi*. What happened to you?' She touches Layla's face and arms, gently, inquiringly, as if she is feeling for breaks.

But there are no breaks. There is only loss. Ziad and Joe and Dog, all lost. Dog lying dead in the car, and an ache heavy as rock in her chest. 'I'm fine.'

Mama moves to hug her, but Layla steps back.

'You'll get yourself covered in it.'

But Mama hugs her anyway, holds her so tight Layla can barely breathe. A good, safe tightness. She buries her face in Mama's shoulder. She is full of tears, but not a single one falls.

Baba puts his arm around her. 'Are you really all right, darling?'

'Yes.'

'God, Layla, we've been worried sick,' says Mama. 'We were up all night calling anyone who might know anything. Except that half the phone lines are down.'

'What happened?' asks Baba, looking down at the state of Layla's clothes as she and Mama come apart. 'What is this? What are you covered in? And how on earth …?'

'The sea. It was in the sea. The water … it turned black.'

'Jiyyeh.' Baba swallows. 'It was just on the news. They targeted the power plant at Jiyyeh. Heavy fuel oil spilled into the sea. You should, you know, get washed, get it off you.'

Mama takes hold of Layla's filthy oil- and blood-stained bandage. 'You're hurt.'

'I'm okay.'

'Has a doctor seen it?' asks Baba.

'A paramedic bandaged it.'

Baba frowns, trying to fit all the pieces together and make sense of what she is saying. He squeezes her shoulder. 'We'll get it looked at.' She's not sure whether he's talking to her or to himself. Already, he is heading towards his shoes.

'No, Baba, I don't want to. I'm too tired.' She turns to her mother. It is difficult to say it: 'I searched for him, Mama, I did. But I couldn't find him.'

The expression on Mama's face releases a sadness in Layla that wells up like flood-water. Staring down at her blackened feet, she tries to tell her parents what happened, but it's as though she is a baby again forming unfamiliar shapes with her mouth, dropping words from lips that don't feel like her own. Those words convey the information haphazardly. But they convey enough.

Her voice stutters and gives out. Taking out the watch from her pocket, she hands it to Baba.

Baba stares at it, as if a viper has materialised on his palm. Then his face relaxes. 'My son,' he whispers, and Layla sees that the watch has the potential to become even more precious to Baba, imbued with even greater significance than it had before.

Mama has forgotten how to blink. Then turns and puts her arms around Layla, trying to comfort her. 'It's all right, darling, it's all right.' But Mama's arms are shaking. So are her words.

Baba stutters. 'He … he must have left Dahiye. He must have.'

'Yes,' says Mama. 'Yes. Certainly he wouldn't have

stayed there. And if he'd tried to call, his phone wouldn't have been working.'

'He could have gone to a friend's, or, or perhaps he's trying to get home now,' says Baba. 'Things are such a mess in Beirut. He's probably stuck somewhere, held up.'

'He might be hurt.' Mama looks desperately at Baba. 'What if he's hurt?'

'We'll look for him,' says Baba.

'We can search the hospitals.' In her oil-smeared nightgown and slippers, Mama starts for the door, but Baba holds her back.

'No, no.' He is still working it out in his head. 'We can't. They've started shelling again down there, can't you hear?' Even from this far away, the thud of explosions is clear: loud ones landing in Beirut, and fainter thuds that are falling further off. 'We can't go tonight.' His voice softens. 'Tomorrow. We'll go tomorrow, Meerna, I promise.'

Mama heaves a defeated sigh.

'We'll find him. We will.' Baba, looking pale, pulls himself together. 'Right. I'll phone the doctor.'

'No,' says Layla.

'Of course,' says Baba. 'We've got to get that seen to.'

'But it's late, and ...' Layla can't think up another excuse right now.

'Yes it's late, but he'll see us.'

'But Baba ...' This is the last thing she wants. She wants to stay here in case Ziad calls or walks in. And she doesn't want to think about her hand, doesn't want to see a doctor who might take away whatever little hope is left of her carrying on with her music. Better not to know.

'He's a clever man,' says Baba, already dialling. 'I trust him.'

'Please, Baba.'

But Baba just carries on. She won't win this one. 'All right. I'll get washed.'

'Do you need help?' asks Mama.

'No. No thanks.'

Mama looks around, as if at a loss for something to do. 'I'll make some aniseed tea then.' Her eyes snag on the trail of oily footsteps leading from the kitchen door. 'And clean up.'

Baba is speaking to the doctor. Both he and Mama are in a place of their own now, their attention engaged elsewhere. So Layla goes into the bathroom, still steamy from Mama's shower, and begins to scrub the oil from her arms.

She and Baba take a taxi to the doctor's. They have to, Baba's car is a stinking oily mess on the inside, and bashed up and dusty on the outside. Although, apart from not moving for several seconds when he sees it, Baba makes no comment.

Dr Zgheib has been the family doctor for as long as Layla has been alive. He gave her and Ziad all their inoculations, prescribed medicine when they were ill, and sent her to hospital for an X-ray after she fell and broke her collar-bone at the age of five. She feels guilty for bringing that body to him damaged again.

Dr Zgheib is balding now, his remaining hair grey, but he still has the same round belly and capable manner he has always had. 'So, Layla.' He peers at her. 'What have we done to ourselves today? Hurt your hand, I hear.'

Perched on his examination couch, she feels like a child again. As a child, Dr Zgheib always put her and Ziad at ease by telling them jokes. But there are no jokes today, not even the suggestion of a smile.

He holds her bare hand palm up in both of his. 'Are you left-handed?'

'No.'

Baba is standing slumped against the wall, staring at the floor but evidently seeing only his thoughts.

'That's all right then. Eh, Fadi?'

Baba shakes himself back into the present moment. 'What's that?'

'Your daughter. Not left-handed.'

'Oh. Yes. But as you know, doctor, she plays the piano. She's been studying in London.'

London, where her life waits like a discarded skin that might now never be filled.

'Ah yes, yes. The musical one. Talented, I hear.'

Layla remains silent; watches Baba drift back into agonizing about Ziad; wishes this whole thing was a nightmare.

She doesn't dare try to move her hand or fingers. Where the bandages were, the skin is pale and dead-looking, and the cut below her fourth and fifth fingers makes her think of meat hanging in a butcher's shop. She looks away, down at the fabric stretched across Dr Zgheib's stomach, the tension on the shirt button at that point, and further down at his slippers, which are the only indication that it is half past nine at night.

'Well, you've had the full course of tetanus jabs. Relax your hand – there – just relax it.' He observes it carefully from several angles, as if it might suddenly leap up. 'Mmm.' He feels both radial and ulnar pulses on her wrist.

Baba comes closer to see. 'No vascular damage?'

'None. And it's not swollen.'

Baba nods, his spectacles glinting. There is comfort for him in this conversation, where he understands what is going on. Where the sequence of diagnosis follows a logical order.

'Now for the nerves.' The doctor goes to his desk and rifles about in a jar of pens and pencils, then tips the lot out and picks a paper clip off the desk. 'There are three main nerves that supply the hand,' he says as he unbends the paper clip. 'Now, Layla, close your eyes and tell me if you feel one point of this paper clip or two.'

'Earlier ...' Her skin is clammy with fear. 'Earlier, the feeling in my fingers wasn't ... normal.'

'Well, let's see what you can feel now, shall we? Close your eyes, close.'

For the next few minutes, she feels the point of the paper clip, sometimes one and sometimes two, on the backs of her first and second fingers, and on the webbed part of her palm between thumb and forefinger. But Dr Zgheib concentrates most on her fifth finger.

Finally she is allowed to open her eyes again. He asks her to hold the end of a biro with the tips of her fingers and thumb; then to spread her fingers wide.

'Well,' he says, 'with that cut, the worry was the ulnar nerve, but she's done well. The nerves seem intact.'

Baba's mouth twitches into a quick smile.

'I'll check the tendons. Then we'll examine the wound. So.' The doctor holds down her third, fourth and fifth fingers. 'Can you curl your forefinger?'

The process is repeated for each finger while he holds down the others. She grimaces in pain. But the pain is nothing compared to the panic that flies through her when she can't properly bend her fourth and fifth fingers. It is agony even to try.

'I can't do it!'

261

'Just once more, Layla. Try once more.'

She does.

'Okay.' He straightens up, goes to a cupboard and takes out a vial and a syringe. 'I need to have a poke about in the wound to confirm, but I suspect a partial tendon tear.'

Layla can't speak. She can't even swallow. In an instant, the dreams that held up her life – all their lives – have come crashing down like a house of cards.

'What does that mean?' asks Baba. 'Will she need surgery?'

'It's controversial, but the latest studies show that suturing partial flexor tendon tears will result in weaker tendons, and more likelihood of rupture.' Dr Zgheib prepares the syringe. 'The best course of action is to do nothing. So: this is a local anaesthetic.'

Once the injection has taken effect, Layla doesn't watch him examine the wound. Baba holds her good hand and she looks at him instead, but although he tries to look reassuring, anxiety for his family has turned him ashen.

Dr Zgheib makes little noises as he examines her hand: a tut, a 'hmm', air sucked through his teeth. 'As I thought,' he says at last. 'It's partial. Certainly less than sixty per cent, which is good news.'

Baba nods. But Layla isn't sure just how good such good news can possibly be. She feels limp with exhaustion.

The doctor cleans the wound and closes it with butterfly strips.

'She'll need antibiotics?' asks Baba.

'Yes. And it'll have to be splinted to stop further tearing. But she has to keep it mobile, right from day one. That's important.'

After he splints her hand, Dr Zgheib explains the exercises she has to do, and makes another appointment for her. 'If there's any problem, just call,' he tells Baba. 'Keep her doing those exercises. And don't get the hand wet. Well, you know all of that.'

Baba nods.

'Are you alright, Fadi?' asks the doctor in a low voice. 'Is something else wrong?'

But Baba doesn't want to talk about it.

They shake hands.

Now Layla plucks up enough courage to ask the only thing she has wanted to ask since she walked in. 'Will it be the same as before?'

Dr Zgheib smiles kindly. 'You were lucky, Layla. Very lucky. It's possible that your fingers might never be the same as before the injury, but I'm hopeful. The depth, the location ... I can only say I'm hopeful.'

They walk to the door.

'I forgot to ask about your family,' says the doctor to Baba.

'Meerna's fine, thank you.'

'And Ziad?'

Baba rubs his forehead and adjusts his glasses.

Dr Zgheib looks up sharply. He doesn't say anything more.

It's early when Layla wakes up the next morning. The house is still, and there are no cars on the road. Her body aches in strange places – shins and hips and forearms. She looks down at her splinted hand and feels like a fish out of water: taken away from her element, she knows she will carry on gasping until she finds herself swimming in music again. Except that, by the time her hand has healed, the skill may have left her fingers.

She puts away that fear and gets up. Quietly, she goes down the hallway. Baba and Mama's bedroom door is closed. Further on, the living room is deserted; and the dining room. On the table is a bottle of whisky, and Baba's glass, empty. There is no one in the kitchen either, but the back door is open.

She stops in the doorway. Outside is an utter stillness, yet the porch is not empty. Mama is sitting motionless on the floor with her back against the house wall, and stretched across her lap, his head hanging off one side, is Dog. Last night, Baba wrapped him up in a sheet and carried his body from the car. He has been on the porch all night. Now Mama has pulled the front half of him onto her lap and peeled back the sheet from around his head. On the floor beneath his open mouth are three small black circles where oil has dripped onto the porch tiles.

Layla holds onto the door-frame. Mama hasn't noticed her there, but as she grips the jamb, her fingers touch something. It is a scratch etched into the wood, one of many that have charted her and Ziad's height over the years. Her forefinger is on the spot where the top of Ziad's head reached, aged seven. There he is again aged eight, then ten, and one final mark where he stood at twelve-and-a-half years old. After that, he announced that he was too grown up to participate is such childish things. Softly, she runs a finger over the spot where he last leant against the frame. Already the house is full of ghosts.

Outside, Mama hasn't moved. Mama who, gazing down at Dog in the stillness of early morning, might be a picture or a photograph, except for the tiny movement of tears that roll slowly down her cheeks.

Chapter Eighteen

It is not yet seven o'clock when Baba wakes up. He is puffy-eyed and smells of alcohol, but after three cups of Turkish coffee, he gets up and calls a taxi. He has to phone five different drivers before one agrees to take them to Beirut.

'He'll be here by eight,' he says as he puts down the receiver. 'You get dressed, Meerna, and I'll ...' He clears his throat, adjusts his glasses. 'I'll bury the dog.'

Layla is already dressed. 'I'll help.' Earlier, standing in the back doorway, she was unable to enter the invisible circle around her mother. Instead, she retreated silently, leaving Mama wrapped in her moment of pre-emptive grief.

Baba carries Dog, and she carries the spade down to the patch of pine forest at the bottom of the slope. There, Baba digs a shallow hole and buries Dog hastily, as the birds begin to chirp their welcome to the day. When it's done, he glances at his watch. 'We'd better get going. The taxi'll be here in a few minutes.'

When they get back to the house, the taxi is already

waiting. Baba goes to wash his hands and change his shirt; then they set off back to Beirut. 'The hospitals nearest Dahiye first,' Baba tells the taxi driver.

'There's someone you're looking for?' The man has one arm dangling out of the window, holding a cigarette.

'That's right,' says Baba, but doesn't say any more.

Today, Layla feels hopeful. They will find Ziad and life will have some brightness again.

The taxi driver, a young man with a thick moustache, is talkative. 'It was quieter in Beirut last night. They hit the airport highway again, and Dahiye, but Israel's been too busy blasting what's left of the south, and sending fighter planes to start on the north.' He takes a drag on his cigarette. 'Mind you, Hizballah was shelling Israel all night. And what about that ship they rocketed yesterday? They're saying that four of their sailors were killed.'

Baba remains silent.

'Three days,' says the driver. 'Three days ago, life was normal. Now Hizballah's dragged us into war, whether we like it or not, and Israel blames our government for everything.'

Baba snorts contemptuously. 'Our government can't control the flush on my toilet, let alone this country.' After this proclamation, he sits sullen and tight-faced, chewing on his thoughts and responding to the taxi-driver's chatter only with a brief word or two.

Next to Layla, Mama looks out of the window and grips her handbag with both hands. Layla thinks of the way Najat held tight onto the car door when they were driving to Dahiye; of Joe's face in the rear view mirror, and Dog panting in the back seat; the flash of joy a short while later when she spotted Ziad's red scooter parked on Najat's street.

She slides across the back seat and puts her arm through Mama's.

It's strange returning to Beirut, which feels at once familiar and alien to Layla; where she was so happy, and also so scared. When they reach the outskirts, they find the roads leading out of the city clogged with traffic, and loud with shrieking horns. But once they get past the larger roads, the traffic eases and they head towards the south of the city. The taxi driver stubs out his current cigarette on the outside of the car door, tosses the butt into the road, and falls silent. Slowly, they drive across an intersection flooded with water from a burst mains pipe. Nationalistic music blares from a bakery. Apart from that, there is an eery quiet. In a supermarket window, a large handwritten sign announces that they have run out of batteries and candles. Further on, a butcher is closing his shop, already out of meat.

Baba sucks in his breath. 'There was an overpass here.'

All that remains is two hills of rubble that have been cleared to either side of the road.

'I haven't been down here since mid-week,' says the driver. '*Ya Allah*, what have they done?'

'Where's the smoke coming from?' asks Mama. A thin, dark grey smoke is drifting down the street, sitting in doorways and curling around corners. The few people who are out are walking with handkerchiefs clamped to their mouths.

'It must be from the burning oil terminals,' says Layla, coughing.

The driver winds up the windows and turns on the air conditioning.

Layla gazes up at a block of flats peppered with bullet-holes, but realizes with a jolt that what she is looking at is old damage that has been there since the eighties; the country's last round of destruction still written on its buildings even as fresh damage is unleashed.

'Right.' They are on a clear stretch of road. The driver accelerates. 'Let's get you where you need to go.'

A pair of black eyes peers at Layla out of thick bandages as she follows the nurse down the ward. A child, she can't tell what gender. Mama clings onto Baba's arm as if he is the only thing holding her up, and he has Mama's hand beneath his in a tight grip. Layla is glad they have found each other again, however temporarily.

It has only been a couple of days since the attack began, but already the wards are filling up with casualties – men, women and children of all ages. The wounds are often severe: tears made by shrapnel, limbs crushed by rubble, lungs affected by dust, swollen faces and head trauma. The sight of bloodied children makes Layla feel ill, and somehow ashamed of her own small injury.

The man that the nurse takes them to, who stares at them without recognition, and does not know his own name, is not Ziad.

Downstairs in the foyer, a couple are hugging each other, crying. Outside the hospital, an old man is sellotaping a photograph of a younger man who must be his son on the railing, with a telephone number beneath it.

At the second hospital, Ziad's name is not on the patient list either, but there are some recent arrivals whose details have not yet been registered. Again, a member of staff agrees to take them up to the ward. But Baba says he's going to wait downstairs for Layla and Mama from now on.

'He can't bear what he might find,' Mama tells Layla in the lift. This reversal in the order of things surprises Layla. The possibility of losing Ziad has shaken her father, yet drawn out a steely inner strength in her mother that Layla never knew was there.

Up on the ward, it's the same story. Women weep

over children and husbands. There are bandages and casts and sheared limbs. A doctor is telling a man that his daughter will never recognize him again,; that although she has the body of an adult, she is a child again, and must be cared for the rest of her life.

The nurse stops in front of a bed. In it, a teenage boy lies unconscious. He has a zig-zag tear down the side of his face, an eye swollen shut, one arm and one leg in casts.

Mama grasps Layla's arm. She looks small and fierce. 'If they've done that to him ...'

Layla is startled.

Mama opens her hands, and her fingers curve like claws. All of a sudden she is wolfish, dangerous, her teeth half-bared. 'If someone has done that to my son,' she whispers, 'I'll kill them with my bare hands.'

Layla has never seen her mother like this, and for a moment, just one moment, she is jealous of this savage love.

Downstairs, Baba is pacing back and forth near the hospital entrance looking at a newspaper. As they walk towards him, he looks up, and knows instantly from their faces that his son is not found. When she gets close enough, Layla can see what's on the front page of the newspaper in his hand. Photographs of the charred bodies of children strewn across a road in south Lebanon. In the middle of a field, a little girl lying dead in blue pyjamas. And Ziad's absence, although enormous to them, suddenly shrinks in the face of all this carnage.

At lunchtime, Israeli planes start to hit Dahiye again. Sitting next to Layla in the taxi as they head out of Beirut, Mama trembles and wails to herself that it's the civil war all over again. Layla tries to comfort her. She doesn't feel like arguing. One way or the other, it no longer matters.

The next day, and the next, Baba's pharmacy remains shut while they search the hospitals of Beirut and visit Gendarmerie offices. The fact that Ziad's name is not on any list, however, means nothing. He may not be able to speak, or may not remember his name. People are also being moved in and out of hospitals all the time to make room for the incoming.

But by the third day, it seems to Layla that she and her parents will never be in the right place at the right time; that they are chasing a dream. In the space of those three days, Mama has turned mute, and Baba has become old.

That night, it rains. Layla lies awake listening to the sharp patter on her window, like gravel being thrown against the glass, and tries not to think of everything that has happened.

Early the next morning, she wanders down to the patch of forest and finds that the rain has loosened Dog from his shallow grave. Half a paw is sticking out of the ground, and an ear unfurls from the soil like a new spring leaf. The same ear that, muddy and grainy with silt, was once silky between her fingers.

A while later, she and Baba are standing there again. Baba is no good with anything that involves dirt or the outdoors. He isn't used to doing such a bad job either. In his profession, a bad job can cost someone their life.

'I wish I could help,' she says as Baba digs a deeper hole. After the rain, the earth is softer, more pliable than it was. A rainbow sheen colours the ground where fuel oil has spread onto rainwater. Overhead, the flat crowns of the pine trees scratch the sky. There is the clean scent of pine-cones, and cicadas pulse invisible around them.

Using her good hand, Layla helps Baba to carry Dog, and watches as he lays him gently into the new grave. Rigor mortis has set in, but he still looks like himself. If only he would get to his feet, give a shake, head through to tail, and jump out of that hole, somehow everything would be better. The warmth of him, the scrape of his claws, the excitement of a followed trail alive in his nostrils. But the trail is cold, the hunt over.

Baba clears his throat and tries to sound like his normal self. 'Putrefaction still hasn't begun. Underground, decomposition is slower. He is still in the fresh stage. No

273

smell yet, or bloat.' He starts to fill the hole up. One shovel-load. Two. There are sweat-patches on his pale blue shirt. 'But soon the anaerobic organisms in the body will begin to multiply … and his body … his body will …'

Time grinds to a halt and the moment widens, ripple-like, until it covers everything. Then Baba drops the shovel and folds down onto his knees as if he is about to pray. Except that he is not the praying sort. Instead, he begins to push the rest of the soil into the hole with his hands.

'Baba?' Layla has never seen his hands dirty, but now the mud cakes them up to the elbow; darkens his shirt sleeves and trousers.

He stops. The cicadas thrum on.

'Baba.'

His head droops.

She comes up close to him. His slumped shoulders start to shake – little tremors at first, then stronger, as if he is hiccupping. Baba, a man who never cries, is sobbing and shaking, tears mixed with snot.

'Don't, Baba. Please don't.' She puts a hand on his shoulder. 'There are still two hospitals we haven't been to.' If she hadn't come home, would any of this have happened? Perhaps Ziad wouldn't have felt so deficient that he argued with Baba about it. Then Baba wouldn't be crying like a child, and up in the house, Mama wouldn't be locked inside herself, mouth sealed, her face a blank.

Before Layla and Baba came down here, Layla had gone to her parents' bedroom door. It was ajar, and inside, Mama was pacing in a U-shape around the bed, from one section of wall to the other, her arms wrapped tightly around her belly. And Layla wished that Ziad were still in there, curled up safe, armoured by Mama's ribs and muscle, fed through her veins, her heartbeat thrumming in his tiny chest.

Baba is still weeping. 'If I hadn't argued with him … if I hadn't pushed him so hard …' He hunches over as if he has been punched in the stomach.

A car passes on the road some distance away. In the branches overhead, a bird twitters. The sun pulses down on her in waves of bright heat. Nothing seems real. Again, Layla tells herself that it is all true: Joe, Najat, the feel of the baby in her arms, the clambering over rubble to find Ziad. She reminds herself that all of this has happened. But if they don't find Ziad, this feeling of being lost in time will go on, she knows it will, until one moment of one day, there will come a tipping point. One hand will catch up with the other so that they are both playing the same tune, and it will smash into her that all of it is true. Then she will know that Ziad is dead. And in that moment, the sky will expand and the earth shrink to a pinpoint. Mama and Baba will still be grieving, and she will be able to join them. That is what will happen. But it has not happened yet.

'No.' Layla puts her hand to her forehead and squeezes. Beneath her palm, the skin crumples into folds. It can't be possible that she will never see her baby brother again; it just can't. She has come too far for that. She has fallen in love, found a sense of belonging, realized what she wants from her life, and understood that her family, far from being titanium-strong as she'd imagined, is fragile as fine glass. In the last seven days, there has been a blossoming as well as a shedding, and she has finally grown up. 'This can't be it.'

She looks down into the hole. Soil covers Dog's hind legs, but the rest of him is still visible. And now she notices that there are things moving in his mouth and in the slits of his eyes. Tiny grubs or insects. *Things.* He has been taken over, is no longer what he was, except in her memory. The thick fringe of black eyelashes, short as a doll's, on his top lids. The curves of his nostrils like commas, and the indented line that ran halfway up his brown nose. The way there was a gap beside each canine where the opposite one fitted when he closed his mouth. The almost imperceptible whiskers. The dark ridges like eyebrows that allowed his face to form expressions. The flap of his ears when he ran, and the clatter of his claws on tarmac, *prestissimo.* The feel of his muzzle when he rubbed it against her thigh. The smoothness of his white and brown coat beneath her hand.

'We can't stop.' Dog might be dead, but Ziad is not. Until she has seen him with her own eyes and it has therefore been proved for certain, then he is not yet dead. She will carry on searching until she has an answer.

Baba is still crying. The cicadas stop, then tune up again, always the same note. In the valley, a horn blares and a man calls for someone. Life is carrying on.

Both Layla and Baba have their backs to the house, so neither of them sees her come.

She walks straight past Layla. For days she has been ebbing away from the person they know, but now she is here, standing beside Baba and placing an arm around him.

He looks up, blinking away tears.

Layla hardly dares breathe.

Baba's jaw is slack, his mouth hanging slightly open. He looks shocked. Layla is shocked too, by the sheer fact that Mama is here, but most of all by the way she looks. Because she, like Dog, has undergone a transformation. Since yesterday, it seems that she has been concentrating on something inside herself, but now, like a vision, her head is held high and her shoulders are back, as if a burden has been shed. She is moving lightly, and her features are soft.

'It's all right,' she tells Baba.

He gets to his feet, his eyes fixed on her. 'Has someone called? Have they found him?'

Mama shakes her head.

Baba sags. 'How ... how do you know then?'

She curls her hand into his earth-encrusted one, and her fingers reappear threaded through his. The gold of her wedding ring winks in the sun. 'I just know. I would know if something that was part of my body died.' She searches for a way to explain. 'If my arm fell off, I would know it, wouldn't I? So, if Ziad were dead, I would have felt it in every fibre of me.' She takes a deep breath. 'But I don't feel it. I feel just the same as I have since he was born.'

Baba looks at her strangely. Layla doesn't know what to think. Either way, Mama's assurance stems from a place they cannot argue with.

Chapter Nineteen

'Parents not coming today?' The taxi driver, whose name is Rasheed, has become something of a friend.

'Not today.'

Baba was feeling ill. He looked ghastly pale, and although Mama was torn, she decided to stay and look after him. 'You can't go by yourself,' she told Layla, but there was no real argument. This wasn't something that could be delayed. As Layla kissed Baba goodbye, he whispered, 'Your mother isn't herself. Perhaps ... perhaps it's turning her mind.'

'Okay,' says Rasheed. 'So we're off to the last two hospitals then?'

'That's right.'

'We can double check some of the others if you like. The patient lists are always changing.'

'Thank you.' He's just being kind. He must have sensed her family's hope fading with each hospital visit.

'How are your children?' asks Layla.

'Oh, fine, fine. It's my little boy's birthday next

week.' Rasheed turns a corner, then lets the steering wheel spin slowly back beneath his palm. 'You know what he wants for a present? A toy tank like the Israeli ones he's been seeing on the television.' He sighs. 'I was hoping my children wouldn't learn the same lessons me and my brothers and sisters did.'

The morning light shifts over the mountains. Down on the coast, she can see an Israeli boat out at sea, dim in the smog. As they near Beirut, moments from the past flare like images on a screen.: Ziad standing at the school gate, a skinny boy with a large backpack; Ziad in bed with a fever, sweat beading on his forehead; Ziad having a fit of laughter at some joke; Ziad sitting by himself on sport's day. She cannot bear the thought of her parents years from now, slack and old, thin white hair where there is now thick black hair, and still without a son.

Rasheed pulls up outside the hospital.

Layla knows the procedure by now, but there's a queue a mile long at the front desk, so she waits until no one is looking, then slips into a stairwell.

It is not always possible to identify patients by their faces, she knows that by now. Upstairs, an oxygen mask obscures a man's features, but she can tell from his two healthy legs that he isn't her brother. There is a little girl with no hands, a young man with half a face. Incomplete people.

It's a while before she sees her. She is sitting up in

bed, attached to a drip, with one arm in a sling. There is bruising on her face, and one knee is large with heavy bandaging.

Layla's breath catches.

'Najat!' She hurries to the bedside. 'Najat. You're okay.'

Najat blinks. There is still plaster-dust in her hair. She leans away from Layla, stretching the plastic tube attached to her arm.

Layla forces herself to smile. 'Don't you remember me?'

'I … I don't know.'

'I came to see you – me and Joe. We drove you home from the museum. My brother had been staying with you. Remember?'

Najat gives this some thought. 'No. I don't remember.' From the way she's looking at Layla, it's clear she doesn't know her. Suddenly she takes hold of Layla's shirt. 'Can you take me home?'

'What?'

She gives Layla's shirt a couple of little tugs. 'Home. That's where I want to go.'

What should she say? Should she tell her that she no longer has a home to go to? That her house is a mess of rubble? 'You can't leave the hospital yet.'

Najat's face crumples, and tears gleam in her eyes.

'It's just …' Layla gestures at the bandaged knee, 'you've got to stay here till you're better. You can't walk.'

Najat raises a hand to point down the hallway. 'But that lift. Won't that lift reach to my mother's house?'

'Your mother's …?' She hasn't even been talking about the flat and vine-covered terrace in Dahiye.

Najat mentions the name of a place Layla has never heard of, no doubt a tiny village far from here. Her childhood home. A place of olive groves perhaps, where the sun has dried the earth like the crust on a loaf of bread. Where Najat's infant hands picked up fistfuls of dirt and pine needles and gazed wonderingly at them. The place where she had been born and felt safe.

There is a drop of envy in Layla's pity. Her own childhood home, made up of her, Ziad, Baba and Mama, and compact with safety, has dissolved. Perhaps in her old age, though, when she is lost in dementia, it will exist again.

'Take me home.' The wetness in Najat's eyes turns into tears. 'I want to go home.'

A nurse in a white top and white trousers comes hurrying over. She gets between Layla and Najat and checks the drip. 'What's the matter? Are you in pain?'

Layla retreats into the aisle.

'Is she all right?' she asks when the nurse reappears.

'She's calmed down. She's had head trauma. It takes time.'

'But she'll be all right.'

The nurse shrugs with her mouth. 'Physically? Yes.'

Then starts moving away.

'Wait. Please.'

The nurse turns around. She has long brown hair tied back, and a stethoscope slung around her neck. 'Are you a family member?'

'No, but ... was there someone with her when she came in?' It is worth asking.

The nurse purses her lips.

'Please. I'm searching for someone.'

With a sigh, the nurse indicates further down the ward. 'Down there. A young man on the right. They came in at the same time. Her grandson, maybe. All he'd say is that he went back for her.'

Some people sense when, far away, a loved one dies. They might have a vivid dream about them, smell their scent, hear their voice. Or they might simply feel it in their bones, the same way they know if a person is hiding in the room. Mama is one of those people. But Layla is not. Layla has to see in order to believe.

When she sees him, she stops breathing, as if it's not possible to take in the sight without something else giving in. Then her breath starts to flow again. Her body gentles, like warm milk washing over her. It seems as if she must be dreaming.

Slowly, she moves towards him. He is not awake, but she can make out the slight up and down movement of his chest.

She tries to assess the damage. The main injury seems to be on his torso. There is a dressing across his upper chest, and an uncovered edge of raw red skin suggests that the wound is a burn. Apart from that, there are bruises, some cuts on his hands and arms, and a large scab on his chin. But this, of course, is only what she can see. To look at Najat, she could never have guessed that something inside her had broken.

Silently, she leans over him. His cheeks are flushed, his hairline damp. He stirs; turns his head to one side. A finger twitches, but he does not wake.

She notes the changes since they were last together: his body is longer, his shoulders more broad; his eyebrows are thicker and his jaw is square. He has stubble.

Her heart hurts for his injuries, but at the same times, happiness radiates into every nerve until she feels she is made of light.

There's a chair in the hallway, and she carries it to his bedside. For just a few minutes, she wants him to be entirely hers. So she sits.

Silence is punctured by the beep of machines, the ringing of a phone far away, the ting and grate of the lift doors. The thin white scent of antiseptic in the ward coats a darker animal smell of illness, sour breath and sickly flesh. How could she not have noticed any of these sounds and smells before?

After she calls home, and with the sound of Mama's

relieved crying still in her ear, she continues to sit gazing at Ziad. She sits there for an hour before he stirs again and opens his eyes.

At first he looks at the ceiling, blinking, hazy. Then he sees her.

She tenses, waiting for she doesn't know what.

His eyes haven't changed. Large, slightly pulled down at the corners, and olive-green like Baba's. 'Layla.' For a moment he is glad to see her. Then he looks around, and down at himself lying in a hospital bed. His face twists. 'How did you find me?'

For the last seven days, she has strained to remember what his voice sounds like. And now here it is, still full of sleep, and drug-heavy.

'Does it matter?' she says.

Does she appear different to him too? To what extent has three years of living apart, and a few days of war, altered her?

'I should have been there.' Tears come to his eyes. 'When you came home, I should have been there.'

'It doesn't matter.'

He rubs the tears away. One of his eyes is bloodshot. 'Does Baba know I'm here? Is he angry?' Frowning, Ziad bites down on his lip. 'I ... I lost Jeddo's watch.'

She comes and sits on his bed; puts her hand on his. 'It's not the watch Baba cares about, don't you know that?'

He says nothing, but his face softens.

'Anyway, you didn't lose it.'

'What?'

'I found it.'

Stunned, Ziad takes this in. 'But how? You weren't … were you in Dahiye?'

Layla nods. 'I found out where you'd gone, and I went there.'

'To Najat's house?' He remembers something else. 'Najat. Is she—?'

'She's here. She's alive. But don't think about any of that any more. Don't think at all. Just rest.' She strokes his hair. The pieces of their family can be mended back together. The possibility is there again.

'You came.' Ziad's voice is scratchy with tears and medication. 'You found me.'

'Yes.' She leans over and kisses him on the cheek. 'This time I did my best. And maybe I was too late again, but at least I found you.'

And now the final bit of distance between them closes. His arms are around her, loosely, and she is crying with happiness. It seems as if she must be dreaming. But she is not.

Epilogue

9th September

Rasheed drives me down to Beirut. Again. There, we pass the hotel where Maria's wedding reception took place. Its garden is neglected now, the swimming pool covered over with tarpaulin. Israel's attack is over, and Lebanon's infrastructure is wrecked. Israel's intention of stamping out support for Hizballah, however, has backfired. The party has grown in popularity, that much is clear from the posters and slogans we drive past.

This time, Rasheed doesn't head to a hospital, but east to find a narrow street in Ashrafieh, and in that street a brown block of flats with two giant pots of petunias that are still standing on either side of the main door. He parks and waits while I press the top buzzer and go in.

It can't have been only two months ago since I was last in this foyer. That day has a glowing quality about it like a memory from many years ago, but there's the same broken chair propped up against the wall, and the same scratches on the floor.

Joe has been away, staying with relatives. Of course I texted him as soon as the mobile connections were working again, to tell him that Ziad was alive, and that I had found Najat too. And it was me who suggested this day and time for meeting.

I make for the staircase, but he is faster than me. There's the *pat-pat-pat* of feet flying down the stairs; a thump as he jumps the last two and stops, pink-faced, at the bottom.

In the taxi, I decided what to say when I saw him, but now the words are lost.

He comes towards me.

'I … wanted to … to tell you,' I stutter, 'that I'm sorry, really sorry – you know, for what I—'

But he raises a hand and shakes his head to stop me from saying any more.

When he reaches me, his arms curve round and draw me into him. My forehead presses against his chest. His chin rests on the top of my head. He touches my hair. I inhale him – soap, warm cotton, the particular sweet scent of his skin – and standing in the circle of his arms, sealed away from the world, a feeling of complete contentment falls over me.

Then we kiss, and everything is right.

'I thought I'd never see you again,' he says; the first time I have heard his voice since that day in Dahiye.

'Me too.'

'Jacques and my mother are upstairs. That's why I came down.'

I nod, and kiss him again.

'Is everything okay at home now?' he asks.

'I guess so. Okay but weird. My mother's stopped eating meat. And Baba's like a different person. And Ziad ...'

'Yes, how is he?'

I tell him everything then, and as I talk, his eyes are by turns happy and sad. When I mention my hand, he takes it and touches the scar; leans down to put his lips to it.

'Has it healed now? I mean, can you play?'

'I can play.' I have been practising every day. Sitting close beside me on the piano stool, at first Mama had to play the left hand notes – an unexpected new way of duetting – until my hand improved enough. 'The movement in these fingers still isn't one hundred percent' – I curl the fourth and fifth fingers of my left hand – 'but I'll get there.'

I tell him that there's a truce between Baba and Ziad now; that they move around each other with a new-found respect. 'Ziad's decided that he's going to go to the south and train to clear cluster bombs.'

Joe's astonishment is tinged with admiration. 'Really?'

He must have seen the footage too: the men and

women dressed in khaki, wearing armoured vests, helmets and face-guards, kneeling close together in lines and examining the ground as if searching for ants; or on their feet, passing metal-detectors slowly left and right as they inch their way forwards. The only way of locating some of the four million cluster bombs, most of which were dropped in the final hours of the war.

'What did your father say?'

'Well, they talked about it for ages, about how dangerous it is.' Both Baba and Ziad had seen the pictures of injured adults, but mainly injured children, who, in villages where toys were a rarity, picked up the round, shiny objects, some of them even coloured, that were exactly the right fit for their hands. 'Anyway, Baba didn't shout. And in the end, he just said that if Ziad was sure, then it was alright with him.'

'That's ... that's great.'

'Yeah. Then that same day, Baba picked up the phone and called his parents. The first time they've spoken in fifteen years.' A reconciliation, however strained, was established. 'He asked them if they could help finance my going back to London. That's how come I'm—'

Joe finishes my sentence: 'Going back.'

So far, neither of us has mentioned the fact that outside, Rasheed is waiting in his taxi, with my suitcase in the boot, ready to take me on to the airport.

'Ziad wanted me to stay. What I mean is, he wanted

me to go to London because it's what I need to do, but he also wanted me to stay.'

Joe smiles. 'You're going to be fine, Layla.'

It physically hurts to know that I am leaving. 'Will I ever see you again?'

He strokes my cheek with his thumb. 'Of course you will.'

This brings a little comfort. 'But ... what if I forget?'

'What if you forget me?'

'What if I forget everything?' The winding dirt roads, the pale limestone buildings and small, heat-silent villages. The details of my family's faces. And Joe's. 'And what if you forget?'

Joe shakes his head. 'This, it doesn't go away, you know.'

But I don't know that.

'Wait.' He squeezes my shoulders. 'Stay there. I won't be a minute.'

He goes to the stairs, and I hear him run up them and, a few minutes later, run back down them again. When he reappears in the foyer, he's holding the paper sparrow that I folded in his room on campus. He holds it out and carefully unfolds one of its wings.

'What are you doing?' With its wing out flat that way, the bird looks maimed.

'Look.' He points at the crease-patterns impressed into the paper. 'You can't get rid of those.' I look. The sparrow's wing may no longer be there, but the actions that formed it are. They cannot be undone. A small thing.

In the last two months, a lot of small things have happened that are in reality not small things at all. One day, Mama took a bag of beef from the fridge, stood looking at the pinkish bulge and gathered juices flickering inside the white plastic bag, then quietly vomited into the kitchen sink. Another day, Baba said the words 'all right' to Ziad. On yet another day, I was able to play both hands of Mozart's minuet in F major, written when he was no more than five or six years old.

Before I leave, I hold Joe's face, and after our goodbye, carry the shape of it away with me in the taxi, onto the plane and up into the sky.

Soon there will be a new landscape. The snow-capped mountains and blue sea, the clear sky and blazing sun, the dry hillsides and lean, umbrella-topped pine trees will melt away, and below me I will see a neat patchwork of green and yellow fields, dark clumps of trees, and roads pin-pricked with the headlights of moving cars. A world that functions.

Perhaps I will return. Or perhaps, with the passing years, the distance will widen, as key by key and note by note, I edge my way into exile.

Acknowledgements

Firstly, my thanks to Matthew Martin for your unwavering support and belief.

Thank you also to the wonderful members of my writers' group, Katherine Davey, Jenny Downham, Anna Owen, Patrice Lawrence and Elly Shepherd, for your warmth, encouragement and wisdom.